"All right, Mac, let's get some ground rules straight...

"We're partners on this run," Kara continued, "and that's all we are. I promise not to get rough with you if you promise to keep your hands to yourself. I've driven these rigs for years, and I can handle myself. But you don't want to get me mad, because I can get awful mean when I get mad."

"I just bet you can." His look was measuring.

"I'm glad you believe me. It'll save us both a lot of trouble."

He grabbed her arm, pulling her to face him. "Pretty sure of yourself, aren't you."

"Look, Mac, I told you—"

"Jake. The name's Jake Murphy. Remember it."

"I don't care what you call yourself, Mac, but if you don't get your hand off my arm in the next two seconds, I'll have you off this run, and you can go into the office and complain that the big bad woman threw you out of her truck."

His green eyes narrowed dangerously before he dropped his hand. "Why the hell would a beautiful woman like you want to play truck driver?"

"Why the hell would a nice guy like you want to play macho man?"

Issue March - 88

Dear Reader,

Sophisticated but sensitive, savvy yet unabashedly sentimental—that's today's woman, today's romance reader—you! And Silhouette Special Editions are written expressly to reward your quest for substantial, emotionally involving love stories.

So take a leisurely stroll under the cover's lavender arch into a garden of romantic delights. Pick and choose among titles if you must—we hope you'll soon equate all six Special Editions each month with consistently gratifying romantic reading.

Watch for sparkling new stories from your Silhouette favorites—Nora Roberts, Tracy Sinclair, Ginna Gray, Lindsay McKenna, Curtiss Ann Matlock, among others—along with some exciting newcomers to Silhouette, such as Karen Keast and Patricia Coughlin. Be on the lookout, too, for the new Silhouette Classics, a distinctive collection of bestselling Special Editions and Silhouette Intimate Moments now brought back to the stands—two each month—by popular demand.

On behalf of all the authors and editors of Special Editions,
Warmest wishes,

Leslie Kazanjian
Senior Editor

PAT WARREN
Look Homeward, Love

Silhouette Special Edition

Published by Silhouette Books New York

America's Publisher of Contemporary Romance

To Pat Bova, who makes friendship into an art form,
for all the years of being there for me

SILHOUETTE BOOKS
300 East 42nd St., New York, N.Y. 10017

ISBN: 0-373-09442-6

First Silhouette Books printing March 1988

America's Publisher of Contemporary Romance

Printed in the U.S.A.

Books by Pat Warren

Silhouette Special Edition

With This Ring #375
Final Verdict #410
Look Homeward, Love #442

Silhouette Romance

Season of the Heart #553

PAT WARREN

is a woman of many talents, including a fluency in Hungarian. She has worked for a real-estate firm, a major airline and a newspaper, where she wrote the "Pat Pourri" column. Growing up as an only child in Akron, Ohio, she learned early to entertain herself by reading books. Now she enjoys writing them. A mother of four—two boys and two girls—Pat lives in Arizona. She and her husband, a travel agent, have toured North America, Mexico, Europe, Israel, Jordan and the Caribbean. When she can find the time, Pat also enjoys tennis, swimming and theater.

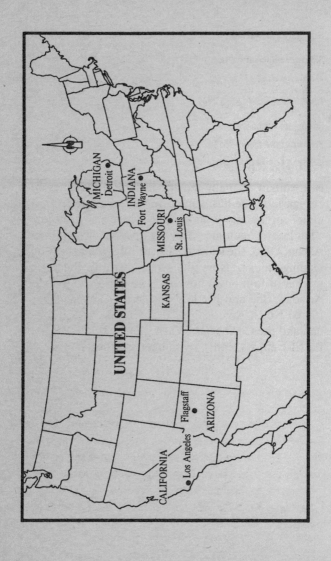

Chapter One

She didn't look like a truck driver. Leaning against his diesel rig, Jake Murphy slowly filled his pipe. He'd watched her drive up in her green sporty convertible, park it alongside the dispatch office and grab a duffel bag from the back seat. He continued to pack his pipe and, from under lowered lids, he saw her reach back into the car for a large canvas purse. She settled the wide strap on one shoulder as she slammed the car door. Her movements were fluid and unhurried.

Her hair was hidden beneath a navy-blue Detroit Tigers' baseball cap, and she wore a light blue man's shirt that somehow emphasized her curves more than a feminine blouse might have. Her skin was the color of honey, her expression behind huge sunglasses unreadable. Quite a package, Jake thought as she came toward the line of trucks.

Suddenly she stopped and reached up to remove her sunglasses. Heavily lashed dark eyes regarded him coolly. He was reminded fleetingly of fire carefully banked. Abruptly she turned and walked toward the office, her long legs under snug jeans hinting at restrained sensuality. Jake glanced at his watch and saw it was only eight in the morning, yet he found himself wishing he had a beer to moisten his dry mouth.

He knew who she was. Louie'd told him that he'd be driving with his niece today. What he hadn't told Jake was how she looked. Like a volatile combination of fire and ice. He clenched his pipe hard between his lips. The day promised to be a long one.

Kara Finelli closed the door behind her, relieved to be out from under the piercing scrutiny of the man's gray-green eyes. She had a fanciful thought that he looked like a pirate, a buccaneer, his beard and mustache bold and brazen in the sunlight. More than arrogance came to mind. Insolent, egotistical, defiant. He was all that and more. A man it would be wise to avoid, she thought as she waited for the woman at the desk to finish her phone conversation.

As usual, Pauly Jones wore faded jeans, a bright floral print blouse and, across her middle, a hand-tooled leather belt with her proudest possession, her rodeo buckle. She'd twisted her pale blond hair into one long braid that hung several inches below her slim waist.

"Listen, Tennessee," Pauly's throaty voice went on, "you just get yourself over here and fast. You overslept again. When I say a load's ready to roll, you can put money on it, you hear? . . . one half hour, see you then." Her bone-thin hand replaced the receiver, and as she turned in her swivel chair, her freckled face broke out in a big smile.

"Kara, honey," she yelped, moving to embrace the younger woman, "if you ain't a sight for sore eyes!" Pauly hugged her in a quick embrace, then stepped back. "Just like old times, seeing you again."

Kara returned her smile. Pauly had worked for her uncle ever since he'd started his trucking company fifteen years ago, and she hadn't changed since that first day Kara had met her. As tall as her own five feet seven, Pauly was lanky as a young boy and unwilling to soften the effects of thirty-nine years of living by adding touches of makeup to enhance her features. Plain described Pauly. Until a person got to know her.

"It's so good to see you again, Pauly," Kara said warmly.

"Two years is a long time. I know you have your reasons, but are you sure you're up to driving again? Those new rigs are something else. I don't think I could do it."

Smiling affectionately, Kara regarded her uncle's right-hand woman. "They haven't built the truck you couldn't drive, and you know it. Is Uncle Louie in?"

"You bet he is. Been here since dawn waitin' for you. Go on in, honey."

Kara smiled her thanks and left her bags on a chair outside his office. She knocked once then walked in. Standing by the window wearing his usual tan slacks and shirt, Louie Santini turned toward the door, his face forming a welcoming smile as he saw who had entered.

Only two years. How could he have aged so much so quickly? she wondered. At fifty-seven, his thinning hair was white when her memory had seen gray. His once ruddy complexion looked more sallow than tan, his tall frame more stooped. Kara hated to think his recent business worries had aged her beloved uncle so noticeably. She smiled broadly and moved into his warm embrace, hoping her face hadn't registered surprise at his appearance.

"Kara, *mia cara*," he whispered, his gruff voice thick with emotion. Because he'd never married and had no children of his own, she'd always been special to him. "I wish you'd have come to see me under other circumstances."

"You don't have time to come to California these days to visit Nona and me, so I had to grab any old excuse to be with you."

"I'm still not convinced it's right for you to do this."

She moved back to look into his troubled brown eyes. "We aren't going to have to go over this again, are we, Uncle Louie? I want to do this, I *can* do it because no one will suspect me, and I *don't* want to hear anymore about it, please. I'm twenty-seven now, not fifteen like I was when I first came here. I can handle it."

He ran a thick hand through his hair and sat down heavily at his old scarred desk. "I know, I know. But I still have my doubts. I have no right to involve you in my problems and risk your safety."

Kara took the chair opposite him, crossing her long legs. "You have every right. Please, let me do this one small thing to try to pay you back for all you've done for me."

"But you're . . . you're a young woman, so small . . ."

"Uncle Louie!"

"Yes, yes, I know. You're independent. Able to take care of yourself. One of a handful of women who can handle the big rigs as well as a man. I know all that." His features clouded over. "But, Kara, we're dealing here with more. Someone, or some group, is trying to put me out of business. Not just me. Other small trucking companies, too. There's sabotage here, maybe danger. There have been several unexplained accidents. Underbidding on jobs. Trucking offices broken into, cargo damaged. What's next? I don't know. But I do know I'm not willing to risk your life to find out.''

Kara leaned forward with a small laugh. ''Uncle Louie, don't be so dramatic. It's not like you. As you said, I can handle the rigs. They'll never suspect me, and I can learn more in one day than you or one of your regular male truckers could in a week. Most of your men know I've worked on and off for you for years while I went back to school so they won't think anything except that I'm back again for the summer to make some quick money. Men loosen up around women, especially women they trust. I can keep my eyes and ears open. If there's a leak in your own outfit, I have a better chance at ferreting out the person responsible than anyone else you could name.'' She gave him a big, winning smile. ''I'll be careful. You know I always am.'' She reached over, touching his clasped hands resting on the desk. ''Uncle Louie, I *need* to do this. I owe you so much.''

''Owe! *Owe* is not a word we use between family.''

Kara sat back, her heart in her smile. ''Maybe not. But all the same, there is a debt here. You and I both know how I feel about indebtedness. I hate to think of all the burdens you've had all these years, and you didn't deserve it. You—''

Louie leaped to his feet, scowling. ''Don't you talk to me about burdens, *cara mia*, not now, not ever.'' His face moved into a paternal smile. ''I'll let you help me, Kara, this one time. But no more talk about burdens. I did what I did because I love you. No other reason. You understand?''

Kara's large dark eyes grew misty. ''Yes, I understand.'' She cleared her throat to hide her emotions. ''But you have to understand, too. I also do what I do because of love. Okay?"

He came around the desk, his arms reaching for her. "Sure, I understand. But you've got to promise me you'll be careful. If something happened to you..."

She grinned through his stranglehold on her. "Nothing's going to happen to me. You worry too much." She moved to sit down again, realizing that Louie was questioning his decision to let her go on this hunt-and-search mission. Yet he had given in, knowing how important it was for her to do this for him, knowing how deeply she felt her obligations. He'd told her on the phone that the dirty tricks had been going on for months, that the police had been little or no help and that the insurance company hadn't been able to pick up a single lead. Perhaps she could.

Kara's eyes followed him as Louie returned to his worn leather chair and picked up a manifest sheet. "So tell me, who are you sending me out with first?"

"His name's Jake Murphy, and he's new with me but not new to trucking. His father owns a big trucking company in California. Jake's been driving these big rigs since he was a teenager."

Kara gave him a puzzled frown. "Why is he working for you if his father has his own company?"

"He had a falling-out with his father five or six years ago. Tom Murphy and I went to college together in California. I've known the whole family a long time. Tom's a shrewd businessman but a tough old bird. Jake doesn't talk about it, but shortly after his mother died, he left his father's place and set off on his own. I thought at first it was just a case of wanderlust, but I believe it's more than that." Louie's voice held a small note of envy. "Jake's lived all over, never in one spot too long. He went down to South America a spell, spent some time in Europe, raced boats, worked as a mechanic somewhere. He lived in France last year. He's a nice fellow and a damn good driver. Just not interested in settling down, I guess."

Kara looked skeptical. "He sounds like a drifter to me. Even though you know his family, he's only been with you a short time. Are you sure *he* isn't our problem? Most of your other men have been with you for years, some from the start."

Louie shook his white head. "Not Jake. Like I say, he comes from good people." He turned to look out the window, his face suddenly nostalgic. "His mother was one of the loveliest, finest women I've ever known. The Murphys are honest and hardworking. His two younger brothers still work in the company. What happened between Jake and his father—it was family trouble, not work problems. They never saw eye-to-eye. Different viewpoints, you know. One day maybe they'll straighten it out. I hope so. I like them both and I trust Jake. You can, too."

Kara leaned back, unconvinced but unwilling to let him see. Louie trusted easily, far more easily than she. "If you say so."

Louie was all business again. "I do say so. He's a big gruff Irishman, and he looks kind of tough with that beard, but he's all right."

Kara sat up straighter. "Beard?" A picture came into her mind of a tall, lean man with hot, hungry eyes. "Is he blond and does he smoke a pipe?"

Louie grinned. "Yeah, that's Jake. Did you meet him already?"

Kara's dark eyes narrowed thoughtfully. "Not exactly, but I saw him outside. Sort of arrogant, I thought.

Listen, why don't I take my first run with someone familiar, like Cowboy or Phil?''

Again, Louie Santini shook his head at her. ''I thought about this a lot, Kara. You haven't been on the road for two years now, and my new trucks are a little different. I want you with Jake first. Even though you'll be senior driver—a fact that doesn't set too well with him, I can tell you—he's the best man to get you broken in again. After this run I'll team you up with the others, alternating so you can see what you can learn.''

''I don't know, Uncle Louie. Jake looks a little conceited to me.''

''Nah. You just got to get to know him, that's all. There's a lot more to Jake Murphy than meets the eye. Now, let me check out this manifest, and you can be on your way.'' Louie bent to his paperwork.

Kara leaned back thoughtfully, considering what her uncle had told her. A lot more to Jake Murphy than meets the eye, she thought. I'll just bet there is. She bristled at the memory of the way his gaze had thoroughly roved over her, feature by feature, when she'd walked from her car to the office. She sighed, making up her mind to get along with Mr. Murphy no matter what. She'd certainly handled his type before. The important thing was she had a job to do, and she was going to do it well.

Crossing her long slim legs, Kara let her mind drift to thoughts of her house on the California coast, the redwood deck she'd worked so hard staining before she'd left, the captivating scent and sound of the sea nearby. She was filled with a rush of longing to be back there, her jeans rolled up high while she walked barefoot on the salt-crusted sand, with her camera in hand and the glorious sun shining overhead. She felt a sense of peace and freedom there in the first real home she'd ever had.

She thought about her photo studio just south of Los Angeles and how well it was finally doing after two long, lean years. Well enough that she'd been able to hire two full-time people last fall and a part-time assistant last month. She'd trained them herself, and she was pleased with their work. Three months. She owed these three summer months to Louie. At the end of August, maybe sooner, she could go home and concentrate on building her photography business. Kara looked up, realizing with a start of surprise that Louie was talking to her.

"I'm sorry, Uncle Louie." She smiled. "You caught me daydreaming." She didn't miss his look of concern as he stood and turned toward the door.

Opening it, Louie impulsively hugged his niece to him. "You be careful, you hear?" he instructed, his voice gruff with emotion.

Her smile was warm, loving. "I will. I'll be in to see you as soon as I return." With a wave to Pauly, who was busy with another call, Kara picked up her bags and walked out into the bright June morning sun.

She looked up and saw that Jake Murphy was still leaning against the red truck, his stance confident, challenging. She took her time, searching for her sunglasses in her bag, all the while studying him surreptitiously. Several inches over six feet, she guessed. Lean and hard, he'd rolled the sleeves of his blue denim shirt up past his elbows to reveal well-corded muscle underneath. His green baseball cap sat atop hair the color of wheat, cut conservatively to his collar. Tight, worn jeans hugged muscular thighs, ending in dusty brown boots, one foot crossed casually over the other. Gray-green eyes regarded her with amused hostility.

Kara swallowed hard and turned toward her car. On the spur of the moment, she decided to take her camera along. She'd seldom done that in the past but perhaps she would need its diversion on this trip. Or the protection of escaping behind those impersonal lenses.

Jake Murphy reached up and opened the sleeper compartment door, tossing in his bag just as Cowboy Adams strolled leisurely toward him from the rear of the trailer. Jake had been with Louie Santini two months, yet he still didn't feel like "one of the boys." Most truckers accepted a new man slowly—except Cowboy. Somewhere in his forties, a hair under six feet and reed thin, Cowboy had a ready smile and a quick wit that made a man feel as if he knew him. Hailing from Texas, he always wore a black Stetson, earning him his nickname.

Cowboy removed his hat, brushed back his mop of thick brown hair with tanned fingers and wiped his damp brow with the back of his hand. "Another humid Michigan morning, right Jake?" he asked in his whiskey-roughened voice.

Jake settled his cap more comfortably on his head before answering. "You got that right, Cowboy."

"I see you're looking over your new 'senior driver.'" Cowboy carefully stuffed a wad of chewing tobacco into the corner of his mouth, squinting at Jake as he watched for a reaction.

Jake's scowl appeared without warning. "I don't agree with this company policy. She may have driven longer for Santini Trucking than I have, but I'll spot her, mile for mile, any day of the week."

Cowboy chuckled, low and deep. "Hell, you know how it goes, Jake. She's got seniority. Besides that, she's the boss's niece. Got to tell you, though, she's one nice lady. And I do mean 'lady.'"

"You've driven with her quite a bit?"

"Sure have. Cross-country. Short runs. You name it. I've been with Louie from the beginning. When she was still in high school, Kara worked summers in the office. Before she was twenty, she drove the rigs."

"Where's her parents?"

Cowboy shrugged his slim shoulders. "Never heard much about her father. Her mother, Louie's sister, isn't worth much from what I hear. She dumped Kara on Louie and his mother when she was a teenager. The kid lived with her grandmother in California, but Louie always treated her like his own daughter. He sent her away to college, but she came back to Michigan every summer. He taught her to drive the rigs because she insisted on earning her own way. She's a damn spitfire about that. You can't even buy her a drink. She'll shove the money back at you. She don't take nothin' from nobody. But she's one hell of a driver. For a woman." Cowboy shifted the tobacco in his mouth and spit onto the dusty ground.

"That so?" Jake asked lazily. Since he'd grown tall enough to reach the brake pedal, he'd been around trucking. He knew that about twenty percent of today's truckers were women. But he'd be damned if Kara Finelli looked like she'd fit the bill. There was something different about her, and yet, he couldn't put his finger on it. All he knew was that his gut reactions seldom led him astray. "Why's she back now?"

"Don't know. Louie said he was shorthanded and Kara offered to come from California to help out for the summer."

"What's she do out west?"

"She's a photographer. Pretty good, I hear."

Jake watched her approach from behind the truck. Sunglasses in place, she carried her baggage. A society picture snapper slumming for the summer. Just his luck. Cool, sleek, mysterious. Another word came to mind—untamed. Even with all but a few strands of her dark hair tucked under that silly cap, that was the way he saw her. He'd bet that a lot of men would give a month's pay to be the one to tame her. He wondered how many had tried.

She greeted Cowboy with a quick, warm hug. "It's good to see you again, Cowboy. You haven't changed a bit."

"*You* have," he said with a grin. "You're better lookin' than ever, Kara. Welcome back."

"Thanks," she said and smiled her appreciation, then turned to face Jake.

In the mirror reflection of her sunglasses, he saw himself in miniature as she stood before him. He felt a nerve under his eye jump in response as she held out a slim hand.

"Mr. Murphy, I'm Kara Finelli." His big hand dwarfed hers. She felt instant heat rise from his touch and struggled to ignore it. Taking a step backward, she withdrew from his grip. "I understand we're driving together. I'd like to check the cargo, please."

He tried to swallow his irritation. "That won't be necessary, Miss Finelli. I've already gone over it, and it checks out to the letter."

She gave him a tiny smile. Some time ago she'd learned that often the best way to handle arrogance was to be one step bolder. "As senior driver, I believe it's my duty to check out the cargo against the manifest sheet on all runs. *If* you don't mind," she stated, reaching out her hand for the trailer key.

He had no choice but to give it to her. But he didn't have to like it. He reached into his pocket, found the key and all but slammed it into her waiting hand. She appeared not to notice.

"Thank you," she said evenly.

As Kara walked to the rear of the trailer, Cowboy cleared his throat, trying not to notice Jake's increasingly dark expression. "Hey, man, don't take it so personal. She's just a stickler for rules."

Jade green eyes narrowed at him. "I don't need a half-pint woman to tell me how to do my job. If I tell someone the cargo is checked, *the cargo is checked*!"

"Yeah, Jake, *we* know that, but *she* don't know that. It's going to be a mighty long week if you don't simmer down. You ever driven partners with a woman before?"

"No, but I imagine it's something like wearing a hair shirt for a week or so."

Cowboy grinned through tobacco-stained teeth. "Oh, man! You sure picked the wrong woman to start off with!"

"I didn't pick anything. Whose crazy idea was this anyway? Damn fool woman...."

Approaching from the rear, Kara narrowed her dark eyes at Jake's back. "This 'damn fool woman' is back from checking the cargo, and, Mr. Murphy, it *does* seem to be in order. Would you care to initial the manifest or shall I?" Kara asked.

Turning to face her, Jake's voice was an exaggerated drawl. "Shucks, ma'am, I'm sure you'll want to take care of an important task like that yourself. A poor *junior* driver surely couldn't handle it as well."

"Probably right," she answered, bending to her clipboard. Cowboy swallowed a laugh and gave a wave as he disappeared around the bend. Jake scowled.

With a casual stride, Kara walked to the office and turned in a copy of the manifest then returned to the cab.

She stretched to reach the sleeper door and opened it to toss in her bags, one after the other.

His stance tense, Jake watched her with flinty eyes. He caught a hint of subtle perfume that seemed out of place coming from a denim-clad truck driver. He felt a surge of heat that surprised and infuriated him.

As Kara closed the door, he suddenly reached toward her in an effort to remove her hat, to throw her off balance. Smoothly she sidestepped him.

Angry sparks flashed from her brown eyes. "All right, Mac, let's get some ground rules straight right from the start. We're partners on this run and that's all we are. I promise not to get rough with you if you promise to keep your hands to yourself. I've driven these rigs on and off for eight years and I can handle myself. But you don't want to get me mad because I can get awful mean when I get mad."

"I just bet you can." He stepped back, his eyes roaming her small frame, his look measuring. He hooked a thumb under his belt defiantly, his other hand braced on a hard hip.

She chose to ignore his challenging arrogance. "I'm glad you believe me. It'll save us both a lot of trouble."

He grabbed her arm, pulled her to face him. "Pretty sure of yourself, aren't you?"

"Look, Mac, I told you—"

"Jake. The name's Jake Murphy. Remember it."

"I don't care what you call yourself, Mac, but if you don't get your hand off my arm in the next two seconds, I'll have you off this run and you can go into the office and complain that the big bad woman threw you off her truck."

His green eyes narrowed dangerously before he dropped his hand. "Why the hell would a beautiful woman like you want to play truck driver?"

"Why the hell would a nice guy like you want to play macho man?"

Unsure of the reason, he let his temper have full rein. The boss's niece or not, he had a job to do, and the last thing he needed was a fancy woman who got her kicks hanging around truckers. First time she got her dainty hands grease stained, she'd probably look to some man to help her out. "Men have been driving these rigs a lot longer than women. Go home, little lady. You're out of your element."

"Bullshit! I'm very good at what I do, and you can believe that or not. I couldn't care less."

"Have you ever been in the Navy?" He watched surprise jump into her eyes.

"The Navy? What are you talking about?"

"You swear like a sailor. I thought maybe you'd worked on the docks, too."

"Bullshit? That's not swearing. It's an observation—a commentary. It uniquely sums up my opinion of your chauvinistic statements. And no, I haven't worked on the docks. But I just might try it sometime."

He gave her an appraising look. "I believe you would. And, for the record, I don't make chauvinistic statements."

"Maybe you don't think you do, but you do. Now look, Mac, are we going to move, or what?"

"I told you, my name is Jake."

"I thought all great big he-man truck drivers were called Mac." She knew she was baiting him, but he'd been so filled with self-righteous indignation at having to put up with her that she couldn't resist exasperating him once he'd shown her how easily she could.

He grabbed the low handle on the door and jerked it open. "After you," he said, his look condescending.

Kara looked up at the yawning distance of six feet or more to the shiny leather seat. She hadn't been up in a cab in two years and never in the newer rigs that Louie now used. Still, she'd be damned if she'd let him see her nervousness.

She hopped up onto the first high step, braced against the fender wall, grabbed the support rod and scrambled up inside the truck's cab with surprising agility. Sliding behind the wheel, she smiled down at him. "Shall I start out or do you want to drive?" she asked with a saccharine smile.

Jake slammed the door hard. Damn fool woman, he thought, walking around to the passenger side. We'll just see if she's as good as she thinks she is. Jamming his pipe tightly between his teeth, he climbed in beside her.

Reluctantly he admitted to himself that she handled the rig expertly, as well as any man he'd driven with. Of course, everything was power now in most of the cabs. An intelligent driver, she made up for her lack of strength with good decisions, her strong, slim hands resting easily on the big wheel.

Jake placed his arm along the back of the seat. He glanced at her canvas purse resting on the seat between them. On top of it was a book, lying face down. Curious, he reached down and picked it up. *Gift from the Sea* by Anne Morrow Lindbergh. Poetry. He replaced the book and turned his head to study her. "Good book," he commented.

Her eyebrows arched. "You've read it?"

"Mmm hmm."

"I'd have thought you more the mystery or western reader."

"I read some of those, too. What else do you like to do?"

"Do?"

"As in entertainment?"

This idle chatter was better than those sizzling looks. Kara let herself relax a bit. "I like little theater, swimming, horseback riding and—don't laugh—I'm addicted to old *Honeymooners* reruns."

His smile was warm this time. "Old Ralph Kramden's a favorite of mine, too."

He just might turn out to be human after all, Kara thought.

Jake couldn't seem to keep his eyes from her. She was lovely, with high cheekbones, an oval-shaped face, skin tan and silky smooth. Her eyes, as she scanned the traffic, were large and dark and distracting, the lashes thick and long. Damn! This wasn't like him at all, he thought. He cleared his throat noisily.

"Why did you come back to driving after two years?" he asked. Normal curiosity, he told himself. That's all it was.

She kept her eyes on the road. "To repay a debt. My uncle's been good to me. He needed help so I came."

"As simple as that?"

"Yes."

"I don't believe you."

Her knuckles whitened on the wheel. "Look, Mac, I don't . . ."

"What about your folks? Don't they care that you're racing around the countryside with all manner of roughnecks?" Her explanation was too simplistic. Cowboy had told him a little about her. He wanted to know more. Occupational hazard, he decided, this being suspicious of everyone.

She took a deep breath, trying to keep her temper in check over his insolent questions. "My father's dead. My mother...my mother is wise enough not to try to run my life. As for roughnecks—" she turned to give him a deliberate, meaningful look "—the only one I've encountered so far seems to be right here in this cab. Have I satisfied your curiosity, *Mr.* Murphy?"

His gaze raked down the length of her then boldly returned to meet her eyes. "Far from it," he answered, his voice deliberately suggestive.

Kara felt her pulse leap. This man was distracting and could undermine her effectiveness. She needed to keep her guard up around his easygoing charm. Only a foolish woman wouldn't. And she was seldom foolish.

Jake knew he'd unnerved her. He'd meant to. He kept his eyes to the front but as the morning moved along, occasionally he felt her cool gaze slide his way, covertly studying him.

A tense silence hung in the air for some time. This was ridiculous, Kara decided. She'd promised herself she'd get along with Jake Murphy no matter what, and she wasn't doing a very good job of it. She needed to win this reluctant trucker over and gain his confidence if she was to be any help to Louie. And, after all, they had a lot of hours to spend together.

"Tell me, Mac, do you ask your barber to cut your hair so that curly lock will fall appealingly onto your forehead or is it sheer boyish coincidence?"

Jake felt the muscles in his shoulders relax with her efforts at a light approach. If she wanted a truce, he'd give her one. He could learn more offering honey than vinegar, he thought, turning to her with a smile. "Matter of fact, I do. He's Italian, a junior Perry Como. Sings while he snips away. He said it would make me look adorable. What do you think?"

"You can't argue with Italians—and win."

"You're Italian, aren't you?"

"Yes."

"I'll take that as a warning then."

She fought to contain a smile but lost, the corners of her mouth twitching in response. Maybe they'd just gotten off on the wrong foot. Lots of men in trucking resented women invading their male domain. If he got to know her, to respect her abilities, perhaps he'd ease up. "You do that."

He looked at her again and leaned closer. "I'll bet *your* hair is adorable, too." Before she could react, Jake reached over and grabbed the bill of her baseball cap, whipping it from her head. Immediately mounds of jet-black hair cascaded down to just past her shoulders, free of confinement. The morning sun flowing through the windows coaxed shiny highlights from the lustrous waves. A flash of answering anger danced in her dark eyes as Jake's gaze feasted on her. God, she was beautiful, he thought.

With an effort Jake thrust the hat back at her. "Here, put it back on." Dumb. That had been a dumb move, he told himself, shifting his gaze out the window. How the hell was he going to be able to keep his concentration where it belonged with her looking like that only two feet away from him? he wondered impatiently.

For once Kara didn't have a snappy comeback. Swiftly she reached for her hat. The man simply wouldn't let up.

Jake took small pleasure in seeing that her fingers shook as she coiled long strands with one hand and stuffed her hair back under the cap.

They rode the rest of the morning without speaking, each absorbed in their own thoughts. When the sun was dead center, Kara pulled off the highway and moved the big rig next to several other trucks in the diner parking lot for their lunch stop. Before she could jump down, Jake was out and around with a hand to help her dismount. Uneasily she placed her fingers in his warm grasp. He didn't release her hand right away but stood looking down at her, his eyes deep gray pools.

She found his closeness disturbing. Pulling free of him she moved back, reached for her bag and flung it over her shoulder. "I'm not hungry," she said, defiance struggling with appetite. "I'm going for a walk. See you later. Have a nice lunch." She sauntered off, swinging her canvas camera case, uncomfortably aware of his eyes on her back.

An Academy Award performance, she told herself as she walked along, trying to quiet her hammering heart. She let out a deep breath, her hands shaking as they searched for her camera. She found it and carefully removed the cover, anxious to lose herself in her photography. Anything to get her mind off Jake Murphy and his surprising magnetism. This was decidedly unlike her. She was not without male friends, and she'd never had trouble controlling her responses around any of them before. How was she going to accomplish the job that she'd come to do with Jake around? she wondered with no small amount of dread.

They'd stopped just outside of Fort Wayne, and for nearly an hour Kara lost herself taking pictures of anything that caught her eye. She straddled an old wooden

fence and adjusted her wide-angle lens so she could capture the lazy beauty of rustic barns and contented cows.
The peaceful farmland scenes soothed her frazzled
nerves.

Returning to the parking area, she entered the restaurant and bought an apple. Walking toward the truck, she
found Jake up in the sleeper, storing several cans of cold
drinks in the small refrigerator under the compact bed.
She stood waiting for him to jump down so she could
climb up. She wasn't really tired, but she thought that if
she went into the sleeper and tried to read for a while, she
wouldn't have to deal with his probing looks and unsettling conversation. Munching on her apple, she waited.

Wordlessly Jake landed at her feet. He looked down at
her from under hooded eyes. "You like apples, I see."

"Mmm. My grandmother used to say: 'an apple a day
keeps the doctor away.' I believed her then, and I still
do."

His gaze roamed her slight frame from her rosy cheeks
to her slim legs. "You do look pretty healthy at that."

Unavoidably her face flushed at his look. She turned
to step up, then felt his hand on her arm.

"What are you *really* doing here, Kara?" he asked. His
hand slid down to examine hers, finding it small, delicate and smooth. "Your heart's not in trucking, and you
don't look like you need the money. What is it, the challenge?"

"I told you once already and—"

"Some people are unable to resist challenges," he went
on, his eyes trapping hers, very aware of her pulse racing
beneath his fingers still on her wrist. "Like climbing
mountains, diving for sunken sea treasures, racing mo-
torcycles. Height, depth, speed. Is that you?" He moved
closer.

She kept her face impassive as she stared back at him.

"You like being mysterious? Well, I like mysteries. I like solving them. And I like challenges."

Kara refused to let him see how his look and his touch were affecting her. Squaring her chin, she looked up at him. "Is that right, Mac?" she asked as coolly as she could manage. She gave a short laugh. "Your imagination's working overtime—or maybe the heat's got you," she shot back. Reaching for her bag, she flung it over her shoulder.

Jake moved out of her way and watched her climb up and close the sleeper door. There was more to Kara Finelli than she let on, he was sure of it. Louie had been brief and vague in explaining her return. Deliberately so. Why? Louie'd trusted him with an important job that had high stakes, and now he'd entrusted him with his niece. Almost like he'd planned it—like a challenge.

Smiling to himself, Jake scrambled up into the driver's seat. He never turned his back on a challenge.

Chapter Two

Jake watched the shimmering heat waves dance along the highway in front of him as he headed into the late-afternoon sun. He drove automatically, his strong hands quietly gripping the wheel, his eyes alert, but his mind on the sleeper compartment occupied by a dark-eyed woman he'd known only a few hours.

He took a deep breath, inhaling the wildflower scent of her. Behind his head, she'd pulled the curtain across the wide window that was another entry into the small room, but he'd been acutely aware of her every movement. The sighing of the bed as she'd shifted restlessly on it, the turning of the pages of a book, the click of the lamp when she'd turned out the light. Now, for well over an hour, there'd been only silence, and he imagined her asleep, curled on her side, with that rich cloud of black hair spread out on the pillow. Jake swallowed and clamped his teeth down hard on the stem of his pipe.

He shoved a tape into the recorder and the low, moody sounds of jazz drifted to envelop him as he roundly cursed himself for allowing Kara Finelli to dominate his thoughts. He was a man used to being in control. So just why was he spending so much time thinking about one small, slightly exasperating woman?

She intrigued him, and he couldn't even explain why. Her reserve, the cool indifference she tried to convey, even her flippancy piqued his curiosity. Why'd she have that great big chip on her shoulder and who had put it there? he wondered.

Louie hadn't said much about her, only that she was coming back and that she was a driver who could hold her own with any man. Louie was unemotional, despite his heritage, a quiet man who kept his own counsel. His niece was another story. A lot of heat simmering behind those huge brown eyes. A lot he'd like to know more about.

Jake put his lighter to his pipe and steadily drew on it as the big semi ate up the miles westward. Despite his curiosity about her, he knew he couldn't afford to get involved. He had a job to do—not an easy one—and he had to give it first priority. He needed a clear head for it. And Kara, with the passion he sensed just under that chilly facade, might make him blow his cover. After this run he'd talk with Louie, get him to pair her with one of the other truckers. He'd never accomplish all he needed to with her around, clouding his mind, fogging his brain.

Ruefully he acknowledged that she was a good driver, very professional. And he ought to know, Jake thought, pulling out into the left lane to pass a slow-moving van, for he'd seen many truckers come and go.

He'd been a teenager when he'd first started driving for his father's company, then just getting off the ground.

"Start at the bottom, son," Tom Murphy had told his eldest son. "Then, when you get to the top, no one will know more than you." And he'd eagerly agreed. He'd taken time out only for school and a little football. But mainly he'd worked with the dedication and tireless strength of youth.

And he'd loved the challenges, the decision making of his work. By the time he finished college, he'd moved into the office and was helping run the company. In time his two brothers joined him and their father. The four of them had lived and breathed Murphy Trucking. What fools they'd all been, Jake thought with a grimace of disgust.

Then, Cindy had entered his life. Jake felt his stomach tighten, his mouth harden into a grim line. But he didn't want to think about Cindy right now. He looked out into the cloudless sky and absently rubbed his beard with one hand, his other resting loosely on the wheel. The company had expanded and thrived under his leadership, while his gentle mother had died. The shock had made him take a look at his life, to see that his single-minded determination to succeed had caused him to neglect his mother, his marriage, even his original goals. His father couldn't, or wouldn't, see the problems. Jake had felt he'd had no choices left. He'd had to leave, to get away. Far away.

He'd wandered the globe for a long while, working odd jobs. He'd wanted no part of ambition or commitment or involvement. Those things had too high a price tag; they wound up costing you too much. He'd wanted to live only for the day, to find peace, to work a little, to play a little, to take time to smell the flowers along the way. And he'd done just that until he'd run into Rob Carter, who'd given him a reason to stop his aimless wanderings and had subtly coaxed him back into the mainstream.

Jake set his cooling pipe in the ashtray and smiled at the thought of his tall, soft-spoken boyhood friend. A good man, Rob Carter. Vice president of a national insurance company, he'd listened to Jake and understood all he wasn't saying. Instinctively knowing a desk job would hold no appeal to Jake's restless nature, Rob had lured him into investigative work for his company. And suddenly Jake found a niche where he felt comfortable again. That had been three years ago.

And now here he was, working undercover, trying to find those responsible for the many unexplained incidents in several small Midwest trucking firms insured by his company. They'd picked Santini Trucking as his cover because Jake had assured Rob that Louie could be trusted to cooperate, to let him use his company as a base and let no one else know his real purpose in driving for him. Though Jake had learned nothing positive yet, he felt certain he would. His record of getting results was unparalleled in the company.

At Santini he was slowly gaining acceptance by the men, moving into their confidence—along with other truckers he met on the routes. Sooner or later someone would make a mistake, and he'd be there. It took patience. Jake was a patient man when he was after something.

But he needed to be alert, his mind free to concentrate on his work, not conjecturing about a woman with soft brown eyes and the kind of thick, dark hair that made a man's hands break out in a sweat with the desire to touch. It wouldn't be easy to step back from Kara, Jake acknowledged as he heard her through the window over his shoulder, shifting restively on the small cot.

On the bunk Kara's jumbled thoughts had her too fidgety to read or rest. This wasn't why she'd left her home, she thought somewhat resentfully, to be cloistered with a man of mercurial moods who kept her tense and too aware of him. Why did he feel it necessary to challenge her constantly, then look at her with those hot green eyes as if he saw deep into her mind and soul? And why did she feel compelled to fire sharp retorts at him as if he were the enemy? This was getting nothing accomplished and was frustrating besides. When they finished this run, she'd persuade Louie to let her drive with someone else, anyone else.

Kara rubbed her arms, sore from the tension of reacquainting herself with the driving she'd been away from so long. It had been only four hours behind the wheel, but she'd put herself under pressure—she hadn't wanted to make a mistake in front of Jake and give him an opportunity to think her less capable than a male trucker.

The not unpleasant aroma of Jake's pipe tobacco drifted to her through the curtained window. Soon it'd be her turn to drive again. They'd decided to alternate every four hours. Rolling over, she closed her eyes, inviting sleep, hoping the time would pass quickly.

It was midafternoon of the next day when they arrived at the receiving dock for their cargo to be unloaded. After her first all-night session, Kara felt even stiffer than the day before. She stretched as she walked about watching the men work. Longing for a bath, she drank a frosty cola and mingled with a few of the drivers who recalled her from previous years. She chatted amiably, hoping someone would say something she might be able to use. Everyone appeared as friendly as she'd remembered, but she sighed with exasperation over learning nothing. When Jake suggested they drive to the

Roadrunner truck stop for a quick shower before eating dinner and starting back, she gladly agreed.

Feeling more like herself after she'd cleaned up, Kara put on fresh cords and a soft pink oxford shirt, pulling her hair back from her face with two ivory combs. She walked across the sawdust floor into the ranch-style restaurant next door to the Roadrunner, hardly noticing the admiring glances following her among the small crowd of truckers and locals. She sat down at one of the empty wooden tables. In the far corner two guitarists and a drummer were tuning up on a small bandstand, holding her attention while she waited for Jake to join her.

She was getting to know Jake, she realized, and reluctantly admitted that she liked what she saw. He'd somehow set aside his earlier reticence the last day and a half, telling her funny stories about his travels, the people he'd met, the things he'd seen. None of it was in the least personal, but it showed him to be more insightful and empathetic to the frailties of others than she'd originally thought him to be. Against her better judgment she found herself watching the entrance.

As Jake came through the door, Kara felt as if a sudden aura of excitement walked in with him. It was a part of him as much as his windswept hair, his sexy beard, his devastating gray-green eyes. She could see that women looked at him and desired him, drawn by his undeniable maleness. Seeming not to notice or care, he just kept walking. She felt the quick stab of an unexpected response. Her dark eyes studied his approach with a mixture of anticipation and annoyance. Even dressed as all the others, in comfortable jeans and a plaid shirt, he stood apart, a man not to be overlooked. No woman could ignore him. Damn, but she didn't want this, she thought with a frown.

As she watched, he stopped at the counter and placed their order before strolling over to join her. He took his time looking her over, missing nothing. Kara found herself almost blushing under his penetrating gaze.

"You clean up pretty good, Mac," she said finally in an effort at easing her nervousness.

Not to be rushed, Jake's eyes continued their assessment of her, aware of her discomfort. At last he gave her a slow smile. "Not half as well as you do, Kara." He sat down. "I've ordered us a couple of beers and a pizza with everything."

"I see you only go first class."

"I'm trying to dazzle you, ply you with alcohol and exotic food."

"It just might work. I'm starved."

The beer was cold and refreshing, the pizza fragrant and spicy, the conversation comfortable and relaxed. In a deliberate effort at friendliness, more to ease their ride home together than anything else, Kara asked Jake careful questions about his boyhood as they ate. He talked fondly and with self-deprecating humor of growing up in California, of his brothers who now ran the family business, of his early years trucking.

The shadow of memories washed over his face, softening the angular lines as he spoke warmly of his mother but didn't mention his father at all. Remembering Louie's remark that father and son had had their differences, Kara avoided mentioning Tom Murphy. There would be no point in raising his dander. Besides, Kara thought, she, too, had a few touchy subjects in her past.

She was a good listener, Jake thought, whether by chance or choice he couldn't decide. However, he felt it was time to switch the focus, get her to talk about herself, maybe satisfy his curiosity.

"Tell me about your father," he began.

"I can't. He died when I was four. I hardly remember him."

"And then?"

He thought he saw a slight tensing around her mouth, but she answered easily enough. "And then I lived with my mother."

"Did she remarry?"

"Yes. Frequently." She toyed with her empty glass, her eyes on the table. A small frown appeared on her forehead.

Go easy here, Jake thought. "I take it you didn't like your stepfather?"

"Stepfathers," she corrected. She gave a small shrug. "Bill was all right. He lasted two years. Hank was a drinker and taught my mother how. I was relieved when he left. After that she stopped marrying them but didn't stop inviting them to live with us."

"Sometimes parents aren't all we wish they were," he said.

She raised deep brown eyes to his. Someone has hurt him, too, she thought. She could hear it in his voice, see it in his eyes. His father? she wondered. "And your mother's dead?"

"Yes. She was a good woman."

"So is my grandmother. Nona's been my salvation. I don't know what I'd have done without her."

"And your mother, is she alone now?"

Her small laugh was bitter. "Probably not. I don't see much of her. She seems to need a man in her life."

"And you don't?"

She gave him an honestly puzzled look. "For what?"

"For what?" he echoed, raising his brows. "Let's start with companionship."

"I've got a dog. Nona lives down the beach from me, and we share him. Figaro's great company, doesn't snore, knows when to keep quiet and never asks me to iron his shirts."

"Figaro? You like opera?"

"Nona named him. Yes, we both like opera."

Well, they had at least two things in common, Jake thought. Opera and Ralph Kramden. Maybe he could find more. "All right, how about support, moral and otherwise? A home to share?" He thought of his warm, loving mother. "Don't you want to settle down, bake cookies in a vine-covered cottage, have someone take care of you, maybe have children?"

"I support myself. I don't need a man to buy me a cottage, vine covered or not." She paused thoughtfully. "I suppose I would like children—one day."

"Okay, what about sex?"

She met his eyes, her gaze level. "What about sex?"

"Women need sex, too."

Kara shook her head as if she were a teacher talking with a slightly slow student. "That's an absurd notion—one that men have perpetuated to get women to fall into bed with them."

He reached over and unexpectedly took her hand, his long fingers caressing the sensitive skin on the inside of her wrist. He watched her eyes grow darker, felt her pulse quicken. "Are you telling me you don't need sex?"

She almost faltered but managed to keep her voice steady. "It's the word 'need' I object to. I never even think of sex unless... unless..." Unless I'm with a man who affects me, she thought. A man like you. She was getting in over her head here.

Turning away from him, Kara gazed with sudden keen interest at several couples shuffling about the small dance floor as Jake studied her profile. "Yes, well, surely one or two men who could move you have wandered across your path through the years?" he persisted, as if he'd read her mind.

"One or two," she answered, deliberately vague. Abruptly, she moved her eyes back to his. "Why don't you forget about my sex life and concentrate on your own?"

His smile was slow and sensuous. He stood, pulling her to her feet, close up against his hard body. "Not a bad idea. Would you care to dance?"

Mistake, her mind clanged in warning. It was a mistake to blurt out off-the-top-of-your-head statements to this man. He had a way of turning them around to his own advantage.

It would have been obvious and insulting to turn him down. Dim amber lighting played across the small dance floor as a slow, sad western tune about unrequited love swirled around them. He was a good dancer, Kara thought, smooth and natural in his movements, holding her much too closely for her peace of mind.

The top of her head came to his chin. She felt the heat rising, his breath warming her suddenly flushed cheeks. There was something undeniably attractive about a man who was so naturally physical. Kara had never before been so aware of a man's body, the way he moved, the effect of his nearness on her senses. It was exhilarating... and frightening.

His hand slid slightly lower down her back, pressing her against the hard length of him. She leaned her head back to look into his eyes, silvery green in the soft shadows. Giving in to an impulse, she did something totally out of character. As if unable to resist, she took her hand from his and brushed her fingers through his tawny beard, something she'd been wanting to do for two days. It felt soft yet bristly. His gaze continued to hold hers as she returned her hand to his. Wordlessly he pulled her closer. This was not smart. This was crazy. This was wonderful. She felt his lips graze her forehead, effectively stopping the flow of her thoughts.

When the band took a break, Jake reluctantly suggested they start the long drive back to Michigan. He walked around the truck, climbed up and crawled into the sleeper. As Kara started out, she placed a familiar classical tape into the cassette player. The star-filled night was a diamond-studded backdrop as she turned onto the highway.

Jake had left the curtain partially open. She inhaled the smell of new leather seats, the lingering aroma of Jake's pipe and his special woodsy scent. Down to her very pores, she was aware of him, lying just inches from her. For a brief moment she allowed herself to remember the warmth of being in his arms as they'd danced, the feel of his beard on her fingertips. With hands shaky on the wheel, she thought about her startling reactions to this virile man and was not pleased with her conclusions.

Despite his cockiness, his self-assurance, his irritating habit of questioning and challenging, she admitted to herself that she liked him. He was good company, intelligent, deeper than he let on and sharp. Very sharp. She reminded herself not to encourage too many good feelings toward him for those emotions had nowhere to go. She was not in the market for Jake or any man at the moment. Certainly not a handsome charmer with a vagabond soul.

Because of their earlier discussion, her thoughts shifted uncomfortably to her mother. She felt depressed at the

picture that came to mind of the near-stranger who'd
given birth to her.

She shook her head. This would never do. The remainder of the trip promised to be difficult enough
without the added burden of struggling with uninvited
ghosts as back seat drivers. She tried to clear her head
and concentrate on her driving. The night stretched out
before her, long and hot and disquieting.

After a full night of driving and a long morning without breakfast, Kara felt tired and hungry. The lunchtime
picnic Jake suggested sounded like a refreshing respite.
Having wordlessly agreed on a truce, fueled by a few
pleasant conversations and perhaps by the memory of the
dance they'd shared, the easing of tensions was welcome
on both sides. The warm noonday sun invited truancy.
They stopped at a highway deli and bought a ridiculous
amount of food then headed for a wooded area by a
small turnoff where they parked the truck.

On foot they followed a gravel path to a shaded clearing on the banks of a stream. After Jake spread an old
blanket, they sat feasting on cold cuts, cheese, crunchy
bread, fruit and iced drinks. In the nearby woods, squir-
rels and chipmunks loudly protested the human invasion
of their playground.

"You look happy," Jake observed as Kara finished her
cola and lay back on the blanket, sighing with contentment. He saw tranquil pleasure on her face as she lifted
it to the warmth of the sun. Unannounced, a shiver of
desire whipped through him.

"I suppose I am. I love peaceful places like this."

He looked at her lush beauty. "Hard to picture you on
a farm."

She shrugged. "Some people are city people and some are country folks."

"And you love the country?"

"Yes. You'd have to bind and gag me to make me live in the heart of a city."

"You surprise me," Jake said, a puzzled frown wrinkling his brow as he lay back and leaned toward her on one elbow. Her reaction had dredged up memories he'd thought long forgotten, of another woman, another beginning. "You look to be more worldly, more cosmopolitan."

"Looks can be deceiving, Jake."

Unable to resist any longer, his hand moved to her hair, his fingers twining around a silken lock. "I still can't believe you'd be content with the simplicity of country living." She returned his look.

"Believe it."

He caressed the smoothness of her cheek with the back of his fingers, then picked up her hand, which rested idly at her side. He seemed to need physical contact, Kara thought, a man whose slightest movement inevitably wound up brushing her hand, her cheek, her hair. The touches seemed impersonal, almost casual, yet she wondered if he was aware how each one affected her. Gently his thumb traced a trembling path along her skin. Everything inside Kara seemed to speed up at his touch. She tried to pull away but he clung. "Jake, please let go."

"You don't like me to hold your hand?"

"It's—very distracting."

"I just want us to get to know one another, become good friends."

Friends. Why is it that friendship didn't seem to be his goal? Someone had to call a halt to this. "I'd say touching is the fastest way to end this friendship before it's be-gun.''

"Oh, it's begun, all right," he continued, with a gleam of mischief in his eyes. "And friendship is only the first step. Then, good friends can become great lovers."

He watched her eyes frost over. Sitting up, she reached for a cluster of grapes and gazed out into the distance as she ate them.

"Do I annoy you, Kara?"

"Annoy, frustrate, infuriate. And that's just the first half of the alphabet." She couldn't put her finger on why she was suddenly angry with him. Or was it with herself for letting him get to her?

"You forgot one." He saw her raise inquisitive brows as she turned to him. "Excite," he said with maddening sureness. He watched as she returned her gaze to the blue sky.

"Who said you excite me?"

He grinned. "You just did."

She sighed, looking off toward the leafy trees over-head. She watched a bird perched on a low-hanging branch cock his head toward her, then chirp hesitantly. "I don't need excitement in my life, Jake," she tried to explain. "I need . . . peace, space and no pressures."

"No, you don't." His gaze roamed over her lovely face, the dark beauty of her hair, the lush figure that jeans and a man's shirt couldn't disguise. "You were made for watching bullfights in Spain, dancing under the stars in Rio, swimming in the nude in Cannes. I believe a woman like you was made for danger, risk, fun." He smiled but his eyes were serious. Was she really as he suspected her to be, or as she insisted she was?

She shook her head. "You don't know me."

He touched her hand again. "*Let* me know you. Tell me more about yourself."

Her sigh was ragged, reluctant. "My life story would bore you to tears."

"I have a feeling, Kara," Jake said, "that you could never bore me."

She gave him a long look, then shifted her gaze toward the gently rolling stream.

Remembering the expensive camera she'd brought along, he decided to try another avenue of approach. "I understand you're a photographer. Did you always want to be?"

She concentrated on the blue of the sky. "Actually I'd always wanted to be a painter. I realized I had an artist's eye, but I didn't have the deep-down talent. Then I discovered photography, and I love it."

"It takes talent to be a good photographer, too. But then, I imagine you'd be good at whatever you set your mind to."

She kept her eyes on the clouds. "I try."

"What are your favorite subjects?"

This was a harmless enough topic, she supposed. Kara searched for the right words. "I have a real affinity for the ocean. I love to photograph its many moods. The sea and children. Both always changing, always new." She sighed deeply. "Last year I found an old house near my grandmother's home. It's on the ocean. I'm in the process of redoing it, room by room. I take a lot of pictures of my house. And my dog and my horse. I like animals better than most people. They're instinctively loyal."

"I take it that means you don't think most people are."

Kara turned to look into his eyes. "A few. Not many."

"Maybe if you had the right traveling companion, you'd change your mind."

"Traveling? Not interested. After this summer I intend to go back home and stay put. I've had all the dragging about, all the running around, all the searching and hunting I'll ever need, and then some. I want to live and work on my little plot of land and watch the world scurry past my door. Spain, Rio, Cannes? Never." She shook her head. "I haven't seen them, and I don't need to. Maybe you do, Jake, but I don't. They don't call to me."

Jake searched her face. Too perfect, he thought. She sounds too perfect. Someone else had once sounded idealistic and honest to him. But she'd turned out to be so much less, wanting much more than he could give her. "Don't rule it out. People change. Never's a long time."

"Like I said, you don't know me."

He got up slowly and pulled her to her feet, holding her hands flat up against his chest. "Not yet I don't. But I'm learning." His eyes moved to her mouth. He touched a finger to her bottom lip and gently traced its fullness. He felt her breathing go suddenly shallow.

"Jake, I . . ."

This was madness, he thought, discouraged with his own lack of willpower. He stepped back from her and glanced toward the sky. "Looks like we might be in for some afternoon rain. We'd better get moving."

Feeling shaken yet oddly disappointed, Kara turned to gather up their picnic things. Jake bent to help her, but she avoided his gaze. Had she wanted the kiss she'd felt sure was coming? Honesty had her gritting her teeth. Obviously she had, maybe more than he, she admitted, a bit chagrined.

In silence they made their way back to the truck. Kara opened the sleeper door and reached for the railing. Close behind her, Jake put his hand on her hair, his touch feather light.

Kara turned her head quickly, realizing too late that it put her mouth dangerously close to his. A shiver went through her as he turned her toward him, bringing them face-to-face. She breathed in the clean, masculine pipe scent of him. *This is stupid,* she reminded herself. *And dangerous.* His beard glinted golden in the sun. She was again tempted to lose her fingers in its softness.

Wary brown eyes searched determined gray. The look held and revealed more than either of them had expected to see. As her blood began to grow warmer, Kara knew she had to do something.

Her voice was low. "Don't push, Mac. I don't take well to pushing."

"I'll make a note of that." He felt a quiver of response ripple along the line of her thighs so very near to his. "You and I will tangle yet, lady. And you know it as well as I do."

With some effort she pushed away from him. Her hand trembled as she grabbed the handrail again and quickly scampered up into the safety of the sleeping compartment. She glanced down at him and tried to look disdainful. "That was both your start and your finish, Mac."

He flashed a self-assured, infuriating smile. "Not by a long shot, lady. And I usually get what I want."

"In a pig's eye, you will," she said, slamming the sleeper door with a resounding thud.

Chapter Three

The early-morning sun was just peeking over the horizon as Kara turned her car into the Santini Trucking parking lot. It had been two weeks since her run with Jake Murphy, two busy hardworking weeks. Within the hour she was scheduled to go out with him again, a fact she faced with mixed emotions.

Louie'd explained it all on the phone to her yesterday, that the only trucker available on the longer California run was Jake. She wanted the exposure of more cities, more stops, more drivers to engage in conversation. If she had to put up with Jake to get it, so be it.

Kara slammed shut the door of her car as her gaze skimmed the lot. Several cabs sat empty, waiting for drivers. A cluster of truckers stood talking and smoking at the far end of the parking area, but she didn't spot the tall, bearded man her eyes had unconsciously sought. She didn't have to. His image was indelibly imprinted in her mind's eye. And therein lies the problem, Kara thought as she stepped into the dispatch office.

Pauly Jones looked up from a pile of papers scattered on her desk and smiled a welcome. "Feeling more like a veteran trucker now that you've got three weeks of runs behind you, honey?" she asked as she motioned Kara to a chair opposite her cluttered desk. She noticed that her friend's usually cheerful smile was slow in appearing this morning, and there were faint smudges of fatigue under her dark eyes.

Kara sighed and dropped into the chair. "I guess so. The new rigs aren't that different. I didn't have any real problem adjusting to them."

Pauly's pale blue eyes narrowed thoughtfully. "It's not the trucks that are bothering you then. Could it be some of the drivers been giving you a hard time? 'Cause if it is, you just tell me which one, and I'll—"

Kara smiled at Pauly's quick protective instincts and shook her head. "No, no, nothing like that. Last week I was with Tennessee Hawkins, and you'd certainly have to go a long way to find a nicer man."

Pauly nodded her head in agreement. "Yeah, he looks like a holy terror with that fiery red hair and that overgrown mustache. And he's so big! But he's a real good family man, nuts about his wife and kids."

"Yes, he is. He called home every chance he got. Did you know his wife's pregnant?"

Pauly frowned. "That'll make four. No wonder Tennessee takes so many extra runs. That man wears himself out trying to make ends meet. He's a former rodeo man, you know."

Kara smiled. "Yes, he told me all about it. He's got this huge belt buckle that he won during his rodeo days— a much larger version of yours. He can scarcely bend over, it's so big. I like him a lot, but I do wish he wasn't addicted to cigar smoking in the cab. You should smell my clothes!''

Pauly, who was in the act of lighting another cigarette from the butt of her last one, smiled sheepishly. "It's a messy habit, all right," she admitted, throwing the butt into an already overflowing ashtray. "I keep meaning to quit but, well, you know."

Kara got up to pour herself a cup of coffee from the pot on the sideboard. "Sure, I know. We all have vices, Pauly."

The thin woman gave her a look of feigned shock. "Not you, too, Kara?"

Kara returned to her seat, laughing. "You bet, me, too. Tell me, when's Uncle Louie due in?"

"Any time now. And how did your run to Kentucky with Cowboy go?"

Kara took a long swallow and leaned back. She felt like saying "disappointing" but knew Pauly wouldn't understand what she meant. Only she and her uncle knew she had been trying to trap a saboteur. But she'd been disappointed again, for she'd learned not one thing from closely observing both Tennessee Hawkins and Cowboy Adams. Nor had she been able to overhear anything suspicious from them or the other truckers she'd run into on any of her runs. Perhaps this week, she thought, trying to swallow her frustrations.

"I guess some things never change," she said in answer to Pauly's question. "And some people. Cowboy's a constant. Driving with him is the same as it's always been. He complains about everything from not enough turnaround time to the rotten food on the road. Every night, he drinks so much I can't imagine he'll be able to find his room much less be able to drive the next day.

And he gambles as much as ever—poker, the ponies, anything. Yet he's fun with his crazy jokes and his off-tune singing. And he's on time, every morning, looking for all the world like he's been sipping mother's milk instead of bourbon.'' She shook her head. ''A hard man to understand but a really fine driver.''

Pauly seemed to let out a long-held breath. ''Did he . . . does he ever mention me?''

Kara watched a faint tinge of pink coloring shade Pauly's face, saw her make a valiant effort to look nonchalant. Lifting her cigarette to her lips with thin, shaky fingers, she busied herself removing a minute speck of lint from her print blouse as she waited for Kara's reply. So that's how it is, Kara thought with sudden understanding.

She'd never seen Pauly and Cowboy together except in the office, but, of course, she'd been away a long time. News of that sort usually got around a company fast yet she hadn't even heard a hint. Who would've guessed that Pauly Jones had more than friendship with Cowboy in mind?

Kara's voice was soft, gentle. ''How long, Pauly?''

Nervously the older woman stubbed out her cigarette. ''Too long.'' She tried a small laugh. ''Forget I asked, will you, honey?''

''Have you told him how you feel?''

''It wouldn't do any good. I been around rodeo men, cowboys and truckers a lot of years, and I should know better. Cowboy's not the marrying type. And I don't want anymore of the other kind.''

There was a sadness, a poignancy to her that moved Kara. She found herself at a loss for words. Acting on instinct, she went around the desk and bent to hug Pauly's thin frame, offering the only comfort she could.

Pauly squeezed her hand, blinked rapidly several times then straightened her shoulders.

"Enough of that. I see by the manifest that you're going out with Jake this morning. What do you think of him? I don't hear you complaining about his smelly pipe."

Kara took her time walking back to her chair, a slow frown on her face. "What do I think of Jake Murphy? I think he's arrogant, demanding, conceited, cocky, argumentative..."

A wide grin appeared on Pauly's small features. "You like him," she stated.

Kara paused a moment then laughed out loud. "Yes. I even like that blasted pipe." She sighed, looking suddenly thoughtful.

Pauly leaned forward, hearing more in her young friend's silence than in her words. "Nona's getting on in years, honey, and I know you're not close to your mom. I hate to sound like Ann Landers, but I do have a little mileage in the men department—if you ever want to talk."

Kara was touched. "Thanks, Pauly, but there really isn't anything to talk about." Not yet there wasn't. How could she put into words what she herself couldn't understand? Mind meanderings, vagrant thoughts, wispy fantasies. It was so new to her, this distracting dreaminess.

"Would you come to me if you needed someone?" Pauly asked softly. She sensed a reluctant need in Kara.

"I...probably," Kara answered vaguely, suddenly anxious to end this conversation. She'd never been very good at girl talk, confiding in people, especially when she was uncertain about her feelings. There'd never been anyone except Nona, and she'd hated to worry her grandmother with her troubles. So she'd learned to cope, to handle her own problems. She would handle this, too, she was sure.

Kara stood, looking at her watch. "Listen, Pauly, I think Uncle Louie's been held up. I've got to get going. Tell him I was in, will you, and that I'll catch him next time. Maybe I'll call him from California before the return trip."

Pauly watched the tall, slender woman make her way to the door and nodded. "Sure, honey. Have a safe trip." She sighed and reached for her cigarettes. Kara had a man on her mind as sure as shootin'. And she'd bet her last dime that it was that bearded pirate. Men, she thought, as she struck a match into flame. We can't seem to live with them, or without them.

As she stepped out into the early-morning sunshine, Kara put on her sunglasses and watched a man raise the flag on the pole alongside the dispatch office. If the weather continued, they'd have a warm Fourth of July weekend, she thought. Walking toward the rigs, her gaze shifted to the right and found Jake. Squatting on his haunches by the truck, he patted the head of a sleek rust-colored beagle.

Again she was surprised at how her heart picked up its beat with just a look at him. The color and texture of his golden hair contrasting with the crisp whiteness of his shirt appealed to both the woman and the photographer in Kara. She longed for her camera to capture him while her fingers ached to tangle in the rough silk of his hair. Already considering angles and lenses, she decided he'd make an interesting subject. Maybe, if she studied the resulting picture long and hard at her leisure, she could discern what it was about him that fascinated her so.

The man was an enigma. Perhaps he was an adventurer, yet she sensed he was more. She knew he was interested only in a brief physical relationship just as she knew she was not. If and when she chose to involve herself with a man, she knew she wanted more. Her mother had never been able to find it. Would she? she wondered. In the meantime she felt content with the life she'd mapped out for herself. Still, she could not deny that she found Jake Murphy very interesting. As she discovered new layers of the man, like peeling paper from a wall to uncover what was hidden underneath, he became more intriguing to her.

She'd thought of him far too often the past two weeks—that she was still thinking about him disturbed her. She was, after all, not a teenager but a grown woman. She could recall exactly the way his hard body had fit against hers as they'd danced, awakening her. And the pleasurable memory didn't please her.

Across the lot their eyes met and held. Each felt the instant attraction, yet sensed the innate hesitation in the other.

Jake rubbed the dog's soft fur, unable to take his eyes from Kara as she walked toward him. He wanted her more every time he saw her. Her face reminded him of forbidden things. That wild mane of hair and eyes the color of melted chocolate. Her gaze was direct, measuring, unwavering, causing a fluttering in his chest. There was a hint of color mixed with her tan, a rosy splash, or was it a reflection from the bright red blouse she wore?

He averted his gaze and stroked the dog's shiny coat. No complications or pressures here, he thought, patting the strong head. Just unswerving loyalty and boundless love. Kara was right. People could take a few lessons from animals, he decided as the dog licked his hand gratefully.

"Well, Mac," her smooth voice said as her shadow fell across him, "are you ready to ride off into the sunset once more?"

His bold eyes traveled up the length of her legs barely outlined in loose-fitting cotton slacks, stopping at his own reflection in her glasses. He was pleased to see a small muscle twitch at her jawline. With a last pat on the dog's rump, he stood, facing her.

"Ready when you are, boss." He reached into his pocket and retrieved a key, holding it out to her. "Thought you might want to recheck the load." His gray-green gaze challenged her.

She thought better of pushing him too far on that point again. "I think I'll trust you this time," she answered, tossing her bags into the back compartment. "I'll start out. You look like you didn't get enough sleep last night."

Jake reached for his sunglasses, partly as a defense from her sharp look, partly to hide his reddened eyes. Pretty funny observation, he thought, coming from the one responsible for his restless nights. He held out his hand to help her up.

He watched her dark eyes study his face as she placed her hand in his. Resting in his rough palm, her hand felt smooth, the skin soft and silky. He wondered how the rest of her would feel—the pulse point at her throat, the satin of her long legs, the sweet swell of her breast. He swallowed with difficulty and reminded himself sternly that this woman could spell trouble.

Kara grabbed the handrail and quickly jumped up into the cab and slid behind the wheel. Jake slammed her door and walked around to take his seat beside her. She adjusted her mirrors and headed the big semi out toward the highway with ease. Driving smoothly, she occupied herself with studying traffic. If Jake wanted to nap this morning—and he did look as if he could use one—she wouldn't disturb him with small talk.

He tried for a while, stretching out his long legs, pulling his baseball cap low over his eyes and crossing his arms over his chest. But it just wouldn't work and he found himself squirming and shuffling all over the seat, trying to get comfortable. At last he gave up and turned toward her, placing his left arm along the back. "How did the past two weeks go for you?" he asked, staring at her profile.

"Fine. And you?"

Jake searched for his pipe. "We had a little incident last week outside of Kansas. You know Big Jim Forester?"

"Sure. He's been with Louie eight or nine years. A good driver. Why?"

"He and I were taking a shipment of auto parts to Denver. The trailer broke away from the cab, veered off and crashed down a gully. It missed us by inches."

"Oh, no! You could have been badly hurt or..." She couldn't complete the thought. Here she'd been so busy with her own thoughts that she hadn't even asked Pauly when they'd talked earlier if there'd been any accidents. This was getting serious.

"We were lucky." Jake ground his teeth in remembered anger. Both he and Big Jim had checked that coupling. It had happened right after they'd had lunch at a popular truck-stop restaurant off the highway. At least a dozen truckers had been there, some he knew, including several from Santini. Had one of them taken a chance like that, messing around a truck in a crowded lot? Someone was getting anxious and more daring.

"And the cargo, was it salvageable?"

He shook his head. "Ruined."

Kara glanced at his hard face. He wasn't as unaffected by the close call as he pretended to be, she thought. Poor Louie. She wondered how long he'd be able to afford his insurance rates with so many claims. When she'd talked with him earlier, he'd mentioned that it was already a problem. "Any ideas on who might be behind it?"

"No, have you?"

"I can't think of anyone who'd want to harm Louie. He's honest and fair with everyone."

Jake busied himself filling his pipe. "It's not happening just at Santini. Ace Trucking, Carson Brothers and several others have all reported problems."

Kara changed lanes carefully, then brought her attention back to their conversation. "They seem to be hitting the smaller companies, the ones with nonunionized truckers. Do you think it's an attempt to unionize?"

His eyes were hooded as he drew on his pipe. "Possibly. But not likely. It's not the usual way union organizers go about things. And these smaller trucking companies have been in business for years. Why now? It sounds to me more like a man with a purpose has found someone with a weakness. Or several someones. It's all been petty stuff so far, but crippling when you add it all up. And costly." His eyes swung to her. "Know anybody with a weakness?"

She continued to stare ahead. "Everyone's got weaknesses, Jake. Of one sort or another."

"Do they now? You, too?"

Oh, yes, she thought. Definitely me, too. Remembering what Pauly had said, Kara hoped those penetrating green eyes of Jake's wouldn't easily spot her weaknesses. "Everyone, Jake. Even you." His sunglasses hid his expression, but she watched him closely as he offered a small smile and continued puffing on his pipe. She adjusted the air-conditioning vents to redirect the smoke and tried again. "What kind of weaknesses did you mean?"

"Someone who could be blackmailed easily, for something in his past. Or someone who likes money and is in desperate need of more. Someone with lots of ambition and no scruples. Or perhaps a man with a grudge to settle, if not with Louie then with another person. Know anyone like that?"

She considered his question a long moment, wondering over his intense curiosity. "Not really. I've known most of the men at Santini from the start. Except Tennessee. And you."

"Could be a woman, you know."

She laughed. "A woman under the truck loosening brakes, uncoupling rigs? Somehow, I doubt it."

"Stranger things have happened," Jake said, shifting in his seat.

Kara sighed. "I wonder if we'll recognize the one responsible if we run across him. He may be among us even now."

Jake felt fairly certain she was right, surprised she'd given it so much thought. But then, her feelings for Louie ran deep. "Probably right."

"If he works for Louie and has his confidence and is accepted by his co-workers, I wonder how we'll ever spot him. I wish there was some sign, some way we could tell."

"Kara, are you so naive that you think good guys wear white hats and bad guys wear black?"

"No," she answered, wondering what color he belonged in, given that designation. She still wasn't a hundred percent convinced he was squeaky clean. "But it would certainly help."

Jake glanced down at the seat between them and found a manila envelope. Picking it up, he asked, "This yours?"

"Yes. They're pictures I took before I left California. I just finished developing them, and since we're headed that way, I thought that I'd drop them off."

"Whose are they?"

"A young couple who live about a half mile down the beach from my house. Snapshots of their two children."

"Mind if I look at them?"

She hesitated only a moment. "No."

He saw a brief frown appear momentarily on her forehead as she agreed. Opening the packet, he studied the photos. The boy was about six, a solemn youngster with deep-set eyes and pale, windblown hair. She'd caught him building sand castles, the sun haloing his head and revealing the intense expression of a young dreamer. The girl was no more than three, chubby and round faced, her blue eyes reflecting her happiness as she chased a wave, watched sand filter through her fingers and happily poured a pail of water on her indignant brother's head. They were good. They were more than good. They captured the special joy of carefree childhood.

"I suppose you know you're very good at what you do?" he asked, putting the pictures away.

His praise pleased her more than it should have. "Thank you," she answered. Satisfaction in her own work was usually enough for her. That and pleasing her clients. When had this man's opinions become important to her? she wondered.

"Do you have an agent promoting your work? A lady like you, full of drive, can go far. But I imagine you already know that."

The frown returned to Kara's face. "No. No agent. I don't think you understand." She took a deep breath, wondering if he ever would. "I opened my photography studio two years ago. We take pictures for people on assignment, an author writing a book or for magazine layouts. We do groups or individuals. I take pictures *of* people *for* people. Sometimes I take pictures of neighbors' children just for fun."

"You have talent. With the right promotion and advice, you could make a lot of money."

"I really don't have the need for a lot of money, just enough so I won't have to rely on others."

"I'd say from the look of things that you do all right." Was she naive or just trying to sound that way?

She glanced at him. "What's that supposed to mean?"

Jake stretched out his long legs before him and didn't look at her as he spoke. "Oh, just putting two and two together. I know a little something about real estate and that house on the California coast that you described doesn't come cheap. You drive a mighty expensive little sports car. You probably have a spiffy wardrobe for when you're not driving trucks, plenty of jewelry. You probably plan to buy a few more Arabians to keep your horse company. You likely have a fur coat or two. Have I missed anything?" He let out a snort of a laugh. "All women love money and the things it can buy."

Her eyes narrowed as she gave him a long, studying look. She couldn't keep a note of disbelief from coloring her voice. "Is that how you see me?" She shook her head, swinging her gaze back to the road. "I own two pieces of good jewelry, this gold chain I'm wearing and the pearl ring Uncle Louie gave me at graduation. You've seen most of my wardrobe, and what's at home is more of the same. I like comfortable clothes. My house was a good buy, not inexpensive but far from palatial. The bank thinks I'm a good risk. Prince is a beautiful chestnut, and I'm still paying for him, too. I have no interest in Arabians. And what would I do with a fur coat in California?'' She frowned, honestly puzzled. ''I'm certainly not the only one who feels like this. Where do you get your information on women?''

''From women. And many are not what they seem to be.''

She sat silently for long minutes as he puffed on his pipe, his chin set, his gaze fastened on the distant horizon. She took the envelope from him and moved it back on the seat between them. ''I didn't realize you were such a cynic. These are going to Marge and Bill—for their photo album. Period.''

Jake took off his sunglasses and turned to her. ''I don't get it. What's your game, Kara?''

''Game?''

''Sure. Game. Ploy. Plan. Everyone's got one. What's yours?''

For the flash of an instant, anger flared in her brown eyes as she met his then disappeared as she turned to face the road. ''You know, I feel sorry for you. I'm exactly as you see me. I can't help it if you won't accept that.''

''Just a simple little small-town girl who wants to spend her life snapping pictures of children playing in the sand, are you?'' Memories flooded his mind, of another time, another woman, making him believe, making him care. Then, when she had what she wanted, she changed her tune. He rubbed his beard in a gesture of annoyance. ''That scenario doesn't fit what I see.''

"And just what is it that you think you see?"

"I see a beautiful woman who's smart enough to know she can have it all. With your looks and talent, all you'd have to do is smile at the right guy and he'd set you up for life. Maybe even marry you. Then, when you didn't need him anymore, you could always dump him. With a full bank account, you could go back to taking pictures for fun."

Thoroughly annoyed and still pushing back the anger, Kara took a deep breath. "Let me tell you a little story," she began, her eyes on the road ahead. "They tell me my father was a hotheaded Italian with more dreams than good sense. He was always chasing a get-rich scheme down a nowhere alley, my mother running after him and dragging me with her. He died penniless when I was four. It took my mother exactly two years to find another dreamer to marry. It took him less time than that to walk out on both of us—and so it went."

Memories flooded back and Kara fought their painful grip. Angry with herself that she'd let him push her into reliving it all, she still needed to make him see. "My mother wasn't good at holding down a job and even worse at managing the little money we had. Soon, there was a succession of men. Mother wasn't good at handling things alone. When I was fifteen, she decided she could do better without the excess baggage and sent me to live with my grandmother."

Unaware that her features had softened, she went on. "Nona and I lived on my grandfather's small pension, but we managed just fine. She offered me spaghetti and stability, home cooking and warm loving. Uncle Louie visited often. He's a nice man, a little gruff, but he has a soft heart. However, times were tough and his business wasn't great. Even with their help, it took me six years to work my way through college. But I made it.

"I've paid Uncle Louie back for every dime he's spent on me, and I never want to be indebted to anyone again. I don't need a man to set me up for life—*or* marry me, thank you. I do just fine on my own."

"I've heard other women say that and not mean it."

She turned her gaze to him, her eyes widening with sudden understanding. She'd thought his father had hurt him, and maybe he had. But so had someone else, she thought. A woman. And she'd done a good job of it. "Not every woman is like her, Jake," she said quietly.

He kept his face hard, expressionless. "You sound like an idealist."

She sighed, wishing she could get through to him. "I'm a realist, Jake. For years I watched my mother play games, and I've seen that it's brought her nothing but loneliness and pain, and it's hurt the people who cared about her, too. It's hard to trust people once you've been hurt, but I think you miss a lot by not taking that risk."

"And if you get kicked in the teeth by someone you trusted, then what? Do you dust yourself off and lead with your chin again?"

"People only take advantage of you if you let them. My mother no longer can. I send her money now because I choose to, out of pity more than anything. She can't hurt me because I won't let her. Someone can hurt you only if you give them permission, if you let yourself become a victim."

They rode in silence, her words hanging in the air. In the reflection of the windshield, Kara saw his frown. That woman had done more than hurt him, she reflected. She'd disillusioned him. Was that why he'd spent the last few years wandering the globe—was he running from a betrayal? It seemed both of them had ghosts riding with them.

Kara spotted a sign heralding a rest stop ahead two miles. "How about some coffee?" she asked. "I think we could stand with a little stretching." She saw him nod, but he was still lost in his own thoughts.

They shared some coffee inside the nearly empty restaurant. Kara walked outside and strolled around while Jake had their thermos filled. She needed to get some air, clear her mind. Conversations with Jake usually left her feeling vaguely uneasy. She'd hoped that when she saw him again, she'd find his appeal diminished. Instead, it had only intensified, and she frowned as she gazed about at the green, hilly landscape.

She'd meant to maintain a casual, friendly attitude toward Jake. She'd purposely avoided him these past weeks and had faced seeing him again with both anticipation and dread. He was trouble. The attraction that had flared so quickly between them frightened her. She'd had little experience with men and even less with emotional involvements. Her head had always been in charge of her heart. But now she wasn't quite sure.

She knew he wanted her, had recognized the signs long before he'd first touched her. She could handle a mere physical attraction. Under other circumstances she might have even enjoyed tangling with him, though he wouldn't be an easy man to handle.

But after some of their conversations, she acknowledged the stirrings of an emotional tugging that worried her. She saw a vulnerability in him that drew her. Professionally, she admired, respected and trusted him. Personally, he scared the hell out of her. Only a shortsighted woman would want to get mixed up with an arrogant man who distrusted women and showed signs of having all the stability of a gypsy moth. She'd always been a long-range planner.

Kara started back toward the truck, distracted by her disturbing thoughts. She nearly bumped into Jake as he jumped down from the cab. "Ready to roll?" she asked, putting on her hat.

Without the barrier of his sunglasses, his eyes were smoky gray and searching. "Not quite," he answered. "I've thought about this for two weeks. I have to taste you." His head lowered, his arms encircled her and his mouth captured hers. Taken aback, Kara's hands clutched at his upper arms to keep herself from falling. Her hat fell to the ground unheeded as she clamped her teeth together, resisting the shattering persuasion of his kiss.

She thought about struggling against him, but before she could react, she was deeply involved. It wasn't the hard, conquering kiss she might have expected from him. It was soft and persuasive, all the more potent in its fervor.

At first Jake tasted anger on her lips and chose to ignore it. Shifting his mouth on hers, he deepened the kiss, taking full possession, tasting, plundering. At last he felt her give up the fight and begin to respond. He felt lost inside of her, his need greater than any he'd known. How could this one small slip of a woman bring him to his knees, weak with desire?

Senses swimming, Kara clung to him. Here was a man with hidden gentleness cloaked in steely strength, and the combination captivated her. She was inexplicably drawn to the streak of wildness she sensed in him, yet his tenderness won her over. With a low-throated groan, he moved her closer, not allowing the sweetness of their melding to diminish for a moment.

Her hands, which should have been pushing him away, moved up his back, curving toward his shoulders, answering his need to be nearer. Desire awakened within her, and she returned his kiss, burying her lips in the softness between his mustache and beard, reveling in the bristly feel of him. It had been so long, so very long since she'd felt so much, wanted so desperately. Or had she ever?

Drawing back from her, he studied her face. He'd promised himself he'd stay in control, and he'd failed miserably. But who could resist her desire-softened eyes, her full mouth that was made for savoring? Feeling her gradually withdrawing, he cupped the back of her head with his hand and pressed his mouth to hers until she was weak and nearly limp in his arms.

Abruptly he released her. He saw that her eyes were slightly unfocused, filled with arousal and confusion. He'd wanted to catch her off guard, and it seemed he had. As she returned to reality, chips of anger flared to a blaze in her brown eyes.

Kara raised her arm, ready to slap him. Watching his face, she saw the hint of triumph in his eyes and knew he'd grab her arm before she could connect. But what really stopped her was the knowledge that she had no right. How could she slap a man for kissing her when she'd participated in that kiss as thoroughly as he had? Furious with herself, realizing she'd responded to him when she hadn't intended to, she took a step back. "Why did you feel you had to do that?"

"I didn't *have* to do that. I *wanted* to do it. I warned you that one day we'd tangle."

She sighed heavily and picked up her hat with trembling hands. "I thought we'd been over all this. We're going to be driving together, probably frequently, all summer. I have a responsibility to my uncle and to his company. I take my work, *any* work I do, seriously. I hope you do, too. There's a lot of other truckers in our company and others we meet on the road. Personal involvements cloud your judgment, and soon you become Topic A for a lot of people. I don't intend to become Topic A, and I don't intend to get involved with you. Not now, not later, not ever. Have you got that straight?''

He arched his brows, a skeptical look on his face. ''Not ever, as in never? I don't think you mean that.''

''I don't care what you think as long as you stay on your side of the seat and behave yourself.''

He stood with the thumb of one hand hooked in the belt of his jeans, his stance defiant, his eyes challenging. His smile was maddeningly confident. After the contemplative morning, his arrogance had returned full force. ''You'll change your mind.''

''I most certainly will not!''

''Yes, you will. I can be a very patient man.''

She saw red. ''You're a very infuriating, egotistical—''

''Now, now. You should watch that temper of yours.'' He took a step closer. ''But then, you usually do, don't you, Kara? Always in control, so cool, unapproachable. You like it that way so no one can get close enough to hurt you. You respond like a hot, passionate woman but underneath it's all chipped ice, isn't it? You talk to me about trust, yet you're afraid to feel, to let yourself care about someone. It doesn't fit into the game plan you say you have for yourself, does it? You're afraid if you let someone get close to you that you'll turn out like your mother, aren't you?''

She released an involuntary breath, as if someone had hit her nicely and neatly in the stomach. Her face went

pale and her eyes turned dark as she pulled free of him
and ran toward the back of the building.

With a muttered oath, Jake went after her. He caught
her easily as she turned the corner. His touch was gentle
as he turned her to face him.

"Let go of me!" Her voice was low, filled with pain.

"Did I hit a nerve? Maybe you needed to hear that."

"Don't tell me what I need!" Her eyes had a wounded
look that aroused both guilt and sympathy in him. He
longed to pull her into his arms, comfort her, take away
the hurt, but he knew she'd never allow it.

"Kara, I'm sorry. I don't usually come on like a herd
of elephants." Perhaps he'd pushed her too far.

She stared into his eyes for a long moment. Seeing his
sincerity, she slowly let go of her anger, swallowed her
hurt. "It's okay. I don't usually overreact quite so dra-
matically."

"Can we have a truce, at least for the balance of this
run?" He saw traces of suspicion in her dark eyes, knew
she'd be even more wary of him now.

Another truce. Why the hell not? She wondered how
long it would last this time. Wordlessly she started back
toward the truck. With his long-legged gait, he quickly
caught up. "Well?" he persisted.

"What do you want, a lifetime pledge of peace between us?"

"Maybe."

She stopped, turning to face him, her eyes unreadable. "I am who I am, Jake, and you want too much."

He watched her walk away. What was she afraid of? he
wondered. She'd told him something of her childhood,
but he felt there was more she wasn't telling him. Perhaps she didn't know herself. And why, he asked himself, was he spending so much time trying to figure her

out? He had a job to do and it did not involve Kara Finelli. Following her to the truck, Jake sighed. It appeared this run would be more unsettling than their last trip had been, if that was possible.

The afternoon dragged by. Kara stayed in the sleeper while Jake drove, his thoughts scattered. A driver he knew casually who drove for Allied Trucking had stopped to chat with him while his thermos was being filled. One of their trucks had been tinkered with, and a crash had been narrowly averted last week. The owners were getting jittery, and Jake couldn't blame them. If only he could get a handle on who and why... When they got to California, he'd check with Rob. Maybe his network of feelers had picked up something they could use.

Jake chewed on the stem of his empty pipe. Unerringly his thoughts returned to another disturbing topic: Kara.

It was sex, he told himself, pure and simple. She was a damned attractive woman, and he wanted her. She turned him on, that was all. He'd win her over, have her and be done with it. Then he'd be free of these unrelenting thoughts. After all, he was thirty-two, and he'd gone around the track quite a few times with all kinds of women. He wasn't some young kid thrown for a loop by the nearness of a beauty. He certainly knew the difference between a passing fancy and a risky involvement. He'd handle Kara. He knew he could.

They stopped for dinner at a steak house just before crossing the state line into Missouri. Kara's nap had improved her disposition somewhat. Though her eyes were still guarded, Jake managed to involve her in polite conversation as they sat in a red vinyl booth by the front window.

Searching for safe topics, Kara asked about the large selection of tapes that she'd seen in the cab, noting that his musical taste ran from classical to pop and even country and western. Finishing their coffee, they were deep in a discussion of jazz classics when a commotion at the register captured their attention. Kara turned to see a husky boy of about seventeen struggling with a slight lad who resembled him enough to be his brother. No more than six, the youngster appeared frightened, his thin face tear streaked and pale under his freckles.

Too far away to hear, they watched in silence as the argument continued. When the teenager slapped the boy sharply across the cheek and shoved him out the door, Kara drew in a quick breath. Jake's hand on her shoulder stopped her from getting up. She started to protest, but he moved quickly past her and out the door.

Through the window she watched as he caught up with the pair, the older one holding the youngster roughly by one thin arm. In the dim twilight she saw Jake's eyes narrow dangerously. As the older boy listened, his eyes grew round with fear. He made one weak attempt at protesting the interference but dropped his hand from the youngster. With a last surly glance, he sauntered toward a beat-up car and climbed in. The tires squealed as he shot out of the parking lot.

Kara saw Jake take out his handkerchief and bend down in front of the boy, gently wiping his face. They talked a moment, then the youngster put his hand into Jake's, and they walked back into the restaurant. Jake signaled to the manager and went to talk with him. Kara picked up her purse and joined them at the register.

The round-faced manager seemed upset. "That kid's just plain bad news," he said, gesturing out the window. "His parents kicked him out, and now he just lives here and there with friends. His brother, Danny here, is staying with his grandparents while his folks are on a trip. The grandparents run a little country store outside St. Louis. Don't know why Kevin dragged Danny all this way.''

Jake looked down at Danny, his small hand still nestled in his big grasp. ''He tells me that Kevin convinced him to go for a ride with him and promised to take him to the movies if Danny brought his piggy bank along. Kevin broke it open, took the money, and of course, there was no movie. I think we'd better call Danny's grandparents and let them know we're bringing him home.''

The manager shook his balding head. ''Can't reach them. It's after six and their store's closed. They don't have a phone in their house.''

Jake's scowl deepened. ''Can you tell me where they live?''

''Sure. Just across the border into Missouri. But maybe you'd better turn him over to the State Police. What if his grandparents already have them out looking for him? You could get in a mess of trouble, taking a kid across state lines.''

Jake's thoughtful gaze strayed to Danny and Kara. With her arm about his thin shoulders, she knelt beside him and helped him put some pennies into a gumball machine. The tiny balls plopped into his small hand, and he laughed with delight. Instinctively the boy trusted them both. When Kara's eyes moved from the child to Jake's face, he reached into his pocket, took out a piece of paper and handed it to the man behind the register.

''Write down their name and address and directions to the house, would you? Police would just frighten Danny further. We'll take him home.''

''Mister, I wouldn't do this if I were you.''

Jake's smile didn't reach his eyes. "But you're *not* me. Write down the address." While Jake paid the bill, the manager did as requested without another word.

Kara settled the boy on her lap as Jake swung out onto the highway. Shyly at first, then more animatedly, Danny chattered about his first ride in a big truck, his blue eyes excited. Evening shadows lengthened as they drove. The steady swaying movement of the ride caused the lad's heavy eyelids to close. As the boy leaned into Kara's softness, Jake watched her shift his weight to a more comfortable position on her lap and touch his fair hair, a gentle smile on her face.

Without forethought, Jake reached over and lightly brushed a strand of hair from her cheek. She raised her eyes to his for a long moment, but she didn't speak. Something's happening here, he thought as he wrestled with a rush of unexpected feeling. Something he wasn't prepared for and didn't want. A quick affair was one thing but anything more meant problems. The last thing he needed in his life now were complications, and Kara Finelli would definitely prove to be a complication.

Her throaty voice cut through the silence. "Why are you doing this, taking a chance? There were alternatives."

He was lost in thought, and a few moments passed before he answered. "Sometimes the chances you take have a price tag, but not taking them has a higher one."

She stared at his shadowed profile long after he'd shifted his gaze back to the road. No one she'd known had ever perplexed her more than Jake Murphy. His hand-tooled leather boots cost more than most trucker's boots, as did the gold Rolex watch he wore. At ease with the men, respected by Louie and admired by several feminine glances she'd witnessed already, he appeared confident and smooth. Maybe too much so.

His conversation, his taste, his manner hinted at a more extensive education than she'd originally suspected. And here he was, the tender champion of a mistreated little boy, shooting holes in his tough-guy image. She'd known him a scant three weeks, quite a few of those days spent closeted mere inches apart night and day as they drove, yet he left her with a bundle of mixed impressions.

Kara studied his large hands on the steering wheel, loosely resting yet alert. They hinted at strength and power, both of which sat easily on his shoulders. Certainly attractive qualities. And, without closing her eyes, she could remember the way his soft, urgent mouth had molded to hers so perfectly, the exciting way he'd made her feel just this afternoon. Then there was that vagabond nature, the wanderlust that had him traveling the world in search of... of what? She'd seen enough free-spirited men stroll in and out of her mother's life to last her a lifetime—two lifetimes.

Every light in the house was ablaze as Jake stopped in front of Danny's grandparents' small bungalow. He jumped down and walked around, opening Kara's door. Standing on the high step, he gazed for a moment at the small boy cuddled in Kara's lap. He saw the gentle expression on her face and noticed how at home she looked with the child. Not as tough as she tried to appear, Jake thought.

Kara angled toward him on the seat as he slid his arms under and around the boy. He saw a wistful look darken the brown depths of her eyes as she reluctantly handed her warm bundle over to him.

Holding Danny, Jake stepped down just as a tall, gray-haired man came out onto the porch, evidently having heard the big semi wheeze to a stop. Kara watched as Jake spoke to the man and gave him the sleeping child. The smile on the older man's face was tinged with gratitude as he embraced his grandson. In moments Jake returned and headed the big truck back toward the highway and on to their destination.

Yes, there was a lot more to Jake Murphy than he let most people see, Kara thought as she settled back in her seat and closed her eyes. Nevertheless, what she saw was a man she'd better keep at a distance.

Chapter Four

The unexpectedly balmy summer weather held up, and so did their tentative truce as they journeyed westward. For the next two days they drove, ate and talked together as a couple of friends might, avoiding any comments that might inflame. Kara dared hope that Jake was backing off as she saw him give her some badly needed breathing room.

On the third morning Kara sat on the passenger side, lost in the scenery and her thoughts, when the sound of a siren close behind them brought her out of her reverie. Angling her head to check in the side mirror, she saw the sheriff's car with red light flashing, signaling them over.

"Were you speeding?" she asked Jake as he slowed to pull over on the shoulder of the highway.

"No, I had the cruise control on," he said with a scowl. "I don't know what they want." Opening his door, Jake jumped down as one of the burly officers approached, hand on his holster. "What's the problem, Officer?" Jake asked.

"Let's see your driver's license," he said without preamble. As Jake dug out his wallet, the other policeman opened Kara's door and ordered her out. She walked over to join Jake, a puzzled frown on her face.

"Your ID, too, please," the first officer told Kara.

From her purse she handed him her chauffeur's license and stood watching as he examined both permits.

"Radio these in, Pete," the burly man said, handing them to his partner. Turning to Kara, he looked her up and down thoroughly, his suspicious eyes missing nothing. Removing a folded paper from his pocket, he studied it a moment, then swung his gaze back to Kara.

Jake had had enough. "Could you tell us what this is about? Have we violated a law? What's going on?"

Ignoring Jake's questions, the officer stuffed his paper back into his pocket and turned to him. "Let me have your cargo key," he demanded gruffly.

Annoyed but unwilling to make a scene, Jake shoved a hand into his pocket and gave him the key.

"Stay right here," he told them as he walked to the back of the truck.

Kara heard him open the cargo door and scramble up into the trailer. She'd been stopped occasionally by State Police or sheriff's deputies in the past when she'd driven for her uncle during her summers, but the officers had always been polite and respectful. These two seemed to have left their manners back at the station. She turned to see Jake thoughtfully studying the tall policeman talking on the patrol car radio.

"I can't imagine why we're being hassled like this," she commented, crossing her arms over her chest and leaning back against the truck. "Do you think it has something to do with some of the trucking incidents?"

"Maybe," Jake answered. The thought had occurred to him, too. He knew he'd kept his speed down, personally checked their cargo and had even gone over their truck this morning as he usually did, just in case. In his line of work, it paid to be cautious. But these surly, nononsense deputies worried him.

At last, the burly cop refastened the door and came back to them. Wordlessly he handed Jake the key, turned and opened the sleeper compartment door and slowly pulled himself up. They stood watching as he carefully and thoroughly searched the compartment, checking out even the refrigerator and running his hands over and under the bedding.

With a tense jaw, Jake stepped back as the officer jumped down and next climbed into the cab, examining under the seat, in the glove compartment and finally studying their manifest. Jake knew better than to challenge a small-town cop with a badge and a gun in a hip holster. But this waiting and wondering was making him jumpy. Were they searching for stolen merchandise? Trucking violations? He could demand more information, but it might involve breaking his cover, and he couldn't risk that. Silently he watched and waited.

The tall officer slammed the patrol car door and walked toward them as the heavier one backed down out of the cab. The two of them moved off to the side, turning their backs to Jake and Kara, conferring in whispers. Jake shoved his hands into his pockets, seething inside, his mouth a grim line.

Standing next to him, Kara touched his arm. He turned his head toward her, feeling the warmth of her fingers, recognizing in her brown eyes that she understood his frustration. Somehow it eased his mood, and he gave her a tight smile.

The shorter deputy turned and, removing his hat, scratched his balding head as he walked toward them. On his face was a slightly sheepish look. "Sorry to hold you up like this, but we've been following you the last twenty miles or so, and we both agreed we'd have to stop and check you out. You're both clean so you can be on your way."

Frowning, Jake jerked his hands out of his pockets and took a step toward the man, mindful of Kara's fingers tightening on his arm but too annoyed to heed her unspoken warning. "Wait a minute. What was all that about? Why were you following us?"

Shuffling his feet, the man looked a shade uncomfortable as his partner turned and walked back to their car. "We were trailing behind you by chance when we got this radio report that a runaway teenage girl had been spotted riding with a trucker, and it looked like he was heading across the state line with her. The description said she's kind of small with long black hair and dark eyes, only sixteen."

He nodded toward Kara. "Pete and I saw you and thought . . . well, we had to make sure."

Indignation pinkened Kara's face as realization hit her. She drew herself up taller and stared him down as she heard Jake's hoot of laughter ring out. "Sixteen? You thought I was sixteen?"

Uncomfortable now, the deputy held up a hand as if warding off a possible attack from her. "Don't go gettin' mad, lady," he said, noting the sudden fire in her eyes. "Nowadays it's hard to tell about women's ages." He glanced at Jake as if looking for corroboration.

But Jake was too busy struggling to hold in a tension-releasing laugh, now that he knew there really wasn't a problem. Though he felt the two policemen had been a bit heavy-handed, he realized they probably had acted in good conscience. Still, he'd let the self-important little deputy deal with Kara's wrath, he thought, stifling another chuckle. Maybe it'd teach him a lesson.

"Officer," she said, her clenched hands propped on her slim hips, her eyes blazing, "I'm twenty-seven, not sixteen, with eight years experience driving these rigs and I..." Running out of steam, she decided to consider the source, and, giving him a dismissing wave, she turned away, mumbling under her breath. "Of all the bumbling, stumbling, nearsighted excuses for police officers I have *ever* met..." Jerking open the cab door, she hopped up and angrily slammed it shut.

The officer watched her departure and heaved a sigh of relief. "Women," he muttered, sending another conspiratorial look toward Jake, looking for confirmation.

Jake decided to come through. Nodding, he gave him a small smile of agreement. Grinning, the deputy replaced his hat and tipped two fingers to the bill before turning back to his patrol car.

Swallowing his smile, Jake climbed up into the driver's seat and shifted into gear. Out of the corner of his eye he saw Kara slouched down in her seat, her arms crossed over her chest, her hat pulled down low over her face. Silently Jake pulled back out onto the highway.

He didn't speak until they'd resumed their cruising speed. "Guess you better give up those boyish clothes and drive in something slinky from now on," he said, the merriment evident in his voice.

"Just drive, Murphy, and don't say another word," she said, her voice low and still fuming.

"Where's your sense of humor?"

"I don't think it's one bit funny. Drive!"

"Right." Feeling better than he had in several days and smiling despite the angry little spitfire next to him, Jake drove.

After the frustrating afternoon it hadn't taken much coaxing on Kara's part to get Jake to agree to stop that evening at a Roadrunner Overnighter. She was glad he didn't fight her because in her present mood she just might have told him where to get off. Declining his invitation to dinner in lieu of a long soak in a hot tub, she felt the private room with bath was well worth the extra money.

As she lay back in the fragrant suds willing the kinks out of her constricted muscles, she thought back on the afternoon's incident and, with a little time and distance, could finally see a bit of humor in the situation. Jake had certainly enjoyed himself at her expense, the clown!

His last remark filtered through her mind as she trailed the warm water along her arms. Was that how he saw her—boyish clothes, youthful appearance, not at all womanly? It certainly didn't seem that way when he'd kissed her. Only once but she remembered it well, her cheeks warming at the memory. And the thought of that stunning kiss and her unexpected response had been returning to haunt her with increasing regularity, much to her annoyance.

She didn't need this, she didn't want this. He was a nice guy. She would even go so far as to say she liked him. And goodness knows he had the uncanny ability to make her skin hum, her heart beat faster, her body go languid and loose with just a look from those lazy green eyes. But he was a drifter, a man chasing a dream. Like her father and those who came after him. Worse. Jake didn't even seem to *have* a dream.

Raising the washcloth, she dripped bubbly water over her breasts, seeing the changes that just thinking about Jake had brought about. She wanted him. Plain and simple. No, not so simple. Back to that again, she thought, sighing. *Damn!* She slid deeper into the water and closed her eyes.

It seemed like hours later when pounding on the door awakened her. Not again, Kara thought, grumbling to herself. It had taken her a long time to fall asleep with the noisy Fourth of July revelers entering and leaving their rooms, laughing, singing in the hallways, knocking on random doors.

"Go away," she yelled, turning over in bed.

"Kara, it's me, Jake. Are you all right?"

Over the music drifting from someone's room, she could hear concern in his voice. She lifted up on one elbow. "Jake? I'm fine. Is anything the matter?"

"Let me in, Kara," he persisted. "I need to see you."

Of all the craziness, she muttered as she got out of bed and reached into her bag for her oversize shirt. This day took the cake. Hastily she buttoned her shirt, ran a hand through her tousled hair and moved to the door.

"Jake, I'm fine, really. I'll see you in the morning." The last thing she needed right now was another confrontation with him to top off this beaut of a day.

His voice was loud, insistent. "Kara, open the door. I want to see you."

Exasperated, she released the chain lock and opened the door a crack. "See, here I stand. All in one piece. What is it that's so urgent?"

He shoved the door open wide and marched in past her. Kara glanced out into the busy hallway and saw a drunken trucker raise his beer to her in a mock salute. Quickly she shut the door. Her arms crossed over her chest, she stared up at Jake, waiting for his explanation.

His gray-green eyes were defensive as he met her gaze. ''The sheriff's men were here earlier, while I was eating dinner with a couple of the guys. They were still looking for that teenage girl. When we got back, this driver from Allied told me that they searched the rooms and came out with a dark-haired girl wearing jeans and a checked shirt, her hands behind her back. I thought . . . well, I didn't know. I just wanted to see for myself that you were all right.''

Was that the reason he'd come? Jake asked himself as his eyes slid over her sleep-softened features. Common sense had told him it probably hadn't been Kara. Was it just that he needed to see her and had used that as a handy excuse?

The pale blue sleepshirt, which came almost to her knees, was thin and nearly transparent in the soft glow of the bedside lamp. He could see she wore nothing under it and felt his body's reaction as his mind moved the frail material aside. Her skin was tanned and smooth and very lovely. Her hair was wild and night-tossed, soft curls framing her face, falling to her slender shoulders. Why was he doing this to himself? he wondered.

Despite herself, Kara felt a smile tug at the corners of her mouth. ''You honestly thought they'd dragged me off, kicking and screaming, in a patrol car? Jake, I've been looking after myself for a lot of years now. But thanks for your concern.''

''Louie'd never forgive me if something happened to you.''

"Hey, we're partners on this run. You're not my baby-sitter. Or my bodyguard."

A shrill voice in the hallway finished telling a story, and a chorus of laughter followed. Jake glanced at the door. "How can you sleep with all that noise out there?"

"It isn't easy. I had to fight one of them off awhile ago."

Immediately, his face darkened. "You what? Who was it? I'll—"

She glared at him. "*Will* you stop this? When I need a champion, I'll call you. For heaven's sake, you're acting like an outraged father! There isn't a woman alive who hasn't had to deal at one time or another with a slightly inebriated man who suddenly thinks he's Don Juan. It was my own fault for opening the door before checking who it was."

She relaxed and smiled at him. "Actually, he was quite funny. He told me he 'don't hold with no sexy broads driving trucks no how.'" She laughed at that, hoping he'd find something comical in her story. Was it his turn to lose his sense of humor? she thought, noticing his still grim face. "As I shoved him out the door, he told me to go find a guy who's man enough to keep me home."

The room was suddenly quiet. Jake watched the smile leave her face as he took a step toward her.

Kara felt her heart leap. He was close enough so that she could smell liquor on his breath and wondered how much he'd drunk. Why on earth had she mentioned that stupid story to him? she asked herself as she saw his eyes darken. "You've been drinking," she said, trying to keep her tone even. This was no time to challenge him. "How much?"

"Not nearly enough," Jake answered, moving closer, his hands sliding along her bent arms.

"Jake," she warned, taking a step backward from him and from the rush of desire that always seemed to accompany his nearness.

"Is there such a man, Kara?" he asked, his fingers moving along the bare skin of her arms. "A man who makes you dream of hot, forbidden nights, who keeps you awake, imagining, wanting."

Suddenly aware she wore only a thin cotton shirt, Kara took another step back, maneuvering him slowly toward the door. "Jake, this isn't wise. You've had a bit to drink, and I'm groggy from being awakened. I think we should wait until tomorrow to talk..."

"You know something... you should think less, let yourself feel more." A breath away, he looked down at her, his eyes dark and challenging.

She raised a restraining hand to keep him from moving closer and found her fingers on his chest, tangling in the crisp hair inside his open shirt. "So you've said before. Jake, I don't want this. Please."

He covered her hand with his, pressing it to the warmth of his chest. "Kara..."

Enough! She stepped away from him, putting some space between them before the weakness could spread further. She wouldn't let herself be ruled by a need—by a man. "No. Please go now, Jake."

"You can't tell me you don't want me. I won't believe you." His sooty eyes bored into hers.

Shrill laughter from the other side of the door, followed by drunken, off-key singing, assaulted their ears. Someone turned up the radio, and a woman's voice demanded a cigarette from a man named Jim. Stale cigar smoke drifted in through the air vents.

Kara dropped her eyes, refusing to look at him, refusing to rise to his challenge or to answer him.

Jake let go of her hand. He had to get out of her room before he pulled her into his arms. And it wouldn't stop there, he knew. Turning to the door, he opened it and glanced down the hallway. "Lock this behind me." For a long moment his eyes roamed her face. Swiftly he raised a shaky hand and lightly touched her hair then placed a gentle kiss on her forehead. "Goodnight, lovely lady," he whispered.

Silently she watched him close the door. She locked it and turned to lean against it. Her hands trembled as they moved to trace her quivering lips, aching for the kiss she'd denied him. And herself.

Even as she admitted the intensity of her feelings, she knew he could hurt her, and she mustn't let that happen. He would stay just long enough to break her heart then walk away. They were different people, very different. She closed her eyes and sighed deeply. Dear Lord, how long was she going to be able to fight this new, this incredible need? she wondered.

Kara looked out the window and saw a struggling sun trying to break through lingering gray clouds. It had rained during the night, heavy and hard, a summer rain without accompanying thunder or lightning. She was glad it had stopped for she disliked driving on slick pavement. She pulled the zippered closure on her satchel and glanced around the room to make sure she'd packed everything.

At a few minutes before eight, Kara hurried out the door. It was quiet in the building now. Most of the truckers had left much earlier. Even though she and Jake had agreed on the departure hour, she didn't want to be late. She didn't know what kind of mood Jake would be in after their encounter last night.

He wasn't around as she walked to their rig, and when she saw it, she was relieved that he hadn't appeared yet. Staring at the truck, she moaned inwardly as she saw that the large tires of the cab were sunk deep in mud. When they'd checked in last evening, Jake had jumped out to arrange for their rooms, and she'd parked near the rear of the building. They'd been late arriving, and all the paved parking had been taken. The steady rain had poured from the roof of the low-slung building, changing the dry hard-packed dirt to a bed of mud. During the night the heavy truck had slowly settled into it.

Drizzling drops of lingering rain fell on her dark head. Kara unlocked the cab door, hoping to free the truck before Jake appeared. How could she have known it would rain? she asked herself, scrambling up into the cab. A mental picture of Jake's eyes turning to frosty silver had her fingers shaking as she put the key in the ignition and started the motor.

"What the hell do you think you're doing?"

Kara recognized the voice, and the sharpness of the tone left her no choice. She rolled down her window and stuck out her head. Jake stopped short of the door and jammed his clenched hands on his hips. She eyed him coolly. "What's it look like I'm doing? I'm going to move the truck."

He shot her an exasperated scowl. "Just a minute. May I ask why you decided to park our truck in this quagmire of mud?"

"Look, it wasn't a quagmire of mud when I parked it here. I don't suppose you noticed that it rained all night?"

"Any fool would know that summer rains come up quickly and that these buildings aren't equipped with gutters!"

She gripped the wheel till her knuckles hurt and gunned the engine, wishing she could run him over and wipe that arrogant look off his face. Nothing was more infuriating than a superior-sounding male lashing out at a woman with a problem. Incensed, she leaned out the window, her brown eyes blazing. "Just get out of my way!"

"Come down from there," he shouted, taking a step closer. "That's not the way to get a heavy truck out of the mud."

She forced herself to take a deep breath as she put the truck into gear. "I put it here, and I'll get it out!"

"Kara, don't be stupid!"

"That did it! I warned you...." She stepped on the gas lightly. The heavy cab groaned and sank deeper. Swearing to herself, she threw it into reverse and gunned the engine, this time with more force. She felt movement, but not much. Shifting into low again, she barely touched the gas pedal, turning as she did so to glance over her shoulder out the window. Mud flew like rain, splattering Jake with generous globs from the top of his dark blond hair to the tips of his once-dusty boots. Oh no! she thought. Hastily she removed her foot from the gas pedal, shifted into park and turned off the engine.

She sat very still for a moment, considering several avenues of escape. None seemed very plausible. With those long legs, he'd catch her in minutes. She dared another peek out the window, swallowed hard and pulled up the door handle. Best to face the music, she thought, her heart pounding.

She climbed down cautiously, landing ankle deep in mire and slowly lifted her eyes. He was standing in the same place but he looked quite different. There wasn't a clean spot on his blue denim shirt. Big, dark globs of brown gunk trailed down his jeans, up and over boots completely covered with mud. Rivulets trailed and traipsed through his hair, dripping off the ends of his beard. On his nose rested a generous chunk. She couldn't read the expression in his eyes. As she struggled to suppress a grin, she twisted her hands in a worried, helpless gesture. "Jake, I'm sorry...."

"Come over here," he said, only his lips moving.

Wary, she held her ground. "Honestly, Jake, I didn't mean to..."

He lifted a hand and pointed to a spot directly in front of him. "Over here. Now."

With a shaky sigh, still suppressing a smile that threatened to break through at any moment, she hesitantly sloshed through the mud and stood before him. Afraid she'd lose her battle to contain her mirth if she met his eyes, she fastened her gaze on the smudged hairs of his chest at the opening of his soaked shirt. His hand moved up, and, with one muddy finger, he lifted her chin, forcing her eyes to meet his.

"You seem to find some humor in this situation." His grin was sudden and diabolical, white teeth flashing through his mud-caked golden beard. "How funny do you think this is?"

Strong hands slipped under her arms and scooped her up as he staggered a few steps backward before depositing her in a messy pond of mud nearly a foot deep. Kara landed on her rear with a mighty splash, showering both of them with a fresh supply of murky mud. Jake lost his footing and followed, nearly landing on her. She lost her battle with control, laughter bubbling out in bright gales as she squirmed against him.

She stole a quick glance at his features and saw he was grinning as he trailed muddy palms down her face. None too gently, he rolled her in the sticky mess.

"You like mud baths, do you?" he asked as he turned her slippery body over easily until she was flat on her back facing him. She tried to wriggle free, closing her eyes against the onslaught, but he was too fast for her. "I hear mud is very good for the complexion," he said with a victorious laugh as he spread a generous handful over her cheeks and along the smooth column of her throat.

Kara shifted and slithered away from him, grabbing a glob of mud. "Two can play this game," she shrieked, stuffing the slime down the back of his shirt.

Laughter pealed from him as he fought to hold her off. Recovering, Jake pinned her shoulders back and held her down with the weight of his body as he lay along the full length of her. "I'd like to know what fool taught you how to handle a truck."

In a flash she freed one hand and smeared a generous portion of mud into the center of his face. "The same fool who taught you how to mud wrestle," she answered. She wiggled out from under him as he paused to scrape the bulk of the dirt from his nose and eyes.

With little effort he caught her arm and pulled her back. She landed unceremoniously atop him. Her laughing eyes challenged him as she held still another handful of mud threateningly near his head. He gave a short laugh of surrender. "I bow to your superior expertise in mud combat," he admitted. She collapsed against his chest in victory, laughing, breathing heavily from her struggles.

Most women, especially a beautiful woman, Jake thought, would be livid at being dragged into a mud fight. Cindy would have killed rather than be caught grappling on the ground, dirtying her lovely body, her exquisite hair, her designer clothes. But Kara Finelli was definitely not just any woman. She was laughing just as hard at herself as she had at him.

She felt his steady heartbeat against her ear. Lightly his hand rested on the back of her neck, her heavy mud-soaked ponytail swept to the side. Instead of quieting, her own heartbeat accelerated as she became aware of his body under hers. It was difficult not to be attracted to a man who laughed at himself despite all the provocation she'd given him for anger. She'd wanted to dislike Jake Murphy. It was safer. But she couldn't. Something deep inside her stirred, something deeper than hunger, more enduring than passion.

Suddenly Kara realized that his touch on her neck had turned to a caress. Slowly she raised her head. He shifted his gaze from the thick overhead clouds to her face. She saw the change in his eyes, knew her own had softened in quiet answer. Her heart resumed its thudding. It was all happening much too fast. She scrambled up, struggling to stand, avoiding his searching look. "I think it's time to hit the showers."

He stood, flinging dripping mud from his hands. "Best suggestion I've heard all day." With two long strides, he reached over and grabbed her, scooping her into his arms. Ignoring her shrieks of protest, he sloshed his way through the mud and in through the Roadrunner door and down the hallway. The place was deserted as he shouldered open the door to the men's shower room.

"Wait! I can manage nicely on my own, thank you," she told him as he deposited her on the tile floor under one of a long line of shower heads. She struggled to pull off her shoes.

Too late! She felt cascades of cold, then warmer water splash over her head and move downward as Jake maneuvered her wiggling body firmly under the spray. Kara closed her eyes and gave up the battle while he ran his hands over her upturned face, down her arms and along her thighs, removing the worst of the soil. She shook her wet head and, with some difficulty, removed the rubber band that had held her hair coiled. She raked her fingers through the thick, matted hair, rinsing out the dirt.

Satisfied that he'd done all he could for her, Jake handed her a bar of soap and stepped to the adjacent shower head. Removing his boots, he directed the spray onto himself.

"Are you always that stubborn?" he asked, lathering his hair and beard.

"Arrogant men who know it all bring out the worst in me," she answered, letting the water pound down on her, rubbing the legs of her jeans. They were plastered tightly to her while the thin cotton of her shirt clung to her breasts. She wished she could strip and rinse off more thoroughly but obviously, with Jake next to her, she couldn't. After he went to change, perhaps she could linger behind and do a better job or return to the room she'd only recently vacated.

As Kara raised her head to the spray, Jake's hungry gaze examined her clearly outlined curves, her nipples straining against the material of her blouse. He tore his eyes from her, and, hoping the chill water would cool his suddenly flaming thoughts, he turned the jets to cold as he took off his shirt and threw it aside. He thrust his face up into the needle spray, only to see her inviting image dance behind his closed eyelids.

Almost at the same moment, they turned off the shower water. Kara straightened and slowly moved her eyes up Jake. Golden curly hair generously matted his tan chest. Droplets of water clung to his blond hair and dripped from his amber beard. Determination settled into the smoky depths of his eyes as he moved toward her.

She knew wanderlust flowed in his veins, mingled with his blood. For the moment she didn't care. Staring at his masculine perfection, she could feel her resistance melting. He made her feel like a woman. She hadn't felt like that in a long, long time. And she *loved* the feeling.

His fingers moved to touch her cheek, his hand shaking as he caressed the soft skin. "What is it about you that excites me?" he asked, searching her eyes for answers. "You're not all *that* beautiful," he said, trying to convince himself. Lazily he traced her brow. "Your eyes are spaced a shade too far apart for perfection." One long finger moved down her small nose and paused at the tip. "And your nose should be longer, more patrician, I think." His touch lingered on her open lips as they trembled apart. He felt her convulsive shudder as her eyes grew dark with desire. "Mouth a bit too full." He ran his fingertip along the soft underside of her bottom lip. "But incredibly soft."

Heat infused Kara's skin, followed by a shiver racing up her spine. Mesmerized by his seductive words, she stood very still, the pounding of her heart hammering in her ears. The back of his hand moved down the curve of her throat, then dipped over the soft swell of her breasts. Her cheeks colored and her eyes widened with his intimate touch. A low moan of pleasure escaped from her as his hand opened and closed over her hungry flesh, the hard peaks welcoming his leisurely stroking.

His voice was ragged. "What do you suppose it is about you that drives me crazy?"

Her chest heaved with the effort of breathing. "I don't know. Please, just kiss me."

Exercising iron control, he bent and lightly brushed her lips with his own, moving with deliberate slowness.

Her eyes flew open in exasperation. She moved her arms up around his neck, drawing him closer. "That's not a kiss," she complained.

His dark eyes smoldered into hers, accepting the challenge. Swiftly he met her open mouth as he pulled her against his hard body. She reeled from the impact as his tongue entered her, probing and exploring. She thrilled at the hunger she felt in him, the raw passion she knew he'd been holding in check.

Vaguely Kara recalled fleeting reasons why she shouldn't kiss Jake Murphy, but her body, perhaps wiser than she, dismissed the thought as unimportant for the moment. She no longer felt the damp clothes that clung to her body nor did she hear a light rainfall begin again outside the open window. She couldn't smell the early-summer morning dampness. She felt only the hard muscles of Jake's back as her restless hands massaged his smooth skin. She heard only the thunder of her own heartbeat as she leaned her body closer into his. She caught the soapy clean scent of him and breathed it only. Without leaving her lips, he changed angles and deepened the kiss. With a soft moan, Kara let a stream of pure pleasure pour through her.

At last he drew back without releasing her, his eyes waiting for hers to open and clear.

"Now, *that's* a kiss," she murmured, her breath mingling with his.

He gave her a tiny smile of satisfaction until his need made him greedy. He moved to cover her face and neck with kisses that spread heat over her skin wherever he touched. But he returned again and again to her waiting lips to experience her special taste, unable to get enough. Each time she met him with her avid, open response. Here was a passion as great as his own, a wildness he'd been wanting to tame.

His hand moved between them, seeking her breasts. The longing to touch her overwhelmed him. Closing over her firm, willing flesh, he swallowed her soft sigh as his mouth lowered to hers once more.

"Mr. Murphy? Mr. Murphy, you in there?" a deep voice called out.

Mumbling a colorful oath, Jake released her, quickly turning and stepping in front of her.

"Glad I found you," the desk man drawled as he came around the stall corner. His fascinated gaze took in the scene, and a grin spread over his fleshy features. "I got the boards you wanted to free your truck. You ready for me to help you?"

Jake allowed Kara another moment to recover as he grabbed a towel and thrust it back at her. Walking toward him, he hustled the curious man away. "Thanks, Sam. Let's go see if we can free her."

They made for the door as Kara shakily wrapped herself in the towel and leaned against the tiled wall. Where, she wondered, would this last encounter have taken them if Sam hadn't chosen that moment to interrupt them? Deeper. She was getting in deeper each day. Sighing heavily, she went to change out of her wet clothes.

Chapter Five

Frowning, Kara drove in the late-morning drizzle. She stole a quick glance at Jake hunched down beside her, his baseball cap covering the top part of his face. But she had her doubts about whether he was sleeping or not and about his recent behavior. And that was what had put the frown on her forehead.

After he and Sam had freed the truck, Jake had cleaned up and changed and joined her for coffee before hitting the highway. Prepared to leave, she'd come out of the rest room to find Jake under the truck. Puzzled, she'd watched a while and when he'd emerged, a heavy wrench in his hand, she'd questioned him. He'd brushed her off with a breezy explanation that he'd been adjusting various nuts and bolts. Without another word, he'd climbed into the passenger side and had seemingly gone to sleep.

There was a tightness in her stomach that she hated to acknowledge. Recent acts of trucking sabotagings had involved snipped wires causing electrical shortages and aborting runs, loosened bolts causing separation of cab from trailer and damage to both cargo and truck, sometimes even drivers. With a heavy heart, she asked herself again, could Jake be involved? Surely he wouldn't be crazy enough to endanger his own life in the bargain! Or was he so clever, so agile that he'd feign sleep until the moment before a crash and then deliberately jump clear? Could he passionately kiss her in the morning and quietly watch her get hurt in the afternoon?

But why? she wondered. Someone with a weakness, a need and no scruples, he'd told her, was likely responsible. But none of those seemed to apply to him. Surely he didn't need money with his family background. Was he working for the larger trucking conglomerates and trying to force the small independents out of business? Had she so misjudged him? Could she be attracted to a man so devious, so cunning?

Kara shook her head and gripped the wheel tighter. *No!* a voice inside her cried. Not Jake Murphy. Or had this attraction blinded her to the truth? Again she shook her head in adamant denial. The truck seemed to handle the same as always. She hadn't eaten dinner last night or breakfast this morning. Was she light-headed and reading more into things than were really there? she wondered.

Why couldn't she get Jake Murphy out of her mind? God knows, she'd tried. But things—too many of them—reminded her always of him. A deep laugh. A lingering smell in the air that brought to mind that somehow appealing pipe. A moment of silence. Silence late at night when doubts shared her pillow and her imagination went on overload.

She was vulnerable away from her home and familiar things. That's what it was. He was near, always near, handy and available. He'd made it clear just how available he was. It hadn't a thing to do with that sexy beard, those watchful eyes on her or the warmth of his touch. No, of course not.

She turned her head to steal a look at him. His strong, bearded jaw jutted forward defiantly, even in repose. His large, strong hands rested in his lap. Earlier their touch had set her blood simmering. And staring at his long, jeans-clad legs, one crossed over the other, she recalled how exciting they'd felt pressed up against her body. Even now, even suspecting him, she longed to reach out, to press her face into the incredible softness of that golden beard, to feel the heat of his skin, to inhale the fragrance of him that smelled like no other. Shakily she returned her attention to the road.

"I suppose you'll be glad to visit your house and get back to nature?" he asked, startling her. She'd make a rotten poker player, Jake decided, sitting up, adjusting his cap and squinting into a pale sky beginning to clear. Surreptitiously he'd been watching her for some moments, aware of her scrutiny and her frown.

"I . . . I thought you were sleeping."

"I was," he lied, "but I'm awake now. So tell me, are you looking forward to seeing your dog and your horse?"

Shoving her random thoughts to the back of her mind, Kara thought of her animals, which brought a smile to her face. Here was a neutral topic. "Yes, I am. I mentioned once that I often find I like animals better than people. And these are special animals. Prince is a beautiful chestnut and Figaro is a beagle of . . . well, of questionable parentage, but that's never bothered him or me. He lives with Nona when I'm away."

He turned in his seat, facing her.

She felt his eyes, his studying gaze. "I can see you don't believe me."

"Oh, but I do. 'I think I could turn and live with animals, they are so placid and self-contained,'" he quoted.

Totally disarmed, Kara shot him a surprised glance, then broke out in a warm smile. A look passed between them, as strong and as real as the passion they'd shared in the shower room.

"Oh, I can't believe *you* would be quoting Walt Whitman. He is such a favorite of mine!"

"And of mine. But I don't know why that should surprise you so."

"I guess I thought . . . I mean I . . ."

"You thought I was a big, dumb truck driver who wouldn't even know who Walt Whitman was?"

She scowled at him. "Oh, hardly, Jake. It's just that it's nice—very nice—to find someone who feels the same as I do about a poet. About animals. Or maybe about anything."

"Perhaps, Kara, if you gave us a chance, you'd find we feel the same about a lot of things."

A shadow drifted unbidden across her thoughts. "Maybe," she said, rather reluctantly.

He smiled at her profile. "I'll accept that—for now."

He bent over and reached under the seat, bringing up a brown paper bag. Rummaging around inside, he pulled out a bright, red apple and tossed it onto her lap.

Kara picked up the apple, pleased. "Thanks. I see I've made you health conscious."

"Not really. I just like apples." Jake stretched his long legs out, one hand searching for something in his pants pocket. As he shifted, his jeans pulled tightly across the lower part of his body, revealing every masculine line.

Kara looked away quickly and took a big, loud bite of her apple, hoping he hadn't seen her eyes follow his movements. Feeling the heat of her thoughts warm her, she tried desperately to concentrate on her driving.

Finding his Swiss Army knife, Jake proceeded to quarter his apple, though his eyes kept glancing her way.

"Hey, what are you doing?" she asked. "That's no way to eat an apple!"

He stopped with a piece midway to his mouth. "You mean cutting it? Why not?"

She shook her head. Grasping her apple in one hand, she brought it to her mouth and took a large, satisfying bite, enjoying the sound of the crunch. "*That's* the way to eat an apple. Only sissies cut their apples into bite-sized pieces. You lose too much juice that way, and that's the best part."

Jake reached into the sack and brought out another apple. Following her example, he took a huge bite of the crisp flesh and chewed thoughtfully. He turned toward Kara and smiled. "It could be that you *can* teach me something, after all," he reluctantly admitted.

She grinned at him. "Maybe so."

Suddenly he moved very close to her and cupped her chin in one hand.

"What . . . what are you doing?" she protested. "I'm driving . . ." Nervously she gripped the wheel harder.

Jake bent forward, and Kara felt his tongue slide across her lower lip scooping up a small drop of moisture before he moved back out of her line of vision. "You had a drop of juice on your lip," he explained. "You did say it was the best part, didn't you?"

Again. He'd done it to her again. Wordlessly Kara swung her gaze to the front and went back to finishing her apple, her heart thudding loudly in her ears.

Jake took over the driving chores in the afternoon while a subdued Kara gazed out the side window, lost in her thoughts. Dusk painted the sky in pale hues of purple and gray as Jake maneuvered the truck into a restaurant parking area off the main highway, about an hour from their destination. The Gypsy Tea Room was an overdecorated, underrated Hungarian restaurant of mouth-watering European temptations whose location and reputation made it popular with cross-country truckers.

Kara swung down from the passenger side, having spent the last two hours struggling with eyes that wanted to close and a busy, troubled mind. "Are you sure this is what we want to do? Frankly I'd just as soon skip dinner and go to the dock so we can make it home at a reasonable hour."

"You need to eat, and I know if I don't see that you do, you won't." He opened the door for her and allowed her to precede him into the dim entryway.

Through the carved wooden archway, the large, old-fashioned dining room beckoned them with its floral print carpeting, mahogany chairs with needlepoint cushions and round tables with snowy white tablecloths. Tangy, mysterious scents teased them as a small, dark-eyed woman led them to a secluded corner table.

The short, buxom waitress wearing a pale blue dress with delicate embroidery came over as they were seated and handed them both menus. "I am Anna," she said. "Please signal me when you're ready to order."

Too tired to make decisions, Kara let Jake study the menu and order for them. She sighed and leaned her head against the high-backed chair, closing her eyes.

"You look beat," he told her.

"Mmm. I think I am."

"And what do you plan to do tomorrow, with half a day of leisure before we start back?"

The thought of a night's sleep in her own bed brought a smile to Kara's lips. "Sleep until I awaken. Probably call Nona and then check on what's happening at my studio. Go for a ride on my horse. Take a walk on the beach. Nothing special."

Jake leaned forward, his elbows on the table. "Except all of it is very special—to you. Isn't it?"

Her eyes opened, and she looked into his. "Yes," she answered, surprised he'd understand. Unconsciously a frown settled on her brow as she studied him.

"What is it?" he asked.

"You see so much. You constantly surprise me. Most people look *at* someone, not *inside* them."

"Is that what I do? Does it bother you that I see you more clearly than some, that I'm beginning to know you as a person, to put all the little pieces together?"

She thought about that a long moment. "Privacy is very important to me."

He nodded. "I understand. Because of the way you grew up, having to share your home with a variety of men your mother brought home."

She sat up straighter. There was something about Jake that always had her revealing more about herself than she'd intended. "Don't feel sorry for me. It wasn't that bad."

Reaching over, he took her small hand in his large one, smoothing the soft skin. "It's not pity I feel. You're a strong woman. I admire that. But it was bad enough that the effects have lingered. Even through today.''

Kara pulled back her hand. It was time to change the subject. ''And what do you plan to do tomorrow?''

He shrugged. ''Go to my apartment in town. Sleep in. Check out the truck.''

She felt a pang of guilt. Should she ask him to come to the beach with her? she wondered. God, no! That would be disastrous. Still, she felt rotten that he'd be stuck in his hot town apartment while she'd have the beauty and freedom of her seaside home. Maybe she should . . . no!

Anna brought the tea Jake had ordered, and he poured Kara a cup. She sipped the hot liquid gratefully. Let this evening end quickly, she prayed as fatigue took a firm hold on her.

They talked lightly as they ate a rich cabbage soup, chicken with tiny dumplings in a mushroom sauce and a wilted lettuce salad. Kara had little appetite but did her best, though she couldn't suppress a sigh of relief when their waitress cleared their plates and placed a dish containing the check on the table.

Anna returned and smiled down at them, her dark eyes dancing. ''Did you enjoy your dinner?'' she asked, her voice heavy with an indefinable accent.

''Yes,'' they chorused as Jake picked up the check.

''I read tea leaves,'' she said, reaching for Kara's empty cup. ''It is part of our service.''

''Oh, you needn't bother,'' Kara told him with a small smile.

Seeing the flash of disappointment on Anna's face, Jake glanced at Kara. ''Let's hear what she has to say.''

Reluctantly Kara nodded, feeling the start of a headache above her eyes.

Pulling up a chair, Anna peered into Kara's cup, her brow wrinkled in concentration. "Ah," she whispered, turning the beam of her smile on Kara. "You are close to home, near the end of your journey. This summer you will find your destiny."

Curiosity warred with fatigue and won. "Destiny?" Kara asked.

"Oh, yes," the woman assured her. "The stranger will take off his mask."

Very poetic, Kara thought. And a shade mysterious and fanciful. Just like the gypsy woman herself. She smiled her thanks, though she thought the meaning of the elusive message as clear as mud.

"And now the gentleman," Anna continued, gazing deeply into Jake's cup at the residue of tea leaves. At last satisfied, she looked up at him. "You will recognize your love in a rose garden. Soon." She noticed Jake raise questioning brows at her. "Very soon," she repeated, replacing the chair and gathering their cups.

Slipping her a folded bill, Jake thanked her, his smile skeptical.

"You don't believe in those silly things, do you?" Kara asked, putting some money onto the check plate.

"Sometimes."

Rising, she gave him a surprised look. "Who'd have pegged you as a romantic?"

Jake added his money to the check. "And who'd have pegged you a cynic?" he asked, getting up and walking toward the cashier.

After a moment Kara slung her purse strap over her shoulder and followed Jake. Just two more hours, she thought, and she'd be home. Home where she could snuggle down in her own bed and forget for a short while about trucks and crooks and driving and gypsies and, most of all, Jake Murphy.

Despite her plans to sleep late in the comfort of her own bed, as always, the sea called her. Kara couldn't resist the pull, but she had a few things to do first. After a short visit with her grandmother to say hello and pick up her dog, she checked in with her studio. All seemed to be under control there. Next, she took time to visit her neighbors, Marge and Bill and their children. Over coffee, their words of praise about her pictures warmed her. Leaving them, she rode Prince on the hard-packed sand near her house. As she rubbed him down and nuzzled his long white-streaked nose, she murmured soft, loving words to him and smiled as his ears twitched in gentle understanding.

Then, in cutoffs and cotton shirt, she bundled up her camera equipment and headed for her favorite spot far down the beach where sand, sea and sky blended with the jutting rocks in a profusion of textures, colors and smells. Running down the beach with Figaro, she raised her face to the warm rays of the sun. The eager, rust-colored beagle kicked sand onto her long legs as he raced to beat her.

Feeling wonderfully alive, Kara hugged herself and smiled at the sky. She stood barefooted and ankle deep in the foamy residue of shimmering waves that plunged and retreated tirelessly over the sparkling sand. God, how she enjoyed it here, how she'd missed her sea, her work. She hadn't given herself enough time for this, she thought. Enough time to think and reflect and decipher the direction in which her life was going. Perhaps then, she'd find out what it was that seemed to be missing, why she kept longing for something indefinable.

Setting up her camera, Kara adjusted her large Nova-flex lens. Anxiety pumped through her as she waited to capture the precise moment when the billowy clouds hovered just right in the outrageously blue sky and when the churning white-capped waves crashed over the slick black rocks. Feeling happier and freer than she'd felt in weeks, she lost track of time while she threaded several rolls of film into her camera.

Work, she decided, was the answer. Work was what she'd missed. Work involved her, grabbed hold of her mind, made her forget everything. In her photography she could lose herself, lose the imperfect, everyday world and concentrate on capturing the beauty of nature. Work was comfort, satisfaction, escape, and she embraced it greedily.

An hour later she was taking pictures at the request of another neighbor who'd spotted her on the beach. The little girl with the blond curls and the serious brown eyes climbed onto the rock worn smooth by endless ocean waves caressing it through the years. While she adjusted the focus of her camera, Kara smiled at the adorable four-year-old imp in the pink sunsuit. Plopping down on the rock, the child raised a chubby arm and pointed to a sea gull. Kara clicked away, frame after frame, capturing the childish joy as the little girl smiled and waved at the bird.

Straightening from her squatting position, Kara spotted a weathered and gnarled log up the beach a way. "Okay, Michelle. You were great. Now, let's walk down there so I can take a few more of you on that log." Kara turned to the child's tall, blond mother. "She's a natural, Linda. A beautiful child."

"Thanks, Kara," Linda answered, smiling with pride. "She's a regular little ham, all right." They walked companionably on the hard-packed sand, following the running child. "I can hardly wait to see these. The whole family just loved the last ones you took. I'm so glad I saw you out here today and that you have time to take pictures for Michelle's birthday. No one photographs children the way you do."

Kara acknowledged the compliment with a smile as she changed lenses. Working quickly, she situated Michelle on the log and set up the next sequence of shots. As she focused in on the little girl's face, she wondered if the day would come when she'd be snapping pictures of her own little girl. The unfamiliar longing caught her with a lump in her throat that she quickly swallowed, blinking rapidly at a sudden rush of tears. Impatient with her uncharacteristic emotional reaction, she chewed on her lower lip and crouched, concentrating on her work. What the devil was the matter with her lately? she wondered.

When she felt she had enough, she called to Michelle. The child ran over and hugged her so hard they both tumbled over into the warm sand, wrestling playfully and laughing.

Kara instructed Linda to pick up the pictures later in the week at the studio as she slung her camera bag over her shoulder and folded her tripod. She turned to wave at mother and daughter as they walked down the beach toward their house. Sighing, she started toward her own home.

Jake strolled around to the back of Kara's beach house and glanced at the small, redwood balcony off the back, facing the sea. The house was obviously empty though he heard the rich tones of an opera floating through windows open to the ocean air. She couldn't be far if she'd left the music on. Turning, he glanced down the beach and caught sight of her walking homeward, her dark hair blowing in a light breeze. He started toward her.

Halfway home she spotted a sandpiper standing very still, his head cocked inquisitively at her, his small eyes blinking rapidly. Grabbing her camera, Kara squatted, silently trapping his curiosity in her lens. She snapped several until a sound from down the beach caused the elusive bird to fly away. As she looked up to follow his flight, she saw Jake's long-legged strides bringing him nearer, the sun glinting golden on his beard. She gave in to her impulse and moved behind her camera to capture his image on film as she was unable to do in reality.

Jake walked unhurriedly, hands in his pockets, his eyes never leaving the small figure crouching in the sand. For long minutes he watched Kara's passionate involvement in her photography, and he wondered if she brought the same intensity to bed. He'd known he'd find her here, at one with the sea and the beauty of the day. When he'd spoken to Louie and had learned of a change in driving plans, he'd driven to her house instead of phoning, acknowledging that he was curious to see her in her own element.

He watched her trying to harness her long hair with combs, but the warm caressing breezes whipped it about her upturned face. Her dog nipped at her heels and ran playfully along the shoreline. She stood then, watching him approach, her golden skin reflecting health and vitality, hinting at a sensuality he'd sensed from the start. He'd felt an initial instant attraction in that one quick moment that had passed between them in the parking lot the first day he'd seen her. And it had increased daily, he realized.

Women recognized a man's interest immediately, he knew, and tended to take advantage of it at their earliest opportunity. He had scars to remind himself of what happens to men who forget to keep up their guard. He wanted Kara, of that he was certain. But he didn't intend to drop his emotional guard again, not even for Kara Finelli. Instinctively he knew that he would not walk away easily from this one.

Kara felt the sun warm her skin as her dark eyes watched Jake draw nearer. He was not a man that a sane, thinking woman would choose. He was devilishly charming, with a warm sense of humor. At times he showed a sensitivity she'd not suspected earlier. But he was also arrogant, opinionated, somewhat chauvinistic. He was a vagabond at heart, a cynic with a romantic soul, a man who likely loved many and left them all. She doubted if he was capable of a lasting relationship. By his own admission he wanted to spend the rest of his life wandering the world. That was the last thing she would do. And she wanted him with all her heart.

He stopped in front of her. "Hello," he said.

His eyes seemed to borrow the blue of the sky, mingling it with his own gray-green tones in an intriguing combination that she found fascinating.

"Hello, yourself. I took your picture," she said unnecessarily. Why, she wondered, did his presence reduce her to speaking so inanely?

"So I saw. Are you going to make me a gift of the photographs or will you keep them?"

She squinted up at him. As always his nearness played havoc with her even breathing. "I haven't decided yet. Is it time to leave? I often lose track of the hour out here."

"There's been a change. I talked with Louie. I'm to take the rig back alone. He wants you to double up with Cowboy. A short run to Tulsa and then back to Michigan."

Disappointment washed over her. Kara fought to not let it show as she gathered up her camera and bag and glanced up at him. His face was as hard as granite, inscrutable. "Is there some problem you haven't told me about?"

"I want you to be very careful. Cowboy's a good driver, but he drinks too much." He'd wanted to play it lightly but somehow, he was finding it difficult. In his investigative work he'd been involved in dangerous assignments before where others had also faced risk. He'd allowed and even encouraged them to do what was necessary to get to the truth, to complete the job. But this was different. He'd never before wanted to make love to someone he'd exposed to a threatening situation. And it was tearing him up.

As they walked back toward her house, she saw him clench his jaw tightly, as if he were holding himself in check. What had happened to the laughing man who'd wrestled with her in the mud only yesterday morning? she wondered. "I'm always careful."

He stopped, grabbed her arm, whirling her to face him. "Dammit, Kara, don't go defensive female on me. This isn't a game. Don't you know the dangers you face out there every day?"

Her voice was low and quiet. "Of course I do. I'm not an idiot, nor a novice. And I can take care of myself."

"Now you listen . . ."

"What?"

"Nothing." Abruptly he dropped her arm and resumed walking. Puzzled at this sudden angry side of him, Kara marched along beside him, wondering just what it was that Jake Murphy was not telling her.

Jake paced outside the twenty minutes it took Kara to close up her house and get into his car. They rode to the loading dock in strained silence, Kara pondering Jake's oddly protective behavior on the beach.

Arriving at noon, she was even more disturbed at Cowboy's behavior. Unable to locate him at first, she finally found him in his room, dead drunk to the world. She knew he drank heavily but never had she seen him in such a condition. He'd always handled his liquor. While she was wondering how to sober him up, Tennessee arrived and said he was taking the Tulsa run with her on Uncle Louie's orders. Cowboy was obviously going nowhere.

A black scowl on his face, Jake hovered around as she loaded her gear, but he spoke hardly a word to her. She was grateful when Tennessee pulled out onto the highway and they left Jake standing on the dock, his thumbs hooked in his belt loops, his frown deepening. In an effort to put his disturbing disapproval out of her mind, Kara let her thoughts return to Cowboy as she glanced over at Tennessee.

"I just don't know why Cowboy drinks so much," she said, on her face a look of concern.

The big man shrugged. "Trucking's a lonely life. But then, I've heard he's always been a loner. If it weren't for my wife and kids—hell, I don't know if I wouldn't be passed out right alongside him."

"I'm sure he could have any number of women, if he wanted. When he's not drunk, he's funny and interesting and . . ."

Smoothing his bristly red mustache, Tennessee shook his head. "Not *women*," he corrected. "What Cowboy needs is *woman*. One woman who is all his and no one else's."

Kara's mind flew to Pauly and how soft and vulnerable she'd looked when they'd discussed Cowboy. "Maybe there is one woman like that who cares about him if he'd just look around and notice."

Picking up speed, he slid his eyes quickly to Kara, then back to the road. "You mean Pauly? I don't give that match much chance."

Surprised, Kara shifted in her seat, turning toward him. "I wasn't aware you knew she cared about him."

Chuckling, he nodded. "Hell, anyone with two eyes could see that. But I don't think Cowboy's buyin'. Told me just the other day that he had to break away from her 'cause she was always after him, questioning, wanting to change him."

"He could use some changing from what we've seen today."

"Maybe so. Trouble is, most men don't want a woman who wants to change him. And most women don't know when to back off, let a man be."

Sighing, Kara crossed her legs and swung her eyes back to the road. There was a lot of truth in what Tennessee was saying. And it occurred to her that perhaps it applied to her situation with Jake as well. We all want to do the changing and yet not change ourselves, she admitted ruefully.

Her thoughts absorbed Kara so thoroughly that not until the first stop did she remember that she hadn't checked the cargo. Tennessee assured her that the manifest had been initialed, but Kara felt uncomfortable despite his reassurances. She nagged until he finally pulled over. Handing her the key to the cargo compartment, Tennessee laughed at her worrying ways. His laughter stopped as they discovered the key didn't fit the lock. After a short debate Tennessee broke the lock, and they climbed into the trailer. Within a few minutes of checking the numbers on the crates with the manifest, they realized nothing matched.

A sinking feeling came over Kara as they waited for the State Police to arrive. Stolen goods. She made her decision by the time the police pulled up. Unknown to Tennessee she tore a strip off the bottom of the manifest that he'd never examined. The manifest that had been checked and initialed back in California. The notation read: "J.M."

The police confiscated their cargo, made out a report and let them go. Tennessee found a phone and called Louie who instructed them to return to Los Angeles. During the gloomy, silent drive back, whether she had her eyes open or closed, Kara pictured those damning initials on the screen of her mind, the torn slip of paper hiding accusingly in the pocket of her jeans. Uncle Louie trusted Jake. The truckers, every last one of them, respected him. And Kara Finelli, she asked herself, what does she feel about him?

Lord, she no longer knew, if she'd ever known. She only knew something didn't add up. She didn't usually jump to conclusions, but the evidence pointed to the one man she hadn't wanted to believe capable of deception, much less worse. Perhaps he had a good explanation. She wanted desperately to believe he did.

It was dusk when Kara arrived at her house and called Louie in Michigan. He'd already had a complete report on the incident, and there was concern in his voice as he spoke, though he tried to cover it.

"You had a little trouble, eh?" he asked.

"A little," Kara answered just as cautiously. "What did the police tell you?"

"Not much. They're investigating."

She frowned into the phone. "They certainly didn't seem awfully concerned. They just took down the information, hardly questioning us."

Louie sighed with exasperation. "That's how they are here, too, every time I report a new incident. It's just another form for them to fill out."

"Is something else bothering you, Uncle Louie?" she gently prodded.

Though he hesitated, he finally confided that a larger rival firm underbid him on a big contract.

"Is it possible someone found out what your bid was and deliberately undercut you?" she asked.

"I don't see how," he answered, struggling to keep the sound of defeat out of his voice.

"Where do you keep copies of the bids?"

"In the files, next to Pauly's desk. And don't you tell me she'd sell me out. That woman's loyal to a fault."

"No, not Pauly," Kara agreed. "Is the filing cabinet kept locked?"

"Nah. I never had reason to lock it. Not till now. Who would do such a thing?"

"That's what we're trying to find out. Who had access to those files last week?"

"Only me and Pauly. One or both of us is always in the office. Kara, I already thought about all this."

"Uncle Louie," she persisted, "are you sure you were both there every minute?"

There was a thoughtful silence. "Except a week ago Monday, for maybe an hour. I sent Pauly home in the afternoon. She had a miserable headache."

"So the office was empty for a while that Monday?"

"No. Jake came in and stayed while I went to grab some lunch."

Kara felt her heart sink. "Jake?"

"Yeah. When I got back, he was sitting and talking with Cowboy. You know, Kara, I'm really going to have to talk to Cowboy seriously. I may have to put him on suspension if he won't straighten out. He's been with me from the beginning, a good man, but he's let this drinking take him over. One more incident like today and he's through."

Kara's mind was racing. "But for a while that day Jake Murphy was in the office, alone with your unlocked files?"

"You're on the wrong track, Kara. I told you, I trust Jake. You're just not used to his kind of man. In California you got used to college men. Jake's a little rough around the edges, but he's okay. He'd never hurt me." She could almost see the gentle smile on her uncle's face as he answered her. One thing about Louie Santini was his undying loyalty. Had Jake taken him in, too? she wondered.

Kara was worried. Was this just another coincidence? Should she tell Uncle Louie about the scrap of torn manifest before she had a chance to talk with Jake? Chances are, her uncle wouldn't believe her anyway. She decided to go slowly, but cautiously. "Uncle Louie, I'm not 'used to college men,' as you put it. Besides, I think Jake Murphy's been to college for whatever difference that makes. And I'm not accusing him or judging him."

"I think maybe you are, a little. The kind of life Jake has led has given him a certain assurance, maybe a cockiness. He's had to live by his wits. Just because a man's at ease with himself and avoids pretension is no reason to think he lacks intelligence, to suspect his every move. Or to underestimate him."

Kara's dark eyes widened and her voice was firm. "I assure you I would never underestimate Jake Murphy."

He gave her a warm smile. "Good. I'm glad we got that settled."

"Uncle Louie," she began in her most persuasive tone, "I want you to schedule Jake and me on the next long run."

He sighed, a raspy sound. "You're still not convinced, I see."

"Maybe not altogether. Let me do this my way, please? I need to prove it to myself."

Louie's voice became indulgent. "All right. You know I have trouble refusing you anything. You always did have to learn your lessons the hard way. Jake's in L.A., not scheduled to leave till morning. I'll get a hold of him."

"Good. Then I can have dinner with Nona tonight. I didn't get a chance to see her yet."

"Give her my love. I've got to make time to get out there and see her soon."

"She'd like that," Kara said, knowing as well as Louie that he couldn't leave until this mess was cleared up.

"One more thing before you go." His voice was gentle. "You know I don't usually say much, Kara, but it seems to me you're spending a lot of time worrying about Jake. For a woman like you, I'm not sure it's smart to get mixed up with a free spirit like him. I'd hate to see you make a mistake."

Kara turned to look out into the face of the setting sun, her eyes suddenly luminous. "It might very well be," she admitted softly, "that I've already made one."

Chapter Six

"Oh no, please, Nona, no more! If I eat another mouthful, I'll burst," Kara protested as her grandmother prepared to heap another mound of fragrant pasta on her plate. Nona was a small woman who stood only a few inches taller than Kara as she sat at the sturdy kitchen table. As long as Kara could remember, Nona had worn her sparse salt-and-pepper hair pulled back from her face and caught in a bun at the nape of her neck. Despite the lined face of an eighty-two-year-old, her brown eyes were clear and alert. Her smile for her only granddaughter was always warm and filled with love.

"Listen, Kara *mia*," she answered in her low, lightly accented voice, "you should eat more. Look how skinny you got since you left my house! I tell you this every time you come home, but do you listen? No! You young girls today, you think men only want to hug skin and bones."

Kara's laugh was light. "Tell me, Nona, what do men today want?"

"Ha," the old woman scoffed, resuming her seat beside her granddaughter, "the same like they always wanted. A little meat with the bones." She took Kara's slim hand in her firm grip. "And smiling eyes, maybe. The last thing you already got."

"And what would that be?" Kara asked.

"The loving heart. So much to offer, my sweet Kara has. Why is it you don't find some good man to give it to?"

"Haven't you heard, Nona? A good man is hard to find." Kara reached over and hugged her grandmother's small frame, feeling the fragile bones of her back through her print housedress. Nona seemed smaller every time she returned for a visit. She remembered how round, almost portly Nona had been just a few years back. With a heavy heart, as she reached over to kiss the soft powder-scented cheek, she realized Nona wouldn't always be around, that time and age were drawing her away.

Nona's dark brown eyes, so like her own, searched her face. "What is it that puts the sadness in your eyes, Kara? Tell Nona."

Kara looked away a moment. Even after years of not living together, Nona had the uncanny ability of seeing into Kara's heart each time they were together. She felt the love flow from the tiny, dear woman and sensed her concern. Always before, she'd laughed away Nona's gently prodding questions. She didn't feel like laughing tonight.

She turned back to see her grandmother studying her intently. "I'm having trouble sorting out my feelings lately, and there's... well, there's this man," she finished simply. She glanced up and saw no change of expression on Nona's face. "You're not surprised?"

The old woman smiled calmly. "Why should I be surprised? You are a very beautiful young woman."

"Ah, but not a very wise one, Nona. I haven't known many men, not really, and in any case, he's nothing like the few I've spent time with."

"You mean not like the college boys you know or those truck drivers at Louie's place?"

"Nona, I've been out of college for years. And the truckers are mostly older, more like uncles or big brothers."

"So tell me, what is so different about this man? He is special, yes?"

Kara's full lips unconsciously formed a smile. Special. That was a good word for Jake. "Yes."

"But where is the happiness I should be seeing then? Where is the joy?" Her small, fine-boned hand rubbed Kara's cold fingers, as if to infuse them with her own warmth.

Kara dropped her eyes to the table and shook her head, unwilling, unable to say more.

Nona's touch was gentle, caring. "Tell me, Kara *mia*, please."

Kara took a sip of Nona's strong espresso coffee. "There isn't much to tell. He's very tall and has blond hair and a nice beard. He's broad shouldered, quite strong." She was unaware her eyes had softened as her mind slipped to the past few weeks. "He can be funny or silly and can laugh at himself," she said, thinking of how they'd wrestled in the mud, "and he likes poetry. He can be very caring," she went on, recalling the evening they'd taken Danny back to his grandparents. "He isn't afraid of anything."

"Do you love this man, Kara?"

"No!...yes...I don't know." Kara got up and walked to the back door of the cozy kitchen and stood looking out into the gathering dusk shading Nona's garden.

After a moment the older woman spoke softly. "What is it you are not telling me?"

Kara turned to face her, crossing her arms over her breasts. Unused to sharing these new feelings, even with her grandmother, she felt suddenly vulnerable. She searched her troubled mind for the right words. "He's an adventurer, Nona. A man who's traveled the world, lived all over and wants to keep right on doing just that. Right now he's driving trucks for Uncle Louie, but next month he could be off working on motorboats on the east coast. Or somewhere else. We talk a lot, but he's not a man who reveals much of himself. I feel there's something he's holding back, but I can't be sure what it is. I don't think he'll ever settle down. Someone hurt him once and he doesn't really trust women. What he wants is a...a..."

"A playmate?"

Kara couldn't resist a smile. "Where did you learn about playmates, Nona?"

She gave out a quiet chuckle. "Oh, Kara, playmates, they always been around. Maybe people call them other names, but they mean the same thing. And that's not you, am I right?"

"How could I be like that after...after..."

"After your mama." Nona sighed heavily and twisted a napkin absently. "Sure, I know. Your mama's ways left a mark on you, child." Her eyes clouded as she spoke of her daughter. "So this man with the nice beard, he wants you but only for a little while, is that what it is, Kara? And I think maybe, even though for years I hear this independent talk from you, he makes you question what you want. Is that what puts sadness in those big, brown eyes?''

Slowly Kara sat back down. "I don't know myself, Nona. The trouble is I'm becoming more involved with him every time I see him, emotionally involved. I'm beginning to need him, to feel too much, and it scares me. And there are things...things about him that worry me." She shook her head. "I know this whole relationship has nowhere to go."

"Why do you say such a thing?"

"Because, Nona, I've discovered something about myself. I need love. And this man doesn't love me. He just *wants* me. That's not the same thing."

Nona went to stand beside Kara's chair, pulling her against her small frame, hugging her close, her hand caressing her dark hair. "Kara *mia*," she soothed, "nothing ever came easy for you, did it? And now the path of love is rocky, too."

Kara let herself be comforted by the one person who'd always been able to make her feel better. "I don't want to be in love with him, Nona."

Nona smoothed her granddaughter's silken curls and held her close. "I have found, in matters of the heart, often the choice is not ours to make." She kissed the top of Kara's dark head. "Now, enough seriousness. Come, let's put away the food and go out in the garden while it is still light."

Kara's eyes were moist. "I love you, Nona. Thank you."

"I love you, too, Kara *mia*. Don't fret. The answers will come to you, if not today, then tomorrow."

Jake Murphy drove along the winding oceanside road in the deepening twilight and watched as a row of stately royal palm trees dappled the hood of his borrowed red pickup truck with light and shadow. It was another hot and humid July night despite a small sea breeze. He wore his sleeves rolled up, and his khaki shirt stuck to his back.

He'd spent a troubled afternoon, and his mind was busy recapping the events. Accidentally he'd discovered Tennessee Hawkins's faked log entries. He'd gone into the truck depot, grabbed the wrong log book and read several pages before he realized it wasn't his.

Tennessee had recorded that he'd spent eight to ten hours off between his runs, as required by law. But Jake knew Tennessee had been driving with only four to six hours sleep between runs. The impossible schedule was not only hard on a driver but also extremely dangerous.

Jake pulled up to a three-way stop and looked around before resuming his drive along the hilly shoreline street. He'd found Tennessee in the showers, getting ready for another run. Tennessee's eyes were red rimmed, fatigue etched in the lines of his ruddy face. Jake had insisted that Tennessee have coffee with him.

Poor Tennessee, he thought, remembering what the man had told him. He had a lot of problems. Tennessee's face had shown the strains of his worries and his mounting financial burdens as he'd poured his heart out. He had too little time home with his wife who was expecting their fourth child, and she hadn't been feeling well during the sweltering summer months. Their youngest was only a baby of nine months and the older boy, just three, had been recently diagnosed as having a heart murmur. The costly illness was a hardship to an underinsured family.

Though he understood Tennessee's need to make more money and why he'd recorded fake rest periods, Jake warned him that he was headed for trouble. He'd pointed out the possibilities of danger to Tennessee, to Santini Trucking, to his family. What would happen to his wife and children if fatigue took over, and he fell asleep at the wheel of the big semi and crashed? He hoped Tennessee had really listened.

Was Tennessee telling him the truth? he pondered. And, being so vulnerable in his need, could someone corrupt Tennessee, make him do things that ordinarily he would never do? Already he was popping uppers to stay awake. Men under strain often stretched their principles. He'd have to keep his eye on Tennessee.

Jake sighed. What messes people got themselves into, he thought. He'd talk to him again next week. As he drove, Jake wondered if the big, prideful man would consider a loan. Maybe that was one answer. He'd talked to Louie today but hadn't told him about Tennessee. Louie didn't need more worries right now. Perhaps Jake could handle this one for him.

Jake swung around a curve and thought of his conversation that afternoon with Louie. He smiled, remembering Louie telling him that Kara suspected him of the sabotagings. He wasn't surprised. He'd seen her studying him thoughtfully.

Kara Finelli. He sighed, thinking even her name was lovely. Everything about her was lovely. Should he take her into his confidence? he wondered. No, it would serve no purpose at the present time. And, in another couple of months—for surely that's as long as this job would last—he'd be moving on, and Kara would be staying in California for good. He faced that thought with the worst case of mixed emotions he'd ever had to handle.

He was a fine one to ponder the messed up lives of others, Jake thought ruefully. His own needed some straightening out. He'd thought he had everything worked out. His goals had been clearly defined in his own mind. He'd enjoy his job wherever he was. He'd enjoy a life free of attachments. He'd work hard but take time to play, too. And he'd be his own man, answering to no other, not allowing himself ever to get caught again in the rat race as he once had, in his early years.

Thanks to Rob Carter, though he traveled extensively, Jake felt he could remain true to his newfound values. The women who'd shared his bed in the intervening years had come and gone with regularity. Attractive, faceless diversions and nothing more. He'd thought himself a reasonably happy man with a handle on his life. Until this recent job and Kara Finelli. Kara who clouded his mind and made him need again.

He'd known he'd meet a woman one day who'd make him feel again. But was Kara, with her stubborn independence and her drive, the one who could make him settle down, believe again? Instinctively he was drawn to her warmth and passionate responsiveness. Her dark eyes haunted his dreams. But marriage to Cindy had left him a legacy of distrust, and he'd learned his lessons well.

Did he dare believe Kara was different? Jake wondered. She'd once called him a cynic. Was he, or was he just a cautious realist who'd stopped believing in happily ever after? The bottom line—he couldn't seem to stay away from her, and he could only hope something would happen to make him believe she was all he wished her to be.

Jake turned the corner and spotted the small, white frame house set back from the sea in a small cove. Louie had told him Kara'd be visiting her grandmother, and Jake had given in to the urge to see her again, unable to wait for the morning when they'd be driving together again. On the way over he hadn't come up with an excuse to give her for showing up unannounced. He'd think of something.

He parked the truck along the picket fence near the driveway. Alongside the house was a lush garden and vine-covered grape arbor. Probably a great view of the ocean from the backyard, Jake thought as he got out of the car. His heartbeat quickened in anticipation of the sight of Kara as he strolled toward the front.

They were singing, a little off-key, but what did it matter? Kara's slim arm rested on Nona's shoulders as they finished the sweet Italian tune the older woman had crooned to her many times during Kara's childhood. Nona chuckled warmly, then resumed washing the dishes as Kara reached for another plate to dry.

"Ah, you still remember the old songs?" Nona commented.

"How could I forget? All those nights, falling asleep in my room, listening to your soft humming or singing as you sat out here and mended clothes. Good memories, Nona."

"It's nice that you remember the good things, Kara. The bad ones, we should push them aside. It does not help us to think too much on them."

Hearing footsteps on the creaking boards of the porch, they both turned toward the door.

"Now who would be coming here at this hour?" Nona asked. "It's nearly dark."

"I'll go see," Kara offered, laying down the towel. Walking from the kitchen into the small living room, she opened the door, then took a quick step backward in surprise. "Jake! What are you doing here?" His hair was damp, as if from a recent shower, his silver-gray eyes oddly serious. "Is something wrong?"

His smile broke through his golden beard. "Nothing's wrong, Kara. Louie said you'd be here. I asked him for directions to the house."

Kara stood holding the door ajar, conflicting feelings warring inside her. She wanted to confront him, have him explain away the things she suspected. She wanted to lash out at him for her sleepless nights. She wanted to move into his arms and never leave their warmth. She seemed to have lost control of her brain. He looked a little ill at ease, a shade embarrassed, a state she'd never seen him in before. "Did you want something?"

"I just wanted to see you," he said honestly.

She saw a hesitant vulnerability in his eyes, and her heart turned over. With a welcoming smile, she reached to touch him. "Come in. I'd like you to meet my grandmother." Kara closed the door behind him and led him into the kitchen where Nona waited, having quietly watched the two of them talking at the door. "Nona, this is Jake Murphy. We drive together sometimes for Uncle Louie. Jake, this is my grandmother."

"Welcome to my home, Mr. Murphy," Nona said, extending her small hand toward the big man. It was soon lost in his powerful grip.

"My pleasure, Nona," Jake said smiling, not even stumbling over the familiarity. "Please call me Jake." His smoky gaze took in the friendly, neat room with its small, corner fireplace. "What a nice kitchen you have here."

"Thank you, Jake," Nona answered, retrieving her hand, her keen, dark eyes on the rugged features of his face. "It's heard a lot of laughter. And seen a few tears as well."

As if he were an old friend who'd dropped in, Jake picked up a stack of dried dishes. Opening a cupboard, he reached up to put them away. "I noticed your tomato plants at the side of the house," he said conversationally to Nona as she stuck her hands back into the soapy water to wash out a big pot. "What do you use as fertilizer? They're huge!"

Nona smiled at his interest. "Ah, you noticed my prize plants, did you? I will tell you my secret. It's sheep manure. Most people don't use it, but you try it and you will see. Your tomatoes will climb past your windows."

Trying to cover up her surprise, Kara continued drying dishes as she listened to the two of them chatting away like old neighbors. She was absolutely certain Jake Murphy hadn't a moment's interest in raising tomatoes, yet there he stood, captivating even wise old Nona. The man had no shame!

Nona finished the last dish and turned to her granddaughter. "Kara, sit with your friend at the table. I have fresh coffee and apricot cookies."

"Oh, Nona," Kara said, feeling a little closed in by Jake's broad-shouldered presence in the small house, "I'm sure Jake has more important things to do."

In the bright kitchen light Jake's eyes were filled with amusement at her discomfort. "This is your lucky night. I'm free as a bird and I love apricot cookies. My mother used to make them. Tell me, Nona, do you have an apricot tree out back?"

And they're off and running again, Kara thought, seeing Nona's pleased smile as she launched into a discussion of her fruit trees. She moved to get the coffee cups, resigned to being odd man out in this unlikely trio.

For the next half hour Kara listened to Jake and Nona hop from one subject to another with astounding ease, adding only an occasional nod or smile when they noticed her. Finally she got up and gathered the cups, placing them in the sink. Standing by the table, she put her hands on her hips. "Come on, you two," she said, interrupting an intense discussion on the advisability of growing herbs in the shade as opposed to the sun. "Let's go out into the garden. It's so lovely out there."

Nona glanced briefly at the clock then shook her head. "No, Kara. I will finish here. You and Jake go out into the garden. You show him my flowers."

"Leave these few dishes, and I'll do them later," Kara protested. "You come with us."

Nona's small, determined hands opened the back door. "Later. I want to watch a television show first."

"Nona," Kara said with a puzzled frown, "you don't even *like* television...."

"Shoo! Out you go. Enjoy the fragrances and the fireflies dancing in my flowers. I'll be along soon."

Recognizing defeat when she saw it, Kara smiled at her grandmother. Turning aside, she removed a small piece of paper from her canvas bag, slipped it into her pocket and moved through the door.

Close behind her, Jake paused, the back of his hand grazing the old woman's soft cheek before he lowered his head and kissed it lightly. "Thank you, Nona, for understanding." He ducked out the doorway and pulled the screen shut behind him.

So he's won her over, too, Kara thought, walking along a small brick path through the center of the garden. From eight to eighty, he gets them all. She sighed, stepping past the sweet basil, the lush tomato plants straining at their stakes, the rows of cabbage and zucchini. Jake moved alongside her as she stepped through the arches of a heavy grapevine. She sat down on a small wooden bench, inhaling the wondrous scent of nearby rosebushes and glanced up at a full moon playing hide-and-seek with a few wispy clouds.

Jake's hooded eyes roamed approvingly over her lovely face. The soft yellow material of her dress strained over her full breasts and fell in soft folds about her knees as she crossed slim, tan legs. She wore no jewelry; her dark hair hung long and lustrous to her bare shoulders. He plunged his hands into his pockets to keep from reaching out and touching her.

"I knew you had legs if you'd just get out of those jeans once in a while."

"Of course I've got legs," she answered, a bit harsher than she'd intended.

"Are you angry because I came to find you?" Jake asked, sitting down beside her, placing his arm along the back as he angled to face her.

"No," she admitted reluctantly. She *had* missed him, in spite of her misgivings. Yet those worries now brought a frown to her face. "Jake, I need to ask you about something."

"Go ahead," he invited, crossing his legs.

"The cargo that Tennessee and I took to Tulsa—are you aware it was stolen merchandise with phony numbers on the manifest?"

"Yes, I heard about that."

Had she imagined it or had his voice grown a fraction colder? "Do you know who checked the load? Who approved and initialed the manifest?" she asked, turning at last to search his eyes. They were as calm and direct as his voice.

"No. Who?"

"You," she said.

Something flickered in the gray depths of his eyes. "What makes you say that?" he asked.

Sighing, she reached into the small side pocket of her dress and pulled out the damning evidence, the torn edge of the manifest sheet. Wordlessly she handed it to him.

Jake held the slip of paper out and studied it for a long moment beneath a large splash of moonlight. Louie had been right when he'd said Kara suspected him. What neither of them had known was that someone evidently had decided to point a finger at him. Quietly he folded the paper and handed it back to her. "I didn't write that, Kara. I never touched that manifest sheet."

She shoved it back into her pocket. Hugging her arms, she stared out into the moon-drenched flower beds, her thoughts racing around in her head like tiny, disturbed mice caught in a maze. The monotonous hum of crickets filled the ocean air, mingling with the steady pounding of the surf behind them. Leaves rustled with night birds, and she sensed the movements of small, furry animals scampering about. Fireflies winked and blinked like miniature candles in the velvet sky.

"You don't believe me," Jake said. It was not a question.

"I don't know what to believe, Jake," she replied honestly.

"Some things you just have to take on faith, Kara. I can't help you with this one. I respect, admire and like Louie Santini, and I wouldn't hurt him. You either believe me or you don't."

Kara turned to face him, studying his eyes. They looked sincere and honest. She wanted badly to believe him.

Jake watched the play of emotions on her face as she struggled with her feelings. Was he trying to test her by not bringing her in on the truth? He didn't know for sure. But he did know he shouldn't touch her. Not if he wanted to talk with her. Because once he touched her, the fire would take over, and there'd be no more talk. He couldn't stop himself. He reached out, ran his hand along her silken shoulders, up under her heavy hair, caressing her neck. He saw her eyes change, her body suddenly relax as she leaned slightly toward him.

"Hold me, Jake, please," she asked. "I need to be held."

Strong arms encircled her and pulled her against him. Slow warmth flooded her senses, a feeling of familiarity. Jake held her head against his heart, stroking her hair as she closed her eyes.

She'd known him such a short time, Kara thought, yet it was like coming home to return to his embrace. He had to be a good man, an honest one. He held her heart in his hands as surely as he held her body.

"Your grandmother's quite a lady," Jake said, leaning back, his silvery eyes finding hers. "She doesn't miss a trick." His hand on her back traced a slow path up and down her spine. It felt so good to sit here and hold her, talk with her. Once, he'd never have believed he'd feel so content just *being* with someone.

Kara smiled warmly. "Nona's very special." A sudden sadness swept over her. "I can't bear the thought that one day she won't be here and that I can't do anything to stop that."

"Who supports her?"

"She has a small pension from my grandfather. And Louie helps out. I do what I can when I can."

"And your mother?" he asked. He saw her shrug in the pale moonlight, her gaze moving to the far corner where fragrant bougainvillea climbed along the fence. "You and Louie, right? You don't give yourself much breathing room, do you, Kara?" He felt her burrow into

Silhouette's

Best Ever "Get Acquainted" Offer

Look what we'd give to hear from you

6 **FREE GIFTS** 6

Return This Sticker
and Get 6 Gifts—FREE
Compliments of Silhouette

▲ **GET ALL YOU ARE** ▲
ENTITLED TO—AFFIX STICKER
TO RETURN CARD—MAIL TODAY

This is our most fabulous offer ever...
AND THERE'S STILL
MORE INSIDE.
Let's get acquainted.
Let's become
friends—

Look what we've got for you:

Get 4 FREE full-length Silhouette Special Edition® novels.

Plus a handy compact umbrella

Plus a surprise free gift

▼ PLUS LOTS MORE! MAIL THIS CARD TODAY ▼

Silhouette's Best-Ever "Get Acquainted" Offer

Yes, I'll try the Silhouette preview service under the terms outlined on the opposite page. Send me 4 free Silhouette Special Edition® novels, a free compact umbrella and a free mystery gift.

235 CIL R1W3

PLACE STICKER FOR 6 FREE GIFTS HERE

NAME _____ APT. ____

ADDRESS _____

CITY _____

STATE _____ ZIP CODE ____

Gift offer limited to new subscribers, one per household. Terms and prices subject to change.

PRINTED IN U.S.A.

Don't forget...

...Return this card today to receive your 4 free books, free compact umbrella and free mystery gift.

...You will receive books before they're available in stores and at a discount off retail prices.

...No obligation. Keep only the books you want and cancel anytime.

If offer card is missing, write to: Silhouette Books, 901 Fuhrmann Blvd., P.O. Box 1867, Buffalo, NY 14269-1867

BUSINESS REPLY CARD

First Class   Permit No. 717   Buffalo, NY

Postage will be paid by addressee

Silhouette® Books
901 Fuhrmann Blvd.
P.O. Box 1867
Buffalo, NY 14240-9952

No Postage
Necessary
If Mailed
In The
United States

him as his hand caressed her. "Such small shoulders for such big burdens. Why do you take on so much?"

She spoke into his chest. "It's important to me or I wouldn't do it. Nona raised me, almost by herself. My mother can scarcely take care of herself. She...she can't make it alone. What would you have me do—walk away from her? And I owe Louie this summer. Then it'll be my turn. I can spend my days at my studio. It'll be *my* time."

"Got it all figured out nice and neat and orderly, haven't you?"

"Yes." She remembered what Louie'd said about Jake walking away from a good job and all responsibility to live his life his own way. She didn't want to argue with him, not tonight. But she felt they were worlds apart in their viewpoints. "I feel comfortable with debts repaid, order in my life. Don't you?"

Jake knew she was asking more than the simple question implied. He wasn't sure how to answer her without revealing more than he wanted. He took his arm from around her, leaned over and plucked a fragile pink rose. He held it just under her nose. "Smell it," he instructed.

Eyes closed, she inhaled deeply of the rich fragrance. "Mmm, lovely," she murmured.

"When was the last time you did that, Kara? Took time to sit in a garden and smell a flower—and not feel guilty about not doing something else more important?"

She thought for a moment of her musings that morning while walking on her beach, thinking she should take more time to enjoy the things she liked to do. In many ways she knew Jake was right. "A very long time," she answered him.

He pulled her close within his arms again, his chin resting atop her head. "I was like you once. Working my

tail off. Doing everything that everyone expected of me
Being all my father wanted me to be. And I didn't ever
notice that my mother was dying, that my marriage wa
falling apart.''

She leaned back to look at him, remembering an ear
lier conversation they'd had when she'd been sure a
woman had once hurt him. "You have a wife?" she
asked.

"*Ex*-wife. I'll tell you about it sometime, though it'
not exactly a pretty story. She was wrong for me, but
was wrong about a lot of things, too." His eyes scanned
hers. "Be careful, Kara. It's okay to want things, be full
of ambition, but sometimes life has a way of passing u
by. We wake up one day and realize we've been dream
ing the wrong dreams."

Kara struggled with her jumbled thoughts about he
strong attraction to this puzzling man, the possibility tha
he might be hiding something, perhaps be involved
somehow in Louie's problems and the knowledge that she
couldn't seem to stop wanting him. "What do you do
when your dream dies?" she asked.

He shrugged. "You get another dream."

She sat up, uncertain. "I'm not much of a dreamer
I'm a realist. I've always had to be."

Jake took her by the hand, walked her to just under the
tangled grapevines and pointed up at the night sky full of
stars dancing around a pale yellow moon. "Look up
there at that shiny star. Make a wish. That's how you
start a dream."

She followed his gaze and stared for a long moment
then closed her eyes.

He held her loosely in his arms until finally, she opened
her eyes, luminous in the silvery light. "Gardens are
loveliest in moonlight. So are beautiful women," he told

her, his arms pulling her closer. "You *are* very beautiful, you know, with the most expressive eyes. A man could get lost in them." His eyes softened as he studied hers. "I think I already may have."

They stood in the shadow of the grape arbor, hidden from view of the house and road, and gazed silently at each other long and solemnly. Very slowly Jake lowered his head and pressed his lips to hers in a kiss that was as gentle as a summer's breeze, so different from the others they'd shared and, therefore, much more devastating. With limited experience Kara had fewer defenses against tenderness than passion. He took his time, his soft mouth claiming hers with subtle persuasion. The bristliness of his beard rubbing against her face added to the sensations. She clung to the cotton fabric of his rolled-up shirtsleeves, trying to steady her world, but soon gave up and slid her hands over his broad shoulders, up and around his neck, into the thickness of his hair as she rose on tiptoe and molded her body along the length of his.

She parted her lips to receive the welcome invasion of his tongue, sighing as he entered her mouth. Breaths mingled, hearts beat against each other through thin, damp material as their awakening bodies strained for a melding they both desired. Kara felt a passion that had lain sleeping like a threatening storm hiding behind a layer of heavy clouds until Jake had brushed away the wispy barriers. They were gone now, all gone.

He moved his mouth over hers, deepening the kiss, his tongue teasing and tasting. Her anxious, questing hands moved to caress the strong muscles of his shoulders and forearms, gripping his shirt tightly as she moaned his name. Wanting him, needing him, her mouth was avid and seeking. She was his.

Jake broke away and bent his head to give his full attention to the lovely column of her neck as she clung to him, her breathing ragged, her body quivering with her need. She pulled his head back, closing her eyes, inviting his lips to claim hers again.

Abruptly he released her and stepped back, his arms loosening their hold on her. "No," she protested his withdrawal and urged his mouth back to hers. For a wild, beautiful moment, his mouth bruised hers, his special taste flooding her senses, then he wrenched away. His hands on her shoulders were strong and firm.

Her confusion, her need, her willingness were naked in her eyes, staring out at him, accusing him. Jake's oath was fierce as he turned away. "I'll see you in the morning, Kara."

"Wait. What . . . I . . ." her voice was ragged, low in its pain.

He made himself turn and look at her and wished he hadn't. He hated himself for what he was doing to her but knew that he had to do it fast and leave her. "Kara, one of us has to be sensible."

"Sensible!" She sucked in a harsh gulp of air. "I've been six times sideways sensible all my life. For once I don't want to be, and you turn and walk away!"

"I don't deny that it's my fault. I'm sorry."

His matter-of-fact tone scraped at Kara's pride even as it triggered her temper. Her voice filled with anger as she ran shaky hands through her hair and stared off into the night sky. "I don't want your damn apologies."

Through the maze of his own uncertain feelings, Jake was relieved she was angry with him. He could handle anything but seeing the hurt in her eyes. How could he make her understand?

If he held her a moment longer, he'd lose all control, pick her up, carry her to his truck and cart her off to his bed. Only he'd had his fill of one-night stands.

The Hungarian gypsy woman's forecast came back to haunt him. He'd find his love in a rose garden, she'd said. Only he didn't want to fall in love with Kara Finelli. Not this strong, talented, independent lady who, despite her sudden indications to the contrary, wanted no permanent partner, needed no man in her life, especially not a bruised and battered one.

He needed someone all right, someone who believed in him, who wouldn't change on him this time, someone who'd love him always. Someone who could make him believe in forever again. But Kara chased a different dream. How could he ask her to give up hers and embrace his?

She was feeling desire for him now, but that's all it was. In a few weeks she would have enough of playing truck driver, and she'd go back to her beach house, her animals, her camera and never think of Jake Murphy again. Her mother had taught her well. Always was a foolish dream.

She was hurt, thinking he'd rejected her, he knew. But in the long run she would thank him. He'd have to make her see. Desire. That's all they had between them. It wasn't enough, not by a long shot.

Jake ran a hand through his hair and moved to her. "Don't you know what a problem I've had keeping my hands off you ever since I first saw you? If it makes you feel any better, there's nothing I want more than to make love to you all night long." His voice was low, strained.

Flashing eyes met his level, gray gaze. "What exactly is keeping you from doing just that?" she asked.

He turned away, shaking his head in a helpless gesture. "A lot of reasons."

Kara threw back her head and stared angrily at the heavens. "I can't believe I'm actually standing here, begging you, pleading with you, when for weeks you've been... you've been... Oh! This is ridiculous!" She turned and started toward the house.

"Kara, wait. You don't understand!"

She whirled back, brown eyes blazing. "No, and I probably never will!"

Chapter Seven

Cool! That was how she was going to conduct herself on this run, Kara decided a week later as she drove through sporadic Monday morning traffic on the way to the truck yard. After that disturbing encounter in Nona's garden, she'd done something she'd not done in all the years she'd driven for Louie. She'd called in sick, and they'd had to get another driver to accompany Jake back to Michigan. She'd spent the day holed up in her house doing absolutely nothing, not even answering her phone, and the following morning she'd taken an early load out with Phil. She hoped Louie'd understand her recent ambivalence, Kara thought with an impatient sigh.

She'd spent the long days and nights of that drive doing a lot of thinking, and now she was scheduled to take the next run with Jake. She was annoyed to realize she still didn't feel much better about it. Vacillating between hurt and anger, she'd tossed and turned half the previous night, reliving the events of her last evening with Jake. She'd decided to pretend that he hadn't gotten to her, that she didn't care, that *he* didn't matter to her.

Liar! her mind screamed as she stopped just in time for a red light. All her life she'd wanted to be her own person, to depend only on herself, to be free to do as she pleased. She'd worked hard, and she was almost there. And then Jake Murphy had strolled into her life and had her questioning everything.

She must be crazy, Kara decided, entertaining thoughts of love. Perhaps it was the moonlight in Nona's garden. The last thing she needed was to fall in love. Being in love, she knew from firsthand observation, was something like having your feet firmly planted in shifting sand. She'd always preferred solid ground.

Thoughts of love frightened her, as they always had. What she'd seen of her mother's life and some of her friends' had shown her that loving meant dependence, losing control of your life, acquiescing. She couldn't handle that. Jake had overwhelmed her from the first with feelings too powerful to trust and then had proceeded to frustrate her at every turn. She'd discovered that she didn't frustrate well.

The last time she and Jake had been together, she'd practically thrown herself at him, and he obviously didn't want her. From now on, she vowed, she'd keep herself in control, not let him see that he was affecting her. Two could play this game.

Kara swung into the parking lot in a swirl of dust and turned off the ignition. She glanced at her rig. Through her sunglasses she saw Cowboy and Jake emerging from beneath the cab. They stood talking, Cowboy wiping his greasy hands on a rag while Jake's hooded gaze moved past him and found her.

Feigning indifference, Kara stepped out and closed her door with exaggerated care. She shifted her canvas tote and slowly walked toward the office. As she entered the building, she felt a cooling rush of air greet her, a welcome respite from hot green eyes.

The office was empty. She walked to the coffee urn and poured herself a cup. As she sipped the hot, bracing liquid, she strolled to look out the window. She watched Pauly drive up, park and amble over to Jake and Cowboy. Cowboy turned to her and smiled that slow, lazy grin. He removed his hat and wiped his face with a checkered handkerchief as Pauly stood talking with him, her plain face more animated than Kara had ever seen it.

Her earlier assessment had been wrong, Kara thought with a shock. There is a certain way a man and woman behave with each other after they've been intimate. The closeness shows in the way they touch, in a special look they exchange, in a gesture. As she watched Cowboy and Pauly, she realized they were—or had been—lovers, as Tennessee had hinted the day they'd discussed the two of them. But Kara noticed a slight edge of desperation to Pauly now that she hadn't seen before. Something had occurred between them, something that hadn't pleased Pauly. She wondered what.

As Jake glanced toward the building, she stepped back from the window. The last thing she wanted right now was a confrontation with him. It was bad enough that they'd have to spend hours alone together in the close confines of the cab. But there she planned to keep busy taking pictures. She'd answer him with indifference, turn him off with icy retorts or pretend fatigue and crawl into the sleeping compartment. Yawning expansively, she realized she wouldn't need to pretend weariness. Her nerves on edge, she turned, startled, as the door opened. Seeing Pauly, she gave a shaky smile.

"My, my, aren't you jumpy?" Pauly said.

"I guess so," Kara admitted, taking the chair opposite Pauly's desk. She took a long sip of coffee, avoiding the older woman's eyes. All those years growing up under Pauly's watchful gaze, working with her, laughing and talking with her, she'd never once thought of her as a woman in love. *How shortsighted of me,* Kara realized. Her mind flew to her own problems with Jake. *Perhaps Pauly and I have more in common than I'd thought.*

Pauly poured herself some coffee and sat down at her desk, her blue eyes studying Kara over the rim of the cup. "What are you hiding behind those dark glasses, honey?" she asked in her soft Southern voice. "A couple of sleepless nights?"

Kara set down her cup. "What makes you think that?"

"Oh, nothing much. Except I was just out there talking with Jake, and he's touchy as hell and meaner than a snake this morning. And I find you, looking pale and jumpy as a hen at layin' time. I know you two been driving together, that you're scheduled out again today. My busy mind just put two and two together, that's all." She leaned forward, her eyes serious. "If I'm being too personal, just tell me so."

Kara removed her sunglasses and rubbed the bridge of her nose with an unsteady hand. "It's all right. I didn't realize I was so transparent."

"You're not, honey. Except to those of us who care about you. I told you once before, I'm here if you want to talk."

Kara sighed and shook her head. "I don't know, Pauly. I seem to be confused all the time these days."

"What is it you want, honey? Is it Jake?"

A ragged sound escaped from her throat. "Want him?" she asked, turning to look out the window.

"But you don't *want* to want him, right?" She saw Kara's almost imperceptible nod. "And you want other things more?"

Kara blinked back sudden moisture. "More? I don't know. A drifter like Jake Murphy could hardly understand the kind of life I want. I can't imagine why I've allowed myself to get involved with a man like him in the first place. Stupid."

Pauly glanced toward the window wistfully, then returned her eyes to Kara's troubled profile. "Not stupid, honey. Just human. They don't usually put wisdom, or even common sense, in the same package with love. A teenage boy picks out a car with more care than a woman picks out a man to love. Trouble is, we don't always do the pickin'. He comes along, smiles at us in that special way, and sometimes that's all we need. Maybe it's all in the timing. We were just ready when he walked in the door."

"I'm *not* ready," Kara protested. "I don't want this complication. I want to go back to California, finish decorating my house, take my pictures, ride my horse, listen to my sea. I don't need this now. Maybe, one day, when I'm secure, more sure of myself. Then, I'll be ready."

Pauly leaned back and crossed her long, thin legs. "You and I both know we can't pick the time or place, maybe not even the man. You've been hurt and disappointed by people a lot in the past. You're afraid to trust anyone with your heart, afraid they'll walk away like all them men did from your mama. You simply got to take a chance on lovin', Kara. Maybe Jake's not at all like you got him figured out to be. You need a strong man, honey, and he *is* that. You better not let him get away.''

''How do you know he's all you say he is?'' Kara asked, her face looking suddenly young and vulnerable.

''Instinct. I go a lot on instinct. You got to when you start out as a teenage migrant picker on a hot, Texas farm. I may not have that college degree, but I know people and that's one fine man you got there.''

Kara shook her head. ''I certainly don't *have* Jake. He...''

Pauly's bright laugh broke into the quiet room, causing Kara to glance at her, widening her eyes. ''Oh, Kara, honey, what are we going to do with you? You don't even know when a man is plain crazy about you!''

Unbidden, a small hope flared in Kara's eyes before it died as suddenly as it was born. ''You're wrong, Pauly. Jake doesn't want me. Physically maybe, but that's all.''

''Don't pay no attention to what his mouth says. It's in his eyes. I'd give a lot to have a man look at me the way that man looks at you. If ever in the world I saw someone in love, it's Jake Murphy.''

''Did I hear my name mentioned?'' Jake said from the doorway as both women turned to face him.

Pauly recovered first. ''Sure did. I was just telling Kara she didn't have to worry none driving with you. You're the best there is.''

Jake's expression was unreadable as he came into the room. ''I'll bet you tell that to all the drivers, Pauly. Got 'em all eating out of your hand that way.''

She laughed broadly and winked up at him. ''Looks like you see right through me, Jake.''

Silver eyes slid to Kara. He studied her a long moment as she busied herself adjusting her sunglasses. ''You ready to roll? Cowboy and I did a little checking and everything seems okay.''

Quickly she got to her feet. "Ready as I'll ever be," she said as coolly as she could manage. She smiled at Pauly. "I'm glad we talked. I'll see you when we get back, Pauly.''

"Have a good trip, you two.''

Kara brushed past Jake and moved to the door. He watched her leave. Tipping his baseball hat to Pauly, he followed Kara to the truck in his slow, easy gait.

Pauly picked up her coffee mug and walked to look out the window. Never had she run across two more volatile people. She'd give a week's pay to be a birdie on the dash during that ride, she thought, watching the two of them with a slow smile.

Hearing the door open behind her, Pauly turned to see Cowboy enter and head for the coffeepot. As she resumed her seat, she watched him pour a cup, then smack his thin lips in appreciation. He'd always been crazy about her coffee. If only he cared as much about her as he did her cooking, maybe things could be different, she thought, waiting for him to speak. Cowboy wasn't one to chat. Something was likely on his mind or he wouldn't have come in at all.

"You're looking mighty nice today," he said, smiling at her over the rim of his cup.

Compliments early in the morning. Now she was certain he was after something. Guardedly she returned his smile. "Thanks.''

"I'm surprised Jake's going out with Kara again," he went on, pushing his black Stetson farther back on his head. "Didn't think those two got along.''

Pauly shrugged noncommittally. "We're short-handed.''

"That Kara's some woman," Cowboy said, seating himself across from her and crossing his lanky legs. "Can't say I blame Jake for wanting to be with her, never mind she's a spitfire."

"Kara's a fine woman," Pauly defended. "They don't come no better."

"Maybe. But already, since riding with her regular, Jake's more moody, defensive, apt to fly off the handle. Before he wakes up, she'll probably mess him up real good." He shook his head. "Jake's got a lot to learn."

Pauly leaned back, but her eyes never left Cowboy's face. "Lots of people do. That don't mean they're willing to."

Cowboy stared back at her for a long moment, then stood abruptly. Glancing at the papers scattered on her desk, he picked one up. "This the route Jake's planning on taking? Maybe I'll follow behind, see if I can talk some sense into him before he gets himself burned over that woman." His eyes busily scanned the page until Pauly snatched it from his hand.

"Mind your own business, Cowboy," she told him angrily. "I didn't know Jake was such a *good* friend of yours that you feel the need to butt in where your advice ain't wanted or needed."

Putting down his cup, he shot her a narrow-eyed look. "He ain't. Drives me crazy, matter of fact. Too damn snoopy for his own good. He better straighten up right soon, or someone's liable to teach him a lesson long overdue." Adjusting his hat, Cowboy turned and made for the door.

"Just what do you mean by that?" Pauly asked, a note of suspicion in her voice.

Stopping with his hand on the knob, he stood still for long minutes before swiveling back to her. On his face was a small smile that didn't soften his eyes. "Nothin'. I didn't mean nothin'. I was just thinking of Kara. And Louie. He's not going to like finding out Kara's mixed up with a guy like Jake. If she was my niece, I'd tell her to run like hell from him. That man spells trouble. See you next week." Flicking two fingers to the rim of his hat, he walked through the door.

Pauly sat staring after him, wondering what to make of their strange conversation. First, Cowboy'd ranted about wanting to follow Jake, to warn him about women, then all but told her he didn't like Jake and was only thinking of Kara. Mighty confusing.

Reaching for a cigarette, she lit it thoughtfully. Damned if she'd ever be able to figure out that man. Or the reason why she wanted to. With a resigned sigh Pauly turned to face the workload on her desk.

Kara'd done everything possible through the morning to annoy him, Jake thought as he drove the big semi on the highway westward. He'd tried to get out of this run but Louie was shorthanded and uncharacteristically short-tempered these days. Not that he blamed him. Big Jim had a pulled shoulder muscle, and the long hours had finally gotten to Tennessee. He'd called in sick two days in a row. So he'd had no choice but to drive with Kara. Though his eyes were on the road, his thoughts were centered on the slim woman beside him who was slowly driving him crazy.

Was it deliberate? he wondered. Hard to tell. Take her outfit. It wasn't so much *what* she was wearing, as *how* she was wearing it that annoyed him. Instead of her usual blue jeans, she had on olive drab cotton slacks with large pockets that fit as smoothly as a second skin on her round curves and down her slim legs. And the matching short-

sleeved knit shirt with its scooped neck clearly outlined
her full breasts. Beads of perspiration appeared on his
forehead as he remembered the feel of them under his
hands the morning she'd allowed him to touch her in the
shower. A thin gold chain nestled in the low vee of her
neckline and moved slightly each time she breathed. Jake
swallowed hard.

He knew she was angry with him because he'd walked
away from her in Nona's garden. What she didn't know
was that he *had* to leave—and fast. She'd responded
openly and honestly to him, her desire evident. He'd
wanted nothing more than to take her, then and there,
and make her his.

But he knew once would never be enough with Kara.
He felt more than just physical desire for her, and it had
suddenly made him back off. More honestly, it had
scared the hell out of him. Too many emotions warred
inside him. She was a strong, independent woman but
soft and vulnerable, too. He didn't want to hurt her, but
he knew instinctively that she could hurt him, also. He'd
been glad to drive back to Michigan alone, needing some
time and space.

Jake sighed. For all the good it had done him, he acknowledged wryly. He'd put distance between them, but
Kara had stayed with him, in his daytime thoughts and
his nighttime dreams. And now she was here beside him,
intent on tormenting him, and he was right back to
square one.

She'd neatly sidestepped all of his attempts at conversation. Lazily she removed her boots, tossed them back
into the sleeper with her bag and slipped on sandals.
From the corner of his eye he saw that her pink painted
toenails contrasted beautifully with her tanned skin. Sitting beside him, she brushed her long dark hair until it

shone, then fastened it with a gold clip at the nape of her neck, creating a girlish look that belied the sensuality of her sun-warmed skin and her woman's body. Jake ground his teeth. Yes, definitely, she had a woman's body, one that was too enticing and too near.

Seemingly unaware of his discomfort, she took a small vial from her purse and sprayed small whiffs of cologne on her inner arms, her throat, her neck. He didn't know what scent it was; he only knew that it mingled with the warm woman aroma of her, and it was sending him over the edge. He'd had just about enough, he decided.

"Just what do you think you're doing?" he spat out between clenched teeth.

Brown eyes swimming in innocence swung his way. "What do you mean?"

"You know damn well what I mean. If you're trying to get to me, to punish me for the other night, okay, you win. I acted like a heel, and I'm sorry. What more do you want?"

His voice seemed strained to the breaking point. *Good,* she thought. *Your turn, buster.* She pretended not to notice his discomfort. "I'm sure I don't have the slightest idea what you're talking about." Deliberately she scooted down in her seat, placed her baseball cap low over her eyes and, crossing her arms casually under her breasts, closed her eyes.

Though unspoken words charged the air, the morning passed in silence. At the luncheon stop Kara scooted out and joined Stella and Ray, two truckers she'd known for years. Ignoring the threesome with deliberate nonchalance, Jake walked by the booth they occupied and chose a seat at the counter. As his eyes met hers several times in the mirror behind the counter, Kara noticed his speculative frown.

Taking over driving chores in a light drizzle after lunch, Kara hoped Jake would crawl into the sleeper, but he jumped up into the passenger seat instead and, with seemingly rapt attention, studied the passing landscape. As she tried to relax her tight shoulder muscles, Kara wondered at her wisdom in taunting him that morning. Though she'd begun the game, the strain between them was beginning to take its toll on her. She wasn't even sure what she'd hoped to accomplish. She only knew she'd wanted to jolt him. Maybe he was right, and she had wanted to get even with him for hurting her that night in the garden. She'd never been rejected before, at least not quite so blatantly. It was hard to take, especially from a man she'd wanted desperately. And still did.

Jake was sleeping when the rain became heavier, the wind picking up and unrelentingly slamming gusts of water across the windshield. Kara lessened her speed, and still she felt the swaying of the trailer. After nearly an hour, the rainfall became a full-fledged storm. A broad clap of thunder roused Jake from a deep sleep. He sat up straighter, rubbed his eyes and looked about.

"It's pretty bad out there. You'd better pull over and let me drive."

"I'm doing fine, thank you."

"Don't be stupid. I'm a lot stronger than you."

Fire flashed into Kara's eyes as she gripped the wheel harder. "If you'd care to look in my wallet, you'll find a chauffeur's license in there that states that I am as capable of handling this truck as you are. Why don't you just go back to sleep and let me be."

"Damn but you're a stubborn female!" he roared.

"And you're a bullheaded man who thinks he can do most anything better than a woman. No wonder your wife left you!"

The moment she'd said it, she'd known she'd gone too far. Chips of ice were in his cold, gray eyes as he turned to her. "She didn't leave me. I threw her out. Just like I'm going to throw you out if you don't pull over and turn the wheel over to me."

"Jake," she said, her voice suddenly soft, "I'm sorry. That was wrong of me. I didn't mean it."

He chose to ignore her apology. He was quiet a long minute. "We're coming to a bridge a couple of miles ahead. Stop under it and let's sit it out, at least until the worst of the storm is over."

Kara knew she was a stubborn woman, but not stubborn enough to get them both killed trying to prove a point. She slowed, spotting the low bridge and flicked on her right turn signal. Carefully she eased the truck to a halt under cover of the bridge. She shifted into park, letting the motor idle. Fierce winds threw sheets of rain at them, and, with the windshield wipers off, Kara stared at a gray world through torrents of water, her thoughts as skittish as the errant drops of rain that slivered and slid down the glass. She felt the tension building in the cab as surely as she saw the foggy mist forming on the windows. She was trapped in a cocoon of her own making.

Turning to gaze out the side window, she noted that the storm showed no signs of letting up, the sky as dark as late evening instead of early afternoon. She clutched her hands together in her lap. If only they had reached their stop before the storm had begun, then she'd be alone, separated from Jake, able to ignore the need that his nearness awakened inside her. Could she ever escape that desire now that she'd discovered it? she asked herself, not for the first time.

A large, warm hand closed on her arm. Kara shifted questioning eyes to Jake. He'd moved along the seat closer to her, his eyes smoky and searching.

"What is it you're looking for in a man, Kara?" he asked, his voice as uncertain as she felt.

"I'm not looking for a man," she said, deliberately misunderstanding.

"Answer me," he insisted.

"Who's playing games now?"

"Indulge me."

She narrowed her eyes thoughtfully. "A strong man who's not afraid to be tender. A man who knows how to laugh. A man who would love me completely, with all my faults and imperfections, for what I *am*, not what he might wish me to be."

His eyes probed hers. "And if you found such a man, what would you do?"

"Return the favor," she answered instantly.

"I see something in your eyes," he said, his voice suddenly husky. "What is it you *really* want?"

Kara sighed. Pauly had asked her the same question, the question that Kara had asked herself endlessly, and now Jake wanted an answer. She wasn't experienced enough to know how a man like Jake felt about a woman like her sharing herself with him. Would he know that for her it could never be casual, ordinary—especially not with him? She examined his eyes, realizing she'd never know unless she took the chance. Afterward if he still didn't care about her, at least she'd have something to remember.

"You," she said, letting her need show in her eyes. "Only you."

Something flickered in the silvery depth of his eyes. With a soft moan he reached to gather her to him. He took her mouth with gentle possession. Without a moment's hesitation her tongue sought his. The kiss deepened into a quiet affirmation of mutual need.

Jake lifted his head to look into her face. His hand slid from her waist to expertly encircle her breast as her large brown eyes became lost in his. His sensitive fingers felt her flesh swell through her thin shirt, reaching out to him. He watched her eyes darken with desire as he caressed her, felt her heartbeat pound against his touch. "You are so very responsive," he whispered, his lips placing small kisses along the softness of her cheek and along her jaw.

For a long time she'd doubted that she'd respond openly and freely to anyone. "Only with you," she said, her arms tightening about him, her back arching as she moved away from the restrictions of the steering wheel.

His hands framed her lovely face, his mouth losing itself in hers as her body stretched along the length of his, straining to be closer. He felt her shiver as he devoured her lips. Passion, too long suppressed, exploded behind his closed eyelids. He pushed away from her.

Startled, Kara's eyes flew open. *Dear God, not again. Would these games never end?*

But Jake's eyes were filled with purpose. He lifted her onto his lap. "I know of a place, not far from here. Are you sure?"

Her answer was immediate. "Yes."

Still he hesitated. "I can't promise I won't hurt you."

Her eyes were steady. "I know. I'm not going to fall in love with you, Jake Murphy," she promised, the lie coming easily from her lips.

"A wise decision," he answered. Shifting over, he placed her on the passenger's side and moved behind the wheel.

In less than twenty minutes he'd pulled off the high-way and into the parking lot of a roadside motel that boasted a vacancy. Through the steady rain Kara could see a string of individual cabins dotting a grassy area. The chill wind whipped at his clothes as Jake ran to the office to register. Kara shivered, surprised at how this summer storm had suddenly cooled everything down.

In moments Jake ran back, grabbed their bags and helped her down. Shielding her from the worst of the rain with his body, he led her quickly to one of the far cabins.

A sharp clap of thunder echoed briefly as Jake closed the door behind them. Kara shook excess water from her hair and looked around. Decorated in early American, the room was large, yet surprisingly cozy with a huge four-poster pine bed, a small matching chest and mirror, a wooden rocker resting on the oval braided rug and an inviting red brick fireplace.

Jake placed their bags on the floor and handed her a towel from the bathroom. Wiping his own wet hair and beard, he moved to the fireplace. Kara removed her gold clip and dried her hair. She watched Jake place firewood from the hearth onto the grate, which was already filled with kindling. He threw in a match and poked about until a bright fire blazed. Only then did he turn to her.

Suddenly shy, she looked away from his gaze and walked to the window to close the heavy print drapes.

He came up behind her, gently placing a hand on her shoulder. "I thought we could use a fire."

She turned to face him. "Yes. It's chilly." Her eyes went to his chest. "You're soaked through." Her hands moved to unbutton his shirt. She couldn't keep them from shaking as she pulled it away from his belt. She dragged the wet material off him and let it drop to the floor. Reaching for her towel, she began to rub him dry, his arms, his broad shoulders, the curly golden hair on his chest. Her eyes followed the progress of her hands as she worked, admiring his torso, which warmed under her ministrations. She let her fingers linger in the soft hair, then placed both palms over his nipples and rubbed slowly in a circle. A low, involuntary sound came from his throat.

He stood perfectly still as she shifted her attention to his face. She moved a corner of the towel up and patted dry his beard, then on tiptoe, she draped it over his head and let it absorb the moisture there. Her hands caressed the softness of his beard, reveling in the bristly feel of it. She moved her face into his chin and inhaled his fragrance, sighing with pleasure.

Jake needed to take over. "You're wet, too," he said. "I wouldn't want to be responsible for letting you catch a cold." He felt her draw in a deep breath as his hands moved to her waistline and tugged free the ends of her shirt. He pulled the soft jersey over her head and heard it hit the floor with a plop. His eyes moved to her low-cut lacy bra as it strained to confine her swollen breasts. Her breathing grew labored under his gaze.

She stepped back to look at him. He was neither nervous nor intimidating. He was merely waiting. She knew why. A decision had been made. Mutually this time. No turning back. She looked up at him, her heart thudding, as if it were her first time.

There was a churning ache in the pit of her stomach for him, a quick, dark stab of desire. She wanted him, and she felt no shame. This had been coming on since the first day she'd seen the lean, hard length of him propped against his truck, his hair windblown, his eyes insolent.

Kara wouldn't let herself think beyond this moment and this man she so desperately desired. The past was

gone and tomorrow was uncertain. She stepped closer
letting the points of her breasts brush against the mus
cular wall of his chest. She saw him close his eyes, allow
ing the feeling to take him, while her own knees weakened
with the contact.

Jake moved his head back, his eyes on her face. He
simply wanted to look at her a few moments longer, a
her flushed cheeks, her shining eyes, her eager mouth, her
beautiful breasts. Tenderly he kissed her temples, he
brow, the delicacy of her closed eyelids. He closed his
own eyes, moving slowly, letting his hands and mouth
explore her face through taste and touch. He'd waited too
long to rush this.

Kara's breath shuddered through her as he kissed the
corners of her mouth, his thumb tracing the soft under
side of her bottom lip. He sought to memorize every
curve of her, all her hidden places. Lightning flashed
through a slit in the drapes and rain beat against the
window, momentarily drowning out their low murmur-
ings.

She was a slight woman but with strength. She gripped
his arms, her hands squeezing his flesh, her passion rising. Good, he thought. He didn't want compliance nor
passive surrender. She wrapped about him, seeking, her
mouth hungry, demanding. He'd dreamed of this so
often, wanted her so badly, and now, at last, he would
know her.

Anticipation tingled along Kara's spine like sweaty
needles of need. "Undress me," she whispered.

Fighting his urgency, Jake unhooked her bra with
trembling fingers. As he cast it aside, his fingers trailed
over the smoothness of her back. A shiver took her, but
she stood still as he untied the damp cords of her draw-
string slacks. His hands slid them slowly down her slim

hips. Impatiently she stepped out of them, her hands flying to the fastening of his jeans. Caught up in her anxiety, she fumbled, and he moved to help her. Quickly the rest of his clothes joined hers on the floor.

She thought she saw a moment of hesitation in his eyes. "Are you afraid, Jake? Afraid of me?"

It was too late, and he knew it. She had unwittingly captured him, and he wondered if she could see it. He'd fought the good battle and lost. His eyes, smoky with need, told her the truth. "Afraid?" he asked, shakily. "Of a slim woman, scarcely five and a half feet tall..." He scooped her from her feet. "One I can easily hold in my arms..." His eyes roamed her hair, her face... "One with hair like the midnight sky, skin the color of rich honey and eyes that look right through me? Now what on earth would I have to be afraid of?"

Kara felt the mattress give under their weight as he laid her down and quickly joined her. Eager to learn his body, her hands skimmed the taut muscles of his back, his smooth shoulders, his furry chest. She felt him shudder in delicious agony as her lazy fingertips trailed along his ribcage. His face was buried in her neck, his teeth nipping at the tender flesh. Already she was lost in a haze of sensation. Then his hungry mouth moved to hers, claiming it.

As his lips learned more of her, his hands moved down the valley between her breasts, brushing the soft underside, cupping their fullness. His avid mouth followed. His moist tongue circled and tasted, and she arched her restless body as the roughness of his beard against her hot skin introduced new sensations. Her seeking hands lost themselves in the crispness of his hair, urging him on.

His quick hand slyly eased off her panties as she lifted her hips to help him rid her of the last barrier. Her stomach quivered under the onslaught of his searching mouth as it traced a heady path downward. His hands moved along her thighs as his lips moved lower. Lost in a mindless need, she moaned his name as his greedy tongue found her, teasing, tasting, driving her to the brink of madness. She was beyond all rational thought, reaching, wanting. Just as he brought her to the edge, he withdrew and moved upward to claim her waiting mouth even as his impatient fingers sought more of her.

She writhed against him as her need grew, but he put her off. "Too soon, beautiful lady," he murmured into the delicate curves of her ear as she twisted beneath his burning touch. His lovemaking was as foreign to her experience as this devastatingly exciting man was. He set a dizzying pace she could only follow in a mist of feeling. His mouth and hands explored, caressed, tasted, worshipped every inch of her as her fingers gripped the sheet. She heard a clap of thunder reverberate then decided maybe it had been her own accelerated heartbeat as Jake drove her to pinnacles of pleasure she'd never dreamed she could reach. Seeking to return the favor, Kara moved under him, letting her hands roam.

Jake's body was throbbing in its ache for her. He felt his need for her in every fibre, every pore. When at last her hands lightly touched him, then more boldly caressed him, he knew she'd taken him nearly past his limits. No longer still under him, her undulations catapulted him further.

He lifted himself over her and gently eased inside. With a low sound he thrust deeply. She wrapped around him as he swept her with him, taking her to peak after peak, in waves of delicious feeling. She clung to him as the storm broke and crashed all around them, wind and water pelting the windows. They didn't hear. They were lost in the wonder of each other.

Chapter Eight

The steady slush of water through a nearby downspout woke Kara. Opening her eyes, she saw she was lying on her side, her head nestled on Jake's shoulder, her leg thrown familiarly over his. Never before had she awakened entwined in a lover's arms. She examined her reactions and decided she felt both satisfied and frightened.

She moved her head fractionally so she could study Jake's face, slowly so as not to waken him just yet. His thick blond hair fell onto his forehead, where her restless, seeking fingers had pushed it during their loving. His golden, obscenely long eyelashes lay on the tanned skin of his cheeks, guarding those gray-green eyes that seemed to see right through her. His mouth that had moved over every inch of her during the night was still now, buried in the bristly hair of his beard. He was beautiful.

I love him, she thought, and the realization sent her mind reeling. Just yesterday she'd promised herself and

Jake that she wouldn't allow herself to fall in love with him. She'd lied—to both of them. Oh, God, how had she let this happen?

She should've seen it coming, Kara thought with a near moan. She'd wanted him desperately. But sex was something she'd learned to handle years ago, as most women did. Sleeping in the room next to her mother with her endless parade of men had given Kara an early education. Curiosity and a healthy libido had filled in the missing pieces in college. She could control her lusty urges as she controlled all her appetites. It was Jake's emotional impact on her that had caused her to lose control. She'd gone from wanting to needing, and it was a giant step.

Kara sighed deeply and trembled with the force of it. Loving was so damn difficult. She hadn't loved many, and those few had cost her—her poor pathetic mother; dear, sweet Nona whom she'd have to let go of soon; Louie, a shadowy force in her life since childhood. The first, she pitied; the other two, she owed respect along with the love. There had been a few men, youthful infatuations before she'd learned to recognize love. And now, Jake.

Loving him would cost her, too, she was certain. Instinct told her he probably wouldn't welcome her love. He would undoubtedly overwhelm her with sensual satisfaction while he was around then stroll back to his vagabond life-style without further thought when the job was done. He'd warned her, told her their coming together wouldn't change anything, that he'd still move on when he was ready. She'd accepted that. And she'd have to let him go when that time came.

They were wrong for each other anyway, all wrong. It wasn't Jake's fault she'd made the colossal mistake of falling in love with him. But he'd never know it from her. She'd make sure of that. She swallowed a sudden lump in her throat. A bargain was a bargain. At least she'd have him until then.

After all, she was an independent, self-sufficient, modern woman. She'd had to be all these years, growing up as she had, without a real home, without the pleasures of a normal childhood. She'd taught herself not to form sentimental attachments to the men who'd strolled through her life during her formative years. She'd learned that they never stayed for long, and they left pain in their wake.

Her first real home, something that was truly her own, was the house that she'd bought herself, on the California coast. She'd decorated each room with infinite care, making it reflect her personality, and she had a way to go before it was finished. While people were unpredictable and often disappointing, the solid presence of her house was a comfort to her. With her education behind her, the work she loved, a place of her own, she had confidence in herself as a woman and as a professional photographer. She hadn't thought she needed anyone. Then she'd met Jake.

At first he'd confused and angered her. He was the only man who'd caused her to question her choices. And now, here she was in love with him, and the relationship had nowhere to go.

Kara closed her eyes and allowed herself to remember his loving of the night before, her skin warming at her thoughts. She wouldn't think about separations or tomorrow. She was a woman in love, and she would just feel and think only of the here and the now.

Hungry again for a taste of what she'd only recently sampled, she pressed her lips to his warm neck. With a revealing whimper of need, she tasted his skin, breathed in the morning scent of him, mingled now with hers, then realized the intimacy of that revelation. Never with anyone else had she felt this wildness rise inside her, this fervent craving to become part of another, this mindless excitement that left her breathless. Wanting him awake, she moved along him and lazily traced his lips with her tongue.

Jake awoke on a soft moan, his lips moving to capture Kara's with unerring instinct, his arms moving around her. The passion was immediate and frantic, arousing him swiftly, the desire he sensed in her inflaming him. Needing to take charge, in a quick movement he rolled her over and pinned her while his tongue moved into her mouth, seeking again her special flavors.

His hand moved along her silken skin, stopping to caress a breast, pausing to linger at the slim line of her waist, moving lower and finding her, already damp and ready for him. She arched to meet his probing reach, stunning him with her avid response.

Everything inside of Kara speeded up, her heart, her blood, her pounding pulse as his hands and mouth intensified every remembered sensation. She'd thought she'd experienced all he could teach her last night, but he had more to show her—much more.

Pulling back to look at her face flushed with passion, Jake saw her eyes close as her body moved against him with a will of its own. She was strong, independent, her own person. Yet he knew when he touched her like this, he had the power to weaken her, to mold, to make her his—if only for a short time. The knowledge urged him on and, desperate now, he moved over her.

Jake found that his always steady hands were now trembling. His constant control was now slipping away.

In short, the man who'd always played a waiting game now found himself impatiently reaching out—for her, for more, for everything. Returning to her waiting mouth, his tongue tormented both of them until all coherent thought was gone. Delirious, he plunged into her with a soft groan of triumph and took them both to the edge of madness.

Jake opened his eyes. The short nap had refreshed him. Or was it loving Kara that made him feel like an awakening tiger? She lay asleep, snuggled loosely into the side of him. Savoring the moment, he studied her. She looked relaxed and well loved, even more beautiful with a rosy hue combining with the honeyed tan of her skin. He was sure she was totally unaware how Cheshire cat satisfied she looked. He'd waited a long time to have her, and she had been worth the wait.

His arms tightened about her and, with a soft mewing sound, she settled more deeply into him. He turned his face into her hair and buried his nose in the wild tangle of her curls. She smelled so good, so damned good. Everything about her, it seemed to him, was good.

He cared about her, Jake finally admitted to himself. The sexual attraction was there, urgent and strong, no denying it. But the surprise was that the urge to hold her, to simply lie here and hold her, was equally strong. He could never remember those two feelings having equal importance with any other woman—not even Cindy. And it confused him.

Caring was one thing. It was difficult *not* to care for a beautiful woman who was warm and funny, able to laugh at herself, intelligent and responsive. But he mustn't make the mistake of falling in love with Kara. She'd made it perfectly clear she wanted to go it alone. She had other worlds to conquer and so did he. She didn't believe in forever any more than he did. He would do well to remember that, to harbor no illusions. They had separate lives to return to after this chance summer encounter. He would take from her what she was willing to give and return to her all he was able, and then he would let her go. It was simple, really, if you kept the rules in mind.

She stirred, and he kissed her fragrant hair and pulled back to look at her. "Good morning," he said, smiling as she stretched lazily. "You know, it's downright sinful."

"What is?"

"That you look so beautiful so early in the morning."

She ran a hand through her thick, sleep-tangled hair and smiled at him. Lingeringly she caressed his bearded jaw with one slender hand. "Mmm, flattery, sir, will get you *everywhere*."

He shifted so she was on her back, and he was staring into her warm brown eyes. "I was hoping that was the case." He brushed her lips with his then captured them, the slow kiss growing deeper. Idly he wondered why he could not lightly kiss her and move away, if he would ever get enough of her. Jake lifted his head. "You're very passionate, very responsive. You surprised me."

She gave a light laugh. "*I* surprised me."

He nibbled gently on her ear.

"It could possibly be," she said, mischief dancing in her eyes, "that I can learn something from you, also."

Jake smiled, remembering her apple-eating lesson. "I'm glad you think so."

She touched her fingers to his lips, tracing their fullness. "I love your smile. It never fails to warm me."

"You're a very special lady, Kara." He shifted onto his back, moving her so she was held close against his chest.

"Jake," she began after a moment, "this probably isn't the best 'morning after' question, but you aroused my curiosity. Yesterday, you said you threw your wife out. Why?"

He sighed and raised one arm, placing his hand under his head. He'd known that one day she'd ask that question. He just hadn't thought she'd ask it so soon. "It's a long story."

She raised herself on one elbow, tucked the sheet around her then turned to look at him, propping her head on one hand. "I'm not going anywhere."

How to tell her? he wondered. Tall, blond, sexy Cindy had teased, tantalized and intrigued him from the start. She'd thrown her bait, hooked him and reeled him in like a poor fish.

"Her name is Cynthia," he began. "I called her Cindy, but she hated that, preferring the more dignified version, as she put it. She was very beautiful, and I was young, lonely and fairly inexperienced. I'd spent a lot of years working almost night and day in the company, and I hadn't spent much time with women. Not women like Cindy. I mistook lust for love. By the time I woke up, it was too late. We were married."

A muscle in Jake's jaw twitched as he ground his teeth, remembering. Why hadn't he seen sooner through Cindy's smooth facade to the mercenary beneath? he asked himself.

Kara's hand rested lightly on his chest. He reached down and covered her fingers with his own, absently smoothing her soft skin with his thumb. "I was ready to slow down then, to make a home for us, to have children. But Cindy had grandiose plans. She wanted us to build this big showplace of a house on the ocean so we could entertain all her friends. She thought an apart-

ꞁent in New York would be nice, maybe a villa in Nice
ꞁ Rome, a condo in Jamaica for the cold winter months.
ꞁe wanted to travel, buy a sailboat, have servants. When
ꞁtold her we didn't have *that* kind of money, she laughed.
ꞁVork a little harder, Jake' was her answer. She knew I
ꞁanted a child. She said I could have what *I* wanted when
ꞁe had what *she* wanted.''

Kara's eyes were huge with understanding. ''Jake, I'm
ꞁrry I asked. The memories obviously bother you
ꞁnd—''

''No, it's all right. I'm over her. When I think of her
ꞁow I feel only emptiness. My father had spent so much
ꞁme away from home, building the business, and he'd
ꞁrsuaded my brothers and I into joining him. My poor
ꞁother was left alone so much. I think loneliness
ꞁontributed to her early death. I never had much of a
ꞁmily life. Cindy put on a good front in the beginning.
ꞁ thought we could have the family I'd always wanted.
ꞁut . . .'' His sigh was ragged. ''She preferred diamonds
ꞁd furs and other such goodies. Women are often like
ꞁat.''

Back to that again, Kara thought. He was over her, all
ꞁght. But he hadn't allowed the damaged parts to heal.
ꞁhe wrinkled her brow at him. ''Are women like that—*all*
ꞁ them? Are you so sure?''

''Most of them. Some hide it better than others. Oh, I
ꞁon't say that a part of what happened wasn't my fault,
ꞁo. The problems in a marriage are seldom one-sided.
ꞁespite my best intentions, the work at the office buried
ꞁe. I'd spent years neglecting my mother—we all had—
ꞁd then I neglected my wife. Not that she minded all
ꞁat much. I soon began to hear rumors that she'd found
ꞁther men to go to parties with when I was working late.
ꞁ was too damn engrossed to notice for a long time. The

company was growing, thriving, under *my* leadership. I got caught up in it and took a certain amount of pride in my accomplishments. Too much, maybe. Soon, that's all I had left. My mother died, my father had a stroke, and I walked in on Cindy in bed with another man—in our home!'' He turned to look at last into Kara's eyes filled with sadness for him. ''So that, beautiful Kara, is why I threw my wife out of my house, and out of my life. I'd warned you it wasn't a pretty story.''

She nodded in agreement, caressing his soft beard as she spoke. ''You're right, it's not a pretty story. So then, after that, you left to wander the world?''

He shifted again, turning so she was on her back, his big body pressing into her, his mouth inches from hers. ''Yes, ma'am. That's when I grabbed a freighter and set out to see the world.'' His eyes were smiling now. ''A vagabond lover with a woman in every port.'' He found a vulnerable spot along her side and feathered his fingers over it, tickling her lightly.

She wiggled and laughed. ''All right, I get it. You don't want to talk about it anymore. But thank you for telling me. It helps me to understand a lot of things.''

''I like the way you laugh. I like the way you listen, too. Matter of fact, I like a lot of things about you, Miss Finelli.''

He started to move from her, to relieve her of the burden of his weight, but she held him fast. ''No, please stay.''

''I'm too heavy on you. I want you to be comfortable.''

Her smile was filled with meaning. ''I can be comfortable anytime. I can't feel like *this* all the time.''

He grinned against the curve of her neck, his lips feasting there. ''I love the taste of you. Like everything sweet and wonderful. Like the best wine . . . like nothing can put a name to." He raised his eyes to hers. "Do you know how long I've wanted you?"

"No. Tell me."

"From the very first day when I saw you get out of that snappy little car—you were hiding behind those big sunglasses and a haughty go-to-hell look."

She smiled, remembering. "You were pretty rude that day."

"I meant to be. I *had* to be. I knew you were too much for me, even then."

She ran experimental fingers over his back, moving lower. "One small woman is too much for you?"

"Yes," he answered, his mouth taking a journey around her upturned face. "I would have cheerfully strangled you many a night. Those nights that I lay awake trying to sleep, unable to get you off my mind."

Her head went back, offering her throat. "Here, go ahead."

"Mmm, suddenly I have other plans for that lovely neck of yours," he whispered as reawakened passion moved within him.

She looked into his eyes, saw them darken with his need. He was hers, for however long he would stay with her, the only man she'd discovered capable of releasing her fire. Slowly she began to move beneath him.

Jake claimed her mouth, knowing he hadn't had nearly enough of her. Contentment had cloaked his desire long enough. He wanted her again, with the same fervor as before. But this time, with more patience than desperation, he made love to her slowly and thoroughly, gently guiding them both to the ultimate shared release.

The dreary gray morning blended into a rain-splattered afternoon as Jake drove along the highway westward, moving with cautious speed to make up for their late departure.

At his insistence Kara sat close alongside him. Not that she'd argued for she loved resting her hand on his thigh, feeling the tight muscles stretch as he moved his leg from the pedals. Making love for a good part of the night and on into the morning had been wonderful. She felt sated and sleepy, and she rested her head on Jake's solid shoulder. A feeling of peaceful lassitude drifted over her as, snuggling close to his comforting strength, she gave up the struggle and went to sleep.

She didn't know how much later it was when she awakened with a start. The truck was sputtering erratically, missing, causing jerking movements that had the cab bouncing and swaying. Trying to climb out of the haze of her wispy dreams, she blinked to clear her foggy mind as she sat up. Though the pavement was slick and the rain still coming down, they were on an open stretch of road. She glanced at Jake and saw annoyance on his frowning face.

"What is it?" she asked, her heart suddenly in her throat.

"I'm not sure," he answered, his eyes scanning the road ahead of them. "It feels like we got some bad gas, the way the motor keeps missing. At first I thought it was just the tires sliding on the wet highway." The engine coughed then followed with a noise that sounded like a backfire. "I've got to find a station to pull into and get it looked at before we stall altogether."

At last the two-lane highway opened up into four and just ahead on the right, Jake spotted a large full-service gas station. His eyes narrowing, he steered the chugging truck around the curve toward help. The trailer swayed dangerously behind them.

"Is there anything I can do?" Kara asked.

"We're almost there," he told her, flipping on the turn signal. With a loud protest the truck eased onto the drive and limped to a stop alongside the low building.

The last few miles had given them a bone-jarring, bouncing ride, and Kara was glad to step down onto firm ground while Jake went to see if a diesel mechanic was on duty. Digging for change, she purchased a cup of something hot that resembled coffee from a vending machine. Seeing Jake bent over the innards of the cab with a man in greasy overalls, she decided she'd only be in the way if she joined them. Finding a bench, she sat sipping as she gazed at the gray sky desperately trying to clear.

It was some time before Jake, tense and frowning, came over to tell her that they'd discovered sugar in the gas tank. They'd have to sit tight while the mechanic flushed everything and steam-cleaned the engine before more serious damage took place. Tight-lipped, he marched back to watch the operation without another word.

Kara sat back down, reflectively finishing her tasteless drink. Convinced that someone had tampered with their truck, her mind was a kaleidoscope of questions. When had this happened? Who had done it and how? Last night the place where they'd stopped had been off the beaten track, miles from the main highway that the truckers usually traveled. No one knew where she and Jake were all night. And it had poured for hours. Who would want to hurt them? Who felt desperate enough to seek them out in the stealth of night, in a blinding rainstorm and sabotage their truck? She shook her head. The more she pondered, the wilder her thoughts became.

It would take about two hours, the mechanic explained, before the rig would be drivable again. Impatiently Jake paced while Kara consumed endless cups of coffee. Then, just to be doubly sure there'd be no other surprises, Jake rolled under and checked out a few things himself. He peered at wires, lines, gauges. He fiddled with screws, tightened, adjusted, making sure bolts and lug nuts hadn't loosened on their own from the bouncy ride. Finally satisfied, he walked over to Kara, wiping his hands on a rag. "Ready to roll?" he asked.

Kara nodded wordlessly, sensing he wasn't in the mood for chatter.

Jake climbed up into the cab, his mind whirling. He and Cowboy had inspected nearly every inch of the truck yesterday morning. Everything had checked out, and it had run smoothly all day. Last night the truck had been parked close up against the motel cabins. He cursed under his breath as he turned the key. Someone had evidently come while he'd been busy with thoughts of Kara. They hadn't dumped in much sugar, thank goodness. A damn teenage trick. Not enough to ruin the engine, just enough to stall, delay and annoy them. And maybe put a scare into them. Only Jake wasn't frightened as much as angry. He started the motor, listening carefully for unusual sounds.

That someone had to have been damn close on their tail, had to have seen them slow down in the storm, stop under the bridge. They had to have followed them to that out-of-the-way motel. The reasons most likely had some connection with the other sabotagings. The who was still a missing puzzle piece.

He'd have the truck thoroughly gone over at the barn when they got to California, Jake decided. This was getting a little unnerving.

Investigative insurance work was often tedious, slow
nd painstaking, filled with details and occasionally
angerous. But Jake didn't see himself as any kind of
ero. He'd never run from a fight, but he'd never dashed
ito danger either. Perhaps they were nosing too close for
omeone's comfort, though the pieces as yet didn't fit
ogether in his mind. As soon as he got a chance, he'd
heck in with Rob Carter and the office. Perhaps if they
ut their heads together, they could come up with some
ossibilities.

Jake turned to Kara, who sat quietly staring ahead. She
adn't panicked, but then somehow he'd known she
vouldn't. "You all right, babe?" he asked softly, touch-
ng her cheek, the worry leaving his eyes as he took in her
oveliness. God, she was so lovely—in the morning, in the
vening, in between. He felt a twinge of guilt about last
ight. Not that she hadn't been a most willing partici-
ant. Preventing what had happened between them
vould have been as impossible as stopping the tides, he
hought.

Kara nodded, letting him know she was fine, and he
aressed her neck, pulling her close for a long, sweet kiss.
'We'd better get moving. We have a lot of time to make
p." He shifted and moved the big rig out.

Kara and Jake switched off, driving and sleeping, fi-
ally reaching home base two days later. The rest of the
rip had been uneventful.

While supervising the unloading, Jake was handed a
nessage that his father had suffered another stroke. Kara
 offered to go with him to the hospital, but, though he
hanked her, he refused her offer. Keeping his face care-
ully masked, he kissed her lightly and took the rig to the
garage, telling her he'd come looking for her afterward.

She knew better than to push. His relationship with his father was one he'd told her little of. Jake was a loner by choice, especially these last few years. He wasn't accustomed to sharing his problems, confiding his thoughts easily, or having someone trail behind him offering unwanted support.

The small amount of pillow talk they'd shared had been the closest he'd come to discussing his past. She couldn't help wanting to know more; but in this, she would be patient. As a private person who disliked anyone to delve into her affairs, Kara understood this need in him to go slowly in opening up to another. But as a woman who loved him, she couldn't prevent herself from hoping he would turn to her if he needed someone.

Reaching her beach house, Kara flung her things inside and went for a vigorous swim in the late-morning sunlight. Afterward, showering in her own bath felt wonderful. Drying off, she called Nona who immediately invited her to lunch. Ordinarily she'd have jumped at the chance. But she was waiting for Jake.

"I'd love to, Nona, but I'm only here for the day, and I have some things to take care of." Running her fingers over the framed picture of her grandmother that sat on her nightstand, she hoped her voice didn't betray her. "How are you?"

"I am well. And Jake, how is he?"

She might have known the sly little lady would not forget so easily. Since the evening he'd come to her home, each time she'd spoken with Nona, she'd asked about Jake. Though she'd known when Kara had come in from the garden, angry and upset, that she and Jake had had words, Nona'd simply told her granddaughter that all lovers quarreled. She'd also told her not to be foolish enough to let Jake get away. "He's just fine," she answered.

A small pause. "He is with you, Kara?"

Shifting her restless bare feet, Kara swung her gaze out her bedroom window, letting it settle on the calming sea. "He's in town, yes."

"No, I mean *with* you."

She paused a moment, absorbing her meaning. "Not exactly. I don't want that. I don't need that."

"Oh, I think you do, Kara *mia*," the old woman said, her voice soft. "For a long time now, I think you need someone—someone who makes the waking up to each new day special. You know what I mean?"

Kara closed her eyes, leaning her forehead against the window frame, remembering the morning she'd awakened in Jake's arms. Oh, yes. She knew *exactly* what Nona meant. The silence stretched on, but she didn't know how to answer her grandmother.

"You are still there, Kara?"

"Yes. Nona, Jake and I are together, but we are *not* together. I can't handle a commitment to someone else right now, and neither can Jake. I have too much to do, obligations, my house, my work. I have to honor the commitments I made to *me* before I make a commitment to someone else. Do you see?"

Nona also took her time answering while Kara fidgeted with the telephone cord. "Yes, I see. Do not be angry at your old grandmother, Kara, but I see a stubborn young woman who does not want to admit she, too, has needs."

Enough. There was a limit to Kara's tolerance for advice these days, even from Nona. "Stubborn women run in our family, I think, Nona. I've got to go to see Prince. I'll call you again soon. Take care of yourself."

"I love you, Kara."

"Me, too. Bye." She replaced the phone with a sigh.
All this excessive rehashing of her problems was wearing. What she needed was a fast and free ride on her
horse to tire her out and to blow the cobwebs from her
brain. Rubbing her hair dry, Kara went to the closet to
dress.

Standing in the afternoon heat, she inhaled the welcome scent of the nearby ocean breeze and the sweet-
smelling hay of the barn. Prince nuzzled her hand as she
offered him a sugar cube and led him outside into the
high, open field. Crooning gentle words of affection, she
swung into the saddle.

Outdoors at last, with his favorite mount astride,
Prince wanted to fly, and Kara was glad to let him. Freedom beckoned to them both, speed exhilarated, motion
mesmerized. The two rode as one as the cool breezes
whipped her hair about her face. Pleasure flowed through
her. She was a skilled rider who trusted her horse, one
who knew his strengths well. Here, she was in control, at
home, alive again.

When, half an hour later, she returned, slowing Prince
as they neared the barn, she sensed his anxiety to con-
tinue as his restless feet shuffled in the dusty grass. "I
know, boy, I know," she told him, her hand smoothing
his sleek neck. "Soon we'll take longer rides together.
Much longer."

Dismounting, Kara walked with him, talking to him,
nonsensical words of reassurance, letting him cool off
after their vigorous run. Hearing footsteps, she looked up
as Evan, the young man who cared for Prince, came
whistling around the corner and into the barn. She smiled
a greeting as he came toward her.

* * *

It was late afternoon when Jake arrived at Kara's. Finding her house empty, he decided to try the barn where she boarded her horse. He walked across the wide expanse of grass toward the weathered wooden building in the distance. His hands thrust deep in the pockets of his khaki slacks, he thought about the hospital visit and the small, shrunken man who was a shadow of what he'd once been. Jake's face settled into a grimace. He wished he'd never gone but how could he not have? There was precious little left between him and his father. Yet he'd hated to see the results of the crippling illness and his father's relentless life-style on the once tall, proud man. Seeing his father had dredged up feelings he didn't want to cope with just now. Even if the old man had been able to speak, Jake realized with sadness that they would have had little to say.

It was good catching up on family news, hearing that Murphy Trucking was doing well under the leadership of his two brothers. Immediately they'd invited him back into the company, saying they could use his help, explaining their plans for expansion. But he'd told them he was quite happy with his investigative work, which they knew little of. Jake wanted to keep it that way.

Afterward he'd gone to his apartment to clean up, stopped to pick up a gift he'd ordered by phone and went to check on their truck. The mechanic was certain about the gas tampering, of course, and suspicious of more, despite Jake's close inspection.

He'd found incorrect lug nuts that could work free easily, screws with the threading worn bare, two wrong-sized replacement parts. The mechanic refused to go on record but said it was possible that these things could have, in time, caused a few too many parts to juggle and wiggle loose enough to cause more problems. It would've had to have been done by someone very familiar with trucks. Someone very clever.

Jake had a hunch, and he was anxious to test it. Maybe he could flush the guy out. And when he was caught, Jake would end his employment at Santini Trucking, which would inevitably end his relationship with Kara. That was the way it had to be. It was the way he'd wanted it. Wasn't it?

Almost at the barn, he saw her standing alongside the chestnut stallion. Wearing faded jeans and a checkered blouse, its tails tied loosely under her breasts, her tanned midriff bare, she looked young and carefree. Yet he knew that behind her Bachelor of Arts degree and under her camera dangling on a strap around her neck beat the heart of a very passionate woman...a woman who could be his. Did he dare believe that this time, with this woman, it would be different? he wondered. Damn but his seesawing emotions were driving him crazy!

Kara turned and saw him. As she smiled, he felt the sun shine; his gloom lifted and a quick surge of desire washed over him, so strong he almost felt himself swaying with the power of it. How did she make him weak with wanting just by smiling at him? How long would this terrible yet wonderful feeling last? He wanted to scoop her up, take her with him, somewhere, anywhere. He wanted to be alone with her and have her make the world go away.

From inside the barn a man walked out to join her. He looked tall, youthful and strong. A bright flash of jealousy both stunned and shamed Jake. Hadn't he insisted there be no strings attached between them? Kara was free to see others, he told himself, as was he. Why, then, did the thought of her with another man stop him in his tracks? Slowly he walked up to her.

Her eyes searched his. "I've been waiting for you," she said. "Are you all right?"

"Yes." His eyes moved to include the tall man in the doorway.

She stepped back. "Jake, this is Evan McCallister. He takes care of Prince for me. Evan, meet Jake Murphy."

Evan stepped forward and offered a callused hand. Jake forced a tight smile and shook hands with him. On closer examination he saw that the man was quite young, closer to college age. Somehow, even that thought did nothing to cheer him. Kara would appeal to men of all ages.

"Evan's my neighbor's son," Kara said, wondering over Jake's frown. "He's working his way through school. He really knows a lot about horses." She stood between the two men, at a loss to explain the tension in the air.

Evan reached for a pitchfork from a hook on the wall. "Got some work to do on the far side." He nodded at Jake. "Nice to see you." He aimed a shy smile at Kara. "See you later, Kara." He sauntered off and disappeared around the corner.

Kara led the stallion into the coolness of the barn and maneuvered him into his stall. The door creaked as she closed him in. Jake looked around. The high-ceilinged barn was a strangely relaxing place, sweet smelling, dimly shadowed. He watched her walk to the side wall and put away the tack. She had a wonderful walk, a walk that set a man to thinking warm thoughts. She removed her camera and set it carefully down before coming back to him.

"You look a little grim. Was it bad at the hospital?"

"Yes, bad. I find I'm not a very forgiving man, no even as I stood there looking down at the pitiful, sick remnants of my father."

"Sometimes it isn't easy to love a parent. Maybe no even possible."

He rubbed a hand across his eyes. "Love? I think it' too late for that. I don't feel much of anything toward him. He hurt my mother. Maybe she'd still be alive if he hadn't . . . if only he'd . . . never mind. You don't want to hear all this."

She moved closer, put her hand on his arm. "Yes, I do. Tell me."

He shook his head. "Not now." His eyes found the ladder leading upward. Stepping back, he looked up. "Well, I'll be . . . a real live hayloft."

"You really are a city boy."

He stepped on the bottom rung. "Yup. Never set foot on a farm in my life." He began to climb. "Come on. Show me what a hayloft looks like."

Glad to see the melancholy look leave his face, Kara followed him, giving in to the mood of the moment. Despite his words, she knew his visit to his father had affected him deeply. A shaft of sunlight slanted in through the weathered boards of the large, closed window, falling on his hair, turning it golden.

"Why's the window latched?" he asked, strolling over.

"It's only open when they pitch down the hay. Otherwise, it would let the rain in, get everything wet."

He moved to a large mound of hay piled in the corner, reached for her hand and fell backward, pulling her atop him. She laughed as she landed on him, her hands pressed against his chest. "Do you spend a lot of time up here when you're home—like maybe with Evan?" he asked, his silver eyes shaded.

Her brows rose in surprise as she studied him. "You've got to be kidding?"

His face was suddenly serious. "Why would I be kidding? You're a very beautiful woman, and he's a young man in the prime of life. Why not?"

His sudden curious jealousy surprised her. Slowly she shook her head. "He's twenty, a kid. He's like a younger brother to me. I've never been up here or anywhere else with him. I'm surprised you'd even think I had."

His eyes searched hers a moment longer, then he pulled her close. "I'm sorry. I'm not thinking very clearly today."

She pulled back, a teasing smile on her face. "Maybe you ought to give up thinking. Take up an action sport instead." She lowered her mouth to his in a hot, urgent kiss that tightened his arms about her.

When she moved back to study him, he shifted, reaching into his shirt pocket. "I have something for you." He brought out a long, thin package wrapped in silver paper.

She laughed in surprise and delight. "Why, Mr. Murphy!" She sat back and opened it quickly. In a mound of cotton lay a fine gold chain from which dangled a small, golden apple. Carefully Kara removed the necklace and held it in her slender fingers, letting the filtered sun play on its delicate beauty.

Brown eyes suddenly misty smiled into Jake's face. "I love it," she whispered. "Thank you."

"So you'll never be without your 'apple a day,'" Jake said, taking it from her and placing it about her neck, adjusting the clasp as she held her hair out of the way. The dainty apple fell low into the separation of her breasts. Jake bent his head and tenderly kissed the spot where it lay. He moved his lips to her ear. "Do you think Evan can hear us?"

She couldn't resist a smirk. "Well, well, what do we have here, Mr. Shy and Modest? I think he's over on the other side, but I can't be sure. Why, do you intend to make a lot of noise?"

"You never know," he said, his mouth moving to hers, his hot tongue outlining her lips, branding her. He shifted her body until she lay close alongside him.

Jake's hand was big and rough, yet gentle on her breast, barely touching, yet searing. He loosened the buttons of her blouse and lowered his head to touch the tip of her breast. She gasped, arching as she felt the heat spread through her. Deftly he savored her, drawing deeply, fully aware of the feelings he was stirring within her. Drifting, Kara dug her nails into his shoulders.

The need to feel flesh against flesh grew unbearable. With trembling fingers, he removed his clothing and hers as desire licked at him.

At the beginning he'd told himself that once he'd known her, once he'd had her, the need would end, and he'd be over her. But he'd been wrong. Each time he was with her, he was ravenous for each separate taste of her, the clean, country scent of her, the wondrous touch of her slender hands.

At last, unable to stay his flow of energy, he grasped her slim hips and rolled her onto her back in the sweetly fragrant hay. He entered her swiftly, the promise of unlimited pleasure close at hand. She wrapped about him as he drove them both, frantically, further and further, until the summit was in sight, and they reached it together, shuddering.

They lay together, entwined, enveloped, engrossed in each other, their breathing melding, a languid contentment stealing over them. Jake gently kissed her closed eyelids, then rolled on his back, drawing her close against his side. Quietly they rested together.

"I did have a purpose in coming here today," Jake said after a while, his rough hand caressing her bare back.

"Mmm, I noticed, and I heartily approve of your purpose."

He chuckled. "No, *another* purpose. I had the truck checked out and it's in A1 condition."

"Had someone tampered with it?"

He hesitated only a moment before answering her. "The sugar, of course. Could be a prank. Louie said we're to go empty to San Diego, pick up a full load there and head back."

"Right now?"

"Tomorrow morning."

"Mmm, good." She snuggled in closer.

Suddenly they heard the barn door below bang shut, and the sound of off-tune whistling drifted to their ears, followed by a man's voice making unintelligible sounds.

"Who's that?" Jake whispered.

"Probably Evan," she answered, unconcerned. "He's come to clean out the horse stalls. He often talks to them."

"That means we can't go down till he's through." He smiled. "How long do you think it'll take him?"

She moved her head to look mischievously into his eyes. "Well, let's see, there's about a dozen horses, give or take a few, plus some empty stalls he'll probably sweep out. A couple of hours, I would say."

Jake shifted her more comfortably in his arms and brought her face up close to his. "What a shame, stuck up here for several hours! We'll have to think of something to do to pass the time. Any ideas?''

She smiled meaningfully into his smoky eyes. "Several," she whispered before she lowered her mouth to meet his.

Chapter Nine

A weak morning sun was trying to push through a cloudy sky as Jake maneuvered his rig onto the approach ramp of the loading dock in San Diego. Squinting at the dash clock, he saw it was nearly ten, and he'd planned on arriving no later than nine. Though he'd awakened early, he'd lingered awhile in bed, then shared a long, playful shower, delaying his departure. He turned to glance at the seat beside him and the lovely reason for his change of plans.

Kara looked happy, relaxed and very beautiful. If getting involved with her was a mistake, he wasn't going to think about that today.

As he pulled the truck to a halt, he noticed Cowboy leaning against his cab, his cargo already loaded and ready to roll. He'd phoned Jake yesterday, saying he wanted to go over a few things with him. Engaging the brake, he saw Cowboy remove his hat and wipe his brow with the back of his hand, his pale eyes in his weathered face watching their arrival intently. What was on his mind now? Jake wondered as he jumped down and held up his hand to assist Kara.

Taking Jake's hand, she landed gracefully at his feet, toe-to-toe, their bodies very close. His eyes locked into hers in silent communication, and Kara wondered briefly if he could read the emotions hidden there. She didn't touch him. She didn't need to. She saw his answering response, her feelings mirrored in his gaze, and knew he understood. This was moth and flame, hunter and prey, a man and a woman. Wordlessly she grabbed their log book and walked toward the dispatcher to take care of their paperwork.

With a hand that shook slightly, Jake slammed the cab door shut and turned. Biting off a chunk of chewing tobacco, Cowboy stuffed the remainder in his shirt pocket as Jake pulled his pipe from his pocket and sauntered toward him. The sly, knowing look he noticed on the veteran trucker's face had him clenching his teeth on his pipe's stem as he stopped in front of him.

"I see you took care of things, Jake," Cowboy said, grinning. "Kara's no longer a thorn in your side."

Jake flicked his lighter and drew on his pipe, his steely gray eyes studying Cowboy through the smoke. He supposed anyone seeing him with Kara might guess their relationship had passed the "just friends" stage. But that's all it would be—guesswork. Neither of them were the kind to go in for public displays, and he didn't want fellow truckers' bawdy conjectures about them. Perhaps the time to stop it was before it began. He could rely on Cowboy to make his feelings known to the others.

"You got something you want to say about Kara and me, Cowboy?" he asked, his voice low and hard. He saw a small flicker of fear flash in the older man's blue eyes before he tried a smile and rubbed his unshaven chin.

"Hey, Jake. I didn't mean nothin'. What'd I say? Hell, I'm glad you two got together. She needs someone like you to—" He stopped, seeing Jake's eyes turn suddenly colder than anything he'd ever seen.

"I'm glad you approve. Now that's the last time I want you to mention anything about us—to me or to *anyone*. You got that?"

Cowboy swallowed uneasily. "Sure, Jake. Anything you say."

Jake's lips parted in a tight smile that didn't touch the rest of his face. "Good. Just so we understand each other." He stuck his pipe into his mouth and leaned casually against Cowboy's truck. "Are you loaded, ready to roll?"

"Yeah. I was just waiting to talk to you. I hear you had a little trouble couple days ago." Cowboy took out a red checkered handkerchief to mop his brow, his nervous eyes watching Jake's face.

"What'd you hear, and who'd you hear it from?"

"Mechanic up L.A. way. Said it looked like sugar in the tank, maybe some loosened bolts, a few lug nuts missing. I thought we checked your rig out ourselves the morning you took off?"

Jake was thoughtful. He'd specifically warned the mechanic who'd worked on the truck in California not to discuss their suspicions with *anyone*. Did the man have a loose tongue? he wondered. Or was Cowboy's interest more than casual? "I thought so, too."

"So what happened?"

Jake shrugged. "We stopped, had everything steam-cleaned and tightened. Hell of a mess."

"Who do you think's been messing with your truck? I didn't see you or Kara at Roadrunner stops along the way, so I couldn't keep an eye on your rig for you."

Jake's direct gaze never left Cowboy's face. It was a cool morning, yet the man was sweating profusely. Was it because he'd come down hard on him about Kara and him—or something else? "I don't know who, but someone tampered with it. I thought at first we just got some bad gas, but it was sugar, all right. We've been stopping at places along the highway when we're not driving straight through. It's too damn noisy to sleep in those Roadrunners." His eyes challenged Cowboy to question why they'd prefer to spend their nights elsewhere.

Cowboy knew better. "Can't say I blame you. You got any ideas about who?"

"Nothing concrete." He squinted at Cowboy through half-closed eyes. "How about you?"

Cowboy kicked at a pebble with the toe of one dusty boot. "Nah. So I guess I won't see you tonight at the truck stop? Too bad. I could help you keep an eye on your cab, and you could help watch mine."

"Thanks, but I'll manage. Funny, you've never been involved in any of the incidents."

"Just been lucky, I guess."

"Looks that way. Well, I've got a friend, Tim Rutledge, who owns a small hotel near Flagstaff, Arizona. Off the beaten track near Highway 40. It's got a big pool, a nice restaurant, and it's real private. I think I'll take Kara there. This whole thing's worrying her, and I don't want to stay with a lot of truckers who might upset her more."

"I think I know the place." Cowboy spit onto the dry ground. "The Rutledge Inn." He wasn't grinning now.

His eyes sincere, he spoke man-to-man to Jake. "You really do care about her, don't you?"

Jake took a long moment to answer. "You were right about her. She's a mighty fine lady. I wouldn't care what the truckers said about me. I can handle talk. But I wouldn't want anything said that could come back and hurt her."

"They'll never hear it from me, Jake. I'd better get going." He reached up to open his cab door. "Guess I won't see you till Michigan then, right?"

Jake watched the thin man jump up onto the seat. "Right. Have a safe trip."

Cowboy slammed his door and grinned down through tobacco-stained teeth. "You, too." He watched Jake turn to walk away, then called him back. "Hey, Jake? I kind of envy you, you know?"

For the first time since arriving, Jake felt a real smile appear on his face. Giving him a mock salute, he went inside to join Kara as Cowboy shifted into gear and headed toward the exit ramp.

The clock on the dash showed eight o'clock when Jake stopped the truck in front of the Rutledge Inn. The two-story white building with stately pillars flanking the double doors looked almost Georgian and slightly out of place in a small, desert town. The building had been in the Rutledge family for three generations and had become a city landmark.

Jake checked them in and learned that Tim Rutledge was out of town on business. Secretly pleased his friend wouldn't join them for dinner and that he'd have Kara all to himself, Jake carried their bags into the large, comfortable room. After cleaning up, they hurried to the spacious dining room before it closed at nine.

On the drive, comfortable with each other, they'd talked about many things, learning more about one another. The peaceful atmosphere prevailed through a leisurely dinner complete with a chilled bottle of white wine, tart to the taste. As they left the restaurant to stroll the grounds, Jake took the half-filled bottle with them. Though it was well past ten at night, the desert temperature was still in the mid-eighties. Soft summer breezes caressed them as they approached the pool area.

"This town goes to bed with the chickens," Kara commented as they closed the gate of the wrought-iron fence behind them and stood looking at the circular wall of rooms facing the pool. "Look, there's only one window with a light showing, and yet there's no vacancy."

"Maybe the guests have discovered there's more interesting things to do with the lights out than with them on," Jake suggested, stooping to drop his hand into the water to test the temperature. He gazed up at her mischievously. "Mmm, like bath water."

She bent to join him. It was quite dark, except for two muted underwater lights reflecting the color of the side tiles and turning the surface of the pool a shimmering aqua. She dipped her hand into the warm water. "You're right. Too bad we don't have our bathing suits. A swim would feel good."

Jake moved to sit on a webbed plastic pool chair and began tugging off his boots. "Who needs a suit? You just said that everyone's asleep."

"A regular flasher, aren't you? Someone could walk out here any minute."

Already stripped to his briefs, he pulled her to him. His big hands yanked her blouse loose from the waistband of her jeans. "No one's going to come out here. Besides, it's dark under water."

Her hands stopped him as he busily unbuttoned her blouse. "I don't know...."

"Come on. Where's your sense of adventure?" He opened her jeans and slid them down her hips as she nervously scanned the darkened windows. In no time he had her down to bra and panties. A firm hand stopped him on the clasp.

"That's enough. I'll go in like this, thank you." She sat on the edge of the pool. "This is bad enough." Soundlessly she slid under cover of the welcoming water.

Holding the half bottle of wine in one hand, Jake quickly joined her. He moved along the edge until he was facing her in about five feet of water. "Well, what do you think?"

"Mmm, it does feel good."

"Here," he said, offering the bottle, "might as well finish this."

She wrinkled her nose, taking the bottle from him with one wet hand. "What class, Murphy, drinking from a bottle." But she leaned her head back and took several long swallows. Jake drank deeply as well, then placed the bottle on the edge of the pool. Quickly he bent to remove his briefs and placed them alongside the wine.

He moved to Kara, his arms encircling her, his mouth capturing hers, sampling her wine-flavored lips. His hands unfastened her bra as his mouth kept her occupied, and soon the bra joined his briefs on the cement edge. He felt her stomach muscles convulse as his fingers slid beneath the waist of her bikini panties. Eyes still closed, she let him remove them and stood there wearing only her gold chain with the apple dangling low between her breasts. Magnificent, Jake thought. Laughing, she broke away from him and swam to the deep end of the pool. He followed her in a lazy sidestroke.

Treading water, he studied her. A private person, she was suddenly wine relaxed, comfortable with him, at ease with herself. She dipped her head back to evenly wet her long hair. It floated about her, glistening beneath a small shaft of moonlight. Jake couldn't think of another place in the entire world he'd rather be than right here beside her.

"Want to race to the far end?" she asked.

"Sure. Want me to spot you a few feet?"

"No, thanks. Want me to spot you a few?"

"So that's the way you want to play! Okay, lady. This one's for blood!" He backed up and aligned himself with the short end wall. He waited until she joined him and gave him a challenging grin. "Ready?" He saw her nod and brace her foot against the wall for a pushoff. "Set?— Go!"

Jake shoved off and put real effort into his strong, overhead strokes. Through streams of water he saw her skim past him, swimming underwater, a good half a length ahead of him. He hadn't realized he was so out of shape. Despite his best effort she reached the end nearly a full length ahead of him. She jackknifed in the shallow water and moved to her back, floating out toward the middle. He heard her victorious laugh echo in the stillness of the night air as he swam out to join her.

"Where'd you learn to swim like that?" he asked.

"I grew up in California, remember? Public beaches, but nonetheless, I was swimming when I was three. It was the only fun recreation that was free. Looks like they didn't teach you much in that country club set you traveled in, fella!"

She was still on her back. He reached up and, with a firm grasp on her ankle, tugged hard and took her under. Before she broke the surface, he grabbed her by the hand and pulled her into the circle of his arms. Sputtering, she came up, shaking her long, wet hair backward and spraying them both.

"I can see they didn't teach you to fight fair either," she said as he maneuvered their bodies closer. She felt her breasts grow heavy as they nestled against the solid wall of his hairy chest. Her heart began to pick up its rhythm.

"You're the one who doesn't know the rules. The first one is that *all* is fair in love and war."

Her eyes were deep, dark brown pools. "Love?" she whispered.

His eyes were a silvery reflection of the moon. "Did I say that?" he asked. He let his gaze roam her face a moment longer, watching her features soften. He took her mouth slowly and gently. The water lapped around them in quiet whispers as mouths and tongues tasted and hands reached out to renew remembered pleasures.

She could stay here forever, Kara thought, bobbing and floating in the buoyant water, while Jake's loving kisses along her throat sent shivers up her spine.

After a long moment Jake lifted his head. "I'll be right back," he whispered, disengaging himself from her.

She sighed and settled back to lean against the pool wall as he swam noiselessly to the far side. Feeling contented, she closed her eyes. A sharp sound, like the crunching of gravel, snapped her eyes open, making her sink under cover of the shimmering water. That's all they needed was someone to join them for a night swim with their clothes piled on the cement edge.

Through the bushes along the fenceline she looked toward the parking lot, catching a fleeting glimpse of someone tall, wearing a large hat. Hunched over, the figure darted between a station wagon and a parked truck. Their truck? She stood and strained, trying to see in the darkness. There was only silence and shadow. They'd reminded her of someone...yet she could see nothing. Perhaps her imagination was on overtime.

Jake returned to her side, brandishing the near-empty bottle of wine. "One more swallow each should finish it," he said.

"One more swallow should finish *me*," Kara told him, feeling a bit woozy from the effects of fine wine and Jake's tantalizing kisses. She smiled and moved back into the warmth of his embrace. "You finish it."

"No. I always share." He held up the bottle.

She took it and drank a small amount, handing it back. "You didn't hear anything odd while you swam over, did you?" she asked.

He finished off the bottle and set it on the cement. "Odd? What do you mean?"

Floating close to him, she wrapped her arms around his neck and wrinkled her brow. "I heard a noise. It sounded like it was coming from over by the truck. I thought I saw someone—I don't know who—but when I stood to look closer, there was no one."

Jake frowned. "Who'd it look like?"

"A figure, kind of tall, wearing a big hat. Perhaps I was imagining it. You didn't hear anything?"

"Maybe I'd better go check." Jake placed both hands on the pool edge and jumped out. He walked over to where his clothes were and dried himself lightly with his shirt. Quickly he scrambled into his jeans then pulled on his boots. He strolled over to the fence and walked through the gate, cautiously glancing about. He disappeared into the near-inky darkness, and Kara could hear the crunch of his footsteps on the gravel. She felt an uneasy shudder go through her.

Several moments later he emerged into a spot of moonlight and reentered the pool area. Walking to her, he bent to lend her a hand out of the water. Reaching for his shirt, he draped it over her dripping form and began to pat her dry.

"Did you see anyone?"

"No."

"It was probably nothing."

"Probably." He handed her her clothes. As she quickly dressed, Jake gazed toward the parking lot.

Carrying her shoes, she reached for his hand. "Come on. I'm sorry if I ruined the mood."

Jake turned to her and placed his arm about her slender shoulders, hugging her to him. He smiled down into her worried face. There was nothing they could do for the moment about whoever or whatever she'd seen, if anyone. He knew just how to take the concern out of her lovely eyes. "You didn't. I'm still in the mood. Let's go up to our room, and I'll show you just how much."

Her sensuous answering smile was enough to make him forget the troubling incident. Almost.

Kara awakened slowly and reached out for Jake. Finding only the lingering warmth of where he'd lain, she sat up. His suitcase was open on the rack in the corner of the room so he hadn't gone far. Stretching lazily, she decided he was probably downstairs getting them coffee. She eased out of bed and walked to the window. The gray light of dawn was just breaking over the jagged mountain chain. She moved to the bath for her shower, remembering she'd agreed to Jake's suggestion that they get an early start.

In half an hour she was dressed, packed, ready to go and Jake still hadn't returned. She went down to look for him and soon found him, feet sticking out from under the rig.

"Finding anything wrong?" she asked.

"Not yet," came the muffled reply.

"I'll go get us some coffee."

Kara had their thermos filled and brought two steaming cups out to the parking area just as Jake slid out from under the truck. He wiped his hands on a rag and gratefully sipped the hot coffee.

"Everything all right?" Kara questioned again.

"Seems to be, as far as I can tell. I'll go get our bags and be right back." He started toward the lobby.

"I'll come help you."

"Not necessary," he said over his shoulder. "I need to make a quick call. Be right back."

Kara leaned against the cab and watched Jake walk away, struggling with her feelings. She felt slighted, rebuffed then chided herself for taking such quick offense. Jake certainly had the right to privacy when making a phone call. She'd give him his rights and his privacy—but that wouldn't stop her from wondering who and why. Sometimes it seemed as though he deliberately tried to be mysterious, she thought, climbing up into the passenger side.

She finished the last swallow in her cup as Jake returned and threw their bags up into the sleeper then climbed in beside her. He'd washed up, combed his dark blond hair and looked a shade apologetic as he turned to her with a slow smile.

"Let's start this morning all over again," he said, scooting over to her, sliding his arm behind her and gathering her close to his body. "Hello." His warm gaze lingered a long moment on her upturned face before he lowered his mouth to hers in a gentle, undemanding kiss.

"Hello, yourself," she said as he lifted his head to udy her face. "Did you make your call?"

"Yes." Leaving it at that, he touched his lips to her rehead before releasing her and starting the truck.

She tried to sound unconcerned. "Anyone I know?"

"Louie. I had a few things I wanted to talk over with im." He leaned forward to squint through the wind- ield at the dazzling blue skyline. "Looks like we're oing to have a nice day." He moved the big rig out onto e highway.

Kara sighed. As usual, the moment he touched her she as ready to forget all her suspicions. Louie! Now why d he call Louie? Questions clouded her mind but she'd e damned if she'd beg for crumbs of information on his onversation with her uncle. She crossed her legs and, ropping one elbow on the window sill, she coolly gazed ut at the passing scenery. She was probably making a ountain out of a molehill again.

It was some time later that Jake broke the heavy si- nce between them. "You know, you resemble your other a great deal."

It took a moment for his words to register. She turned look at him. "What did you say?"

"I said that you resemble your mother a great deal. I w her picture in Louie's office."

Anger, sudden and fierce, flared in Kara's eyes as she hirled to face him. "I'm *not* like JoAnna! Not in the nallest way. You don't even know her. How could you ompare me to her?"

He shot her a quick glance, surprised she was so sen- tive about the subject. She'd given him the impression e'd adjusted. "Easy, there. I wasn't comparing, I was ommenting. She was about your age in the picture, olding a child of about three on her lap, which I assumed was you. She was beautiful, just as you are now even when you're angry."

"And there the resemblance ends!" Kara was so furious her voice trembled. *Damn!* She had thought she was over this, over the need to disassociate herself from any comparisons to her mother. Evidently she had a few wounds of her own that hadn't healed.

"Do you hate her?" he asked, his voice softer. He knew she added to her mother's support, yet there remained so much hostility.

Kara crossed her arms over her chest, directing her flinty gaze out the window. It took her several long minutes to cool down. Finally she let her shoulders relax, dropped her eyes to her shoes. "No. I stopped hating her awhile back. Now I just pity her."

He reached over and slid the back of his fingers along her smooth cheek then cupped her chin to force her to face him. "I'm sorry. I didn't know that would upset you so. I was only trying to make conversation." He watched the distressful look slowly leave her dark eyes.

She brought her hand up to lay on his. "It's okay. I try not to let thoughts of her get to me, but I guess they still do."

"I should have known that about you. Sometimes I'm not a very nice man." He returned his attention to the road.

She continued to study his profile. "I think you are, but I don't think you like being considered one. I wonder why?"

"For such a short acquaintance, you seem to think you know me fairly well. Perhaps I've only let you see the tip of the iceberg."

"What's the matter, Jake? Are you worried I'll tell the world you're a nice man, and then your tough guy im-

ige will be blown?'' He was wearing a dark green shirt
and when his eyes swung to her, they were more green
han gray and softer than she'd thought they would be
after she'd goaded him.

"I'm not nearly as tough as I'd like to be—about you."

"Is that so bad?" she asked, trying hard to understand.

"It could be," he answered as honestly as he knew
how.

They'd been traveling about an hour through a light
sprinkling of early-morning traffic on the main highway
heading east. The sun was shining in a cloudless sky, the
pavement dry and even, and the truck was handling well.
Everything was fine until their route led them uphill and
then down a broken canyon road. It was then that Jake
discovered that the brakes were no longer holding.

Snapping pictures of the stark beauty of the nearby
craggy mountain range, Kara immediately noticed when
the truck swayed and shook more than usual, throwing
her focus off. As they rounded the final curve and started
downhill at a reckless speed, she turned wide and questioning eyes toward Jake.

His face was hard, set in grim lines, his big hands
gripping the wheel with white-knuckled strength, his foot
trying to engage the impotent brake and coax the big rig
to slow down. Kara tore her eyes away from him and saw
the landscape slide by in a hazy blur as their speed increased even more. She glanced backward and saw the
trailer zigzagging, heard the whine and screech of metal
against metal. Even Jake wasn't going to be able to get
them out of this one. "Oh, God," she whispered in un-
conscious prayer as she felt fingers of fear slither down
her spine.

Jake tried the emergency brake. He swore savagely over its useless state. Whoever had done this had done a damn thorough job, he thought as his frantic mind searched for answers. No excuses, no alibis this time. A cup of sugar in a gas tank was an annoyance. A few loosened bolts were a bother. But this was something else again, something very dangerous.

Kara had seen and heard someone in the parking lot last night. Had that someone hidden until both of them were out of sight, then returned to do the job? Brake line cut just right to hold for a while, then snap through as the morning went on. Or brake fluid drained, a slow leak. Which was it? And who had done it?

He couldn't afford to think about the possibilities right now. He tried to move the gears, to jam the gearbox, but nothing budged. He heard the gush of released air as he pumped the brake pedal and got no response. Why hadn't he been able to spot this when he'd been under the truck earlier? he asked himself as he swerved the powerful cab around another treacherous bend.

To the right, the land fell sharply into a deep, rugged ditch. To the left, the rocky side of a craggy mountain bordered the highway. The greatest danger right now, he knew, was if the downward momentum freed the trailer from the hookup and forced it to crash into them. His flinty gaze skittered about the terrain, searching for a level piece of ground to pull off onto before it was too late.

He risked a glance over at Kara. Her face was white, her frightened gaze fastened on the descending road in front of them, her hands clenched in her lap.

Suddenly the road opened up. His heart lurched in excitement as he spotted the huge sandpile around the next bend. "Brace yourself," he yelled to Kara above the noise of the screaming metal. He knew she saw the runaway truck ramp, too. "I'm going to try for it."

Jake's hands held the wheel in a death grip, his feet pressing against the floorboards as he jerked the cab with a great effort off to the right, heading straight for the sandpile looming in front of them. Peripherally he saw that Kara had pulled her legs up on the seat beside him and had buried her head in her hands. With a mighty roar the trailer broke free of the coupling and careened past them, heading for a cluster of scraggly bushes on the far right. Closing his eyes, Jake braced himself against the steering wheel, protecting his face, as they crashed into the sandpile. A dull, thudding sound invaded his ears as somewhere, not far off, the trailer crashed.

Jake was aware of the enormous silence first. He opened his eyes slowly, unsure if the force of their landing had knocked him out momentarily. The windshield was still intact but the light was dim in the cab for sand covered most all of the windows. He sat up, testing arms and legs and realized nothing was broken as he turned to Kara.

She'd pulled her knees up, her face bent into them, her arms shielding her head. She wasn't moving but neither of them had been thrown off the seat, he realized gratefully, for they'd both been wearing their seat belts.

"Kara, are you all right?" he asked, unbuckling his belt and reaching to her.

Slowly she unclamped her arms and lifted her head. Her eyes, when she turned to look at him, were a little dazed but clearing. Relief flooded Jake as she moved her head tentatively and let out a great gush of air. Just had the wind knocked out of her, he decided as he watched her straighten her legs and lean back.

"You okay, babe?" he asked, running his hands over her arms and back. Unbuckling her belt, he could see no damage. Both of them had escaped injury. They'd been damn lucky.

"I think so," Kara answered, her voice a bit shaky.

"It's all right. We stopped," he reassured her.

"Where are we?" she asked, shifting her limbs, suddenly stiff from the pressure of being tightly coiled during impact.

"We managed to hit the runaway truck ramp and crashed into the sand. See, it's all around us. Look at the windows. That's why it's so dark in here. Are you hurt?"

"No, just a little sore." She ran a shaking hand through her hair. Lord, but that had been a close one. As her mind cleared, her eyes flew to Jake's, her hand to his face. "Are you all right?"

"I'm fine."

"What could have caused the brakes to give out? You were under the truck just this morning. You were . . . the brakes . . ." She couldn't finish the sentence, couldn't give voice to the dreadful thought that had jumped into her mind. *No! It couldn't be!*

Jake's expression sobered as he watched the play of emotions on Kara's face. He could follow her thoughts as surely as if she'd spoken them aloud. She believed that he'd tampered with the brakes, sabotaged the truck, endangered her life. There was no way out now. It was time to tell her the truth.

He thought to take her hand but seeing her eyes filled with unspoken suspicion, he decided she'd probably turn from his touch. "I haven't been fully honest with you, Kara," he said. "But there were reasons I couldn't tell you everything."

Huddled in her seat, she hugged her arms tightly about her. "I'm listening," she said in a voice that didn't sound like hers.

"It's not what you're thinking," he said with a tired sigh. "I have to go back a way. After my mother died and my divorce was final, I told you I left California and bummed around awhile. I worked at a lot of jobs, some a few days, some a few months. And it went on like that for a couple of years. Until I ran into an old friend."

He glanced at her, saw that he had her guarded attention. "Rob Carter and I had grown up together, but we'd gone our separate ways over the years. I'd always admired his intelligence and his integrity, and he seemed to return the compliment. It took a little persuasion on his part—I didn't want to give up *all* my freedom—but I finally agreed to work for him."

Jake turned sideways in the seat and faced Kara directly, his eyes looking for understanding. "Rob's a vice president of Central Insurance Agency, the firm that's a parent company for several local insurance agencies. They do a lot of high-level insuring, industrial mostly. Big car manufacturers, the boating business, foreign interests and the trucking industry. Their claims are often in the millions. Most of them are legitimate. Some are not. I'm one of his investigators."

Kara's eyes slowly changed as she digested what he was telling her. "You're an insurance investigator, for the trucking industry?"

Nodding, he continued. "In the beginning some small truckers, mostly in the Midwest, started turning in higher than usual claims, and, though it was noticed, it was accepted...at first. Then the incidents began to increase and so did the claims, spreading westward and getting more serious. Rob assigned me to the case because of my past knowledge of the trucking business and because he thought the best way to discover the truth was if I went undercover. We approached Louie with the idea, and he was all for it.''

Kara rubbed a weary hand over her eyes. It was a lot to take in at once. "You mean Louie was in on all this from the beginning?''

''Yes.''

''So that's why every time I mentioned my suspicions about you to him, he tried to lead me away from that thought. How long have you been doing this investigative work?''

''Three years. As I told you, I like to be free. My work allows me to be my own boss, more or less, to make good money and yet enjoy a measure of freedom. Rob gives me a lot of room.''

''And you go all over?''

''Wherever there's a serious question about a claim. Before this case I was in the south of France trying to determine if a huge, very expensive yacht that mysteriously caught fire was legit.''

Kara shook her head, filled with relief that Jake wasn't on the wrong end of things, yet needing a moment to absorb it all. "I'm sorry about suspecting you. I didn't want to believe you were doing anything wrong. But so many things—your initials on the manifest...your being in the office when obviously the files had been searched...you under the truck this morning.''

''I know.''

She raised questioning eyes to him. "Why didn't you tell me? Surely you didn't suspect *me*!''

He shook his head with a small smile. "Hardly. Louie and I figured the less you knew the better off you'd be. People who know too much often get hurt.''

"Didn't Uncle Louie tell you that the only reason I came back this summer was to try to get a handle on who was doing this to him?"

He gave her a nod and an exasperated look. "Sure he told me. He also told me that he tried to talk you out of it, and so did I. But you're so damn stubborn. We were both afraid for you."

"Someone is deliberately doing all this . . . ?"

"I'm sure of it."

"Do you have any idea who or why?"

He shrugged lightly. There was no point in conjecturing aloud. Her best protection still was if she didn't know too much. "I have a few ideas, nothing concrete."

And he wouldn't tell her if he did, Kara was certain. "He must suspect you're on to him or he wouldn't have tried to...tried to...oh, God, Jake, someone's trying to kill you!" She shook her head to clear it, moving closer. "I think I'm having a delayed reaction. Do you think you could put your arms around me, for about thirty seconds?"

He smiled as he reached for her. "I'll set my watch." Gently he pulled her into his arms, cradling her head against his chest.

"This work you do, Jake, it's dangerous," she murmured into his shirt.

"Not usually," he said, making light of it. "Mostly paperwork, interviewing people, coming to conclusions. I seldom go undercover."

Why was it she didn't quite believe him? Kara wondered. Both of them might have been killed today. She snuggled closer.

A nagging thought invaded his consciousness. "Kara, why didn't you tell Louie, or anyone else, about my initials on the manifest? You know now that I didn't put them there, that someone forged them, but you didn't know it then. Why did you keep it to yourself?''

Slowly she moved her head back on his shoulder and looked up at him. It was time. Too many games were being played, and she was tired of all of them. ''Don't you know?''

''No. You tell me.''

''Because I love you.''

Kara saw his eyes darken, felt his grip on her tighten. ''I warned you not to let this happen.''

''I know you did. But don't worry. I know it doesn't *really* change anything between us.''

He felt a glimmer of impossible hope. ''Love always changes things—if it's strong enough. I love you, too, Kara. And I never thought I'd hear myself say those words again. Maybe we can work things out.''

Kara's sigh was ragged. It wouldn't last. Love really didn't conquer all, not in real life. ''I don't see how. I've worked too long and too hard to give up the life I've made for myself. I like my independence. I can't just drop all that and follow you across the country, the south of France, wherever your next assignment takes you. I'm a simple, country person. I'd die if I had to live out of a suitcase again.''

Jake stiffened. There it was once more, he thought. That damned independence. He *had* misjudged her after all. ''I would never try to persuade you to do something you didn't want to do. We have different priorities, different needs. I understand.''

All her life she'd wanted one special man to love her, really love her, Kara thought. Why did he turn out to be a man who needed his freedom more than he needed her? Averting her gaze, she toyed with an invisible speck of lint on his shirtsleeve. "When our mystery man is caught, what will you do?" She hated the need that made her ask.

She'd told him that she loved him, Jake acknowledged. But she didn't *need* him. She didn't need anyone. Just her damn house, her camera and her privacy. He couldn't—wouldn't—let her see how she was hurting him. He turned to her, his look steady. "Move on—to the next assignment. I've never lied to you, never promised otherwise."

She met his gaze, her eyes unwavering. "I know." With a soft moan she ended the discussion, moving to touch her mouth to his in a deep, desperate kiss. The time for conversation was past. It had been a frightening, emotionally wrenching morning, and her nerves were stretched to the breaking point. The only man she'd ever loved had just confessed his love for her in one breath then shattered her hopes in the next by telling her almost matter-of-factly that soon he'd be leaving. She didn't want to think anymore. She needed to feel.

Wild, unbridled desire whipped through her, more frantic than she'd ever felt. There was a recklessness in her as she sought his mouth, her hot tongue stealing his breath. His response was instantaneous, his roaming fingers sending a path of fire over her damp skin as if he, too, needed the reassurance that only a lover's touch could give him. Her head swam with the power of the kiss as her searching fingers moved to his shirt, loosening his buttons.

Jake withdrew and moved her away. He reached up and pulled back the curtain over the window separating them from the sleeper compartment. "You first," he whispered, his voice husky.

Uncertainty moved into her eyes. "But, what if..."

"Look, we're jammed nose-end into a big pile of sand. It'll take quite a while to push and shove this door open. It's only about ten in the morning. Do you think putting off going for help for another hour will matter?"

She considered the possibilities. A few moments of fulfillment stacked against a lifetime of emptiness when he'd stroll out of her life. And stroll he would—he'd just told her as much. His rough fingers were incredibly gentle when they moved down her cheek, tracing her jaw. Perhaps this would be the last time they'd make love. She made her decision, meeting his eyes. Had there ever really been any other choice?

Kara tried to lighten things with a mischievous smile. "You're giving me *only* an hour? Hardly seems worth getting undressed for!"

He swatted her bottom as she stepped on the seat in order to crawl through the window. "I promise you, lady, I'll make it worth your while." Gingerly he followed her.

The bed was small, meant for one, with scarcely enough room alongside for another person to crouch. Jake didn't care. His need for this woman thundered in his ears as he hastily pulled off his clothes, his labored breathing the only sound in the cab. Matching his mood, Kara'd painstakingly removed her shirt and scooted out of her slacks. Unable to wait any longer, needing to feel her close to him, he lay down and pulled her atop him.

A sense of loss settled over Jake as his arms encircled her. The last time, he thought. This might be the last time. She moaned deeply as his hand moved between them and found her breast, swelling to meet his touch.

Impatiently cursing the cramped quarters, he buried his face in the warmth of her neck, behaving like a starving man who'd at last found nourishment. Sliding lower, he struggled to remove the silken swatch riding low on her lips. A sweet-smelling woman who wore delicate silk under faded denim. It never failed to excite him. Free of all restraints, she braced her arms and leaned down, brushing her suddenly heavy breasts against his chest, her thick hair falling forward and lazily teasing his taut skin, her gold apple dangling and brushing against him.

Suddenly she was in charge, her mouth hot and hungry, streaking over him, kissing, nipping, tasting. She was wild, stunning him with her fervor as she took him beyond reason with her deft movements, her clever hands, her seeking tongue. Damp, with a rosy hue coloring her face, she arched her back and took him inside, filling herself with him. Then, head tossed back, eyes bright and shining, she began to move, a primeval dance of passion that had him gasping.

She was totally his. There was no mistaking it. She hadn't sought this, hadn't thought she'd wanted it. But from the first moment he'd touched her, there'd been no turning back. She'd told herself that loving was damn difficult but had slipped into it with incredible ease. The difficulty came with happily ever after.

His hard hands clutched her hips to him, straining to get closer, ever closer. Breathing hard, delirious, her movements frantic, she forgot about partings and differences and danger. She forgot everything but Jake, his name pounding in her brain, his heart wildly beating against hers, his body fused with hers. Abruptly she crested, surging against him, feeling him heave beneath her while the world around them exploded into a million scattering pieces.

The air smelled lightly of dust particles lingering from their crash into the sandpile. A sliver of sun peeked through a section of window not buried in the dirt. Soon now, Jake thought, he'd have to try to dig them out though someone might already have spotted them and radioed ahead for help. But they were safe, and, for a few moments longer, they were together.

He lay cradling Kara atop him, her fragrant hair spread over his chest. There'd been a bittersweet poignancy to their union. For a short while they'd put off tomorrow, living only today, the two of them reaching for the only magic, the only sanity left for two lovers to share before they sought their separate worlds. He wanted to hold on for a while yet, just a little longer. Too soon it would be over. His arms about her tightened.

Kara moved her head to touch her lips to his skin, the slightly salty taste mingling with her tears, which had quietly fallen unbidden. She felt as though she would remember this moment for a long while, that in days ahead she would need this memory to keep her warm during the cold times that would surely come.

Chapter Ten

Kara swore at the bent runner of the filing cabinet drawer as she struggled to close it. Not for the first time this week, she wished Santini Trucking was doing well enough to afford new cabinets. The locks on these were useless. As the drawer finally closed, she sighed and went back to her typing.

Sitting down at Pauly's desk, she reached for a stack of billings, glancing out the window at the late August day. She had her own ideas on who the guilty party was. If only she could trip him up. Of course, if Jake knew she was still trying to learn something, he'd be furious.

Jake. Kara sat back and rubbed her tired eyes. Vividly her mind recalled a clear picture of him as he'd looked on the day that they'd met. Leaning against his red truck, he'd appeared arrogant, self-assured and ruggedly attractive. Because of her feelings for Jake, she'd agreed to helping Pauly in the office instead of taking more runs.

And here she was on Monday morning of the second week, away from him in fact but not in thought.

She knew Jake loved her as much as she loved him. Yet she had to face the truth about them. They were different people, wanting different things from life. They'd soon go their separate ways. Unable to fight the inevitable, she'd decided to center her thoughts and emotions on finding the saboteur. She felt better able to accomplish that by working in the office.

The door slammed, breaking into her thoughts.

"Hey, Kara, how's it going?" Tennessee's booming voice was a welcome distraction. He strode toward the pegboard on the far wall and glanced at the posted schedules.

"Fine, Tennessee. How's Norma?" she asked, knowing that his wife was having a rough pregnancy.

Tennessee poured a cup of coffee and settled in a chair across from Kara's desk. "About the same. This heat isn't helping. She's pretty miserable."

With an unsteady hand he raised the mug to his mouth. Kara studied the big man. She knew he'd missed a couple of weeks of runs, fighting a recurring case of summer flu. But he'd come back to work with a vengeance, out more than he was home. Worry lines etched his ruddy face, and, since she'd last seen him, he'd lost weight. Her heart went out to him.

As he raised bloodshot blue eyes, she wondered if he'd had good news about his small son's surgery. "Is Jeremy better?"

His eyes brightened. "So far, so good. He's quite a fighter for a three-year-old."

"Then he's out of the hospital?"

Tennessee's large shoulders drooped. "We brought him home. Our hospitalization coverage ran out and..."

Unable to hide his despair, he blurted out, "I've got to get another run today, Kara. I know I'm not scheduled but . . . can you help me?"

Kara swallowed and turned from the plea in the man's eyes. She knew it cost him to have to ask. Turning to stare out the window, she tried to think of a way to help Tennessee and his family. She knew the truckers' fund, which had been started for just such emergencies, had been depleted by too many necessary loans already. Maybe with her savings and Uncle Louie's help, they could lend him enough to see him through this bad time. Not wanting to hurt Tennessee's already bruised pride, she decided on a little white lie.

Leaning forward, she captured his gaze. "I can't let you go out so soon. You've only been back four hours, Tennessee, and you're beat. It'd be terribly dangerous." She saw the spark of hope leave his eyes, and she hurried on. "But I could arrange a loan from the truckers' fund. Would a couple of thousand tide you over?"

"I heard there wasn't any money left in the fund." He ran a hand over his weary face. "Besides, I've already borrowed too much as it is."

She gave him an encouraging smile. "There's still enough left for a couple of loans. We all get in a bind sometimes, Tennessee. I know Uncle Louie would rather see you take a loan than drive when you're overtired." Kara watched a variety of emotions skitter across his face as he thought over her suggestion. "If you're sure . . . I . . . two thousand might make the difference between . . . between . . ."

Trying to ease his embarrassment, Kara began shuffling her papers. "No problem then. You go home and get some rest. I'll have the check ready for you tomorrow morning."

"Kara?" he said, standing near the door.

She turned to look up at him questioningly.

"Thanks." A tentative smile lighted up his florid features.

As he turned and left the room, Kara let out a huge sigh of relief. She'd have to talk to Uncle Louie about the loan right away. At least she'd feel she'd accomplished something this summer if she could ease Tennessee's burdens a bit.

"Was that Tennessee's voice I heard?" Pauly asked as she came out of Louie's office, her arms filled with files.

"Yes," Kara answered, rolling a billing sheet into the typewriter.

Dumping her load on top of the filing cabinet, Pauly sighed. "Not wanting to go out again, was he? That man's working himself to death."

"No, just clearing up some paperwork," Kara said, deciding that the fewer people who knew of the loan to Tennessee, the better. She glanced up at Pauly. She'd been off sick for two days and still looked paler than usual. "Are you feeling any better? Maybe you came back to work too soon?"

Pauly pulled the last cigarette from her pack and lit it with a hand that was none too steady then fought a coughing spell before dropping into the chair opposite Kara. "No use staying home. You can't hide from some troubles."

So it was more than just physical ills that were bothering her, Kara decided, leaning her elbows on the desk and studying the frail woman. "Is it Cowboy?" she asked softly.

Blowing smoke toward the ceiling, Pauly gave her a sad smile. "Looks like you can see right through me these days, honey. I'm worried about him. He don't want me to, but I can't seem to help myself." She hated revealing her pain, but she badly needed to talk with someone, Pauly realized. Lately she'd felt so helpless and alone.

"I'm worried about him, too," Kara acknowledged. More worried than she dared admit to this lady who loved him. Had Pauly become suspicious of Cowboy's recent behavior also? "Have you noticed anything different about him lately?"

Inhaling deeply, Pauly took her time answering. "Not at first. He's always been a hard livin' man. But he used to drink for fun, like a lot of men do. Now, it seems like he's doing it to escape from something that's bothering him." She shook her head, disgusted. "And that gambling. It's like a sickness with him. The minute he's got two nickels to rub together, he's got to bet them on something. It's a real weakness in him."

Someone with a weakness, Jake had guessed weeks ago when they'd conjectured about who could be involved in the sabotagings, Kara remembered...someone with a purpose who's found someone with a weakness. She'd known Cowboy for years, had liked and trusted him, as had Louie. Her mind fought the possibility even as her instincts told her she was on the right track. Cowboy surely had several weaknesses, but who was behind it, who was the man with a purpose exploiting him?

Her eyes swung back to Pauly's troubled face. "Gambling is a sickness, Pauly, and so is abusing alcohol. Cowboy needs help. Do you think he'd listen to you?"

Slowly Pauly stood and crushed out her cigarette in the desk ashtray. "He stopped listening to me weeks ago. He don't come around my place anymore, and when he bumps into me here, he talks about his runs and nothin' more. He already told me he don't want me in his life."

Kara's heart went out to her friend though there was little she could say that would ease her pain. But she had to try. "Aren't you the one who told me not to pay attention to what a man says, but to believe what's in his eyes? Maybe Cowboy's backed off from you for now, while he's wrestling with his problems. But I've seen his eyes follow you. He may deny it, but he cares."

Jamming her hands into her jeans pockets, Pauly moved to the door. "Maybe so, but the man's got problems I can't solve for him. Question is, do I care enough to see him through them?"

"Only you can answer that one."

Nodding, she opened the door. "I know. I'm out of cigarettes. Be right back." Quietly she closed the door behind her.

Thoughtfully Kara turned back to her typewriter. Obviously she wasn't the only one who'd noticed Cowboy's downward spiraling the last couple of months. He needed help. When Louie returned she'd talk with him, she decided. And Jake. It was time to bring Jake in on her suspicions. Three heads were better than one, and perhaps together they'd find a solution that would help Cowboy.

Of course, she could be wrong. Fervently she wished she was, despite a dreaded certainty that settled over her.

Kara had just finished the last billing sheet when she heard a noise behind her and turned, startled to see Cowboy standing inches from her chair.

"Goodness!" she yelped. "I didn't hear you come in."

Cowboy removed his big Stetson and laughed. "I'll bet you thought only Indians could move quietly." He strolled to the coffeepot, poured himself a steaming cup and turned to regard her. "I heard you were in the office these days and that you'd quit driving. Guess plowing into the sandpile sort of scared you out of riding the rigs?''

Studying his thin face, Kara felt a shiver of apprehension travel up her spine. She wished she had more experience at cloak-and-dagger bantering. ''Not really. I trust Jake, and I knew he'd get the truck under control somehow. I just decided to finish up the summer in the office. It's a nice change and Pauly needed some help.'' She arranged the billing forms in a neat stack. ''She hasn't been feeling too well. Have you been over to see her?'' she asked, looking up at him meaningfully.

He took a swallow of his coffee and shook his head. ''Nah. I don't have time for women in my life, Kara. I need to be footloose and fancy-free.'' His smile seemed forced.

''Too bad, Cowboy. Pauly's a special lady.''

His features hardened. ''She been bending your ear about us, telling you things?''

''I thought you knew her better than that, Cowboy,'' she answered, sudden fear for Pauly justifying the slight distortion of the truth. Just then, he'd sounded quite capable of getting even with her for discussing him.

''I know her as well as I need to, I guess.'' He stepped closer. ''And what about you, Kara? Who keeps you warm on a chilly night? Jake Murphy?''

Swallowing a quick flash of anger at his insinuating question, she realized he'd offered the perfect lead-in line for what she wanted to ask him. She'd take advantage of it. Putting on a dreamy smile, she looked up at him. ''Maybe. We had a lovely evening in Flagstaff last week. We stopped at this rustic inn and went for a moonlight swim. You should have stopped there instead of the Roadrunner. You took the same route we did, didn't you?''

His eyes took on a wary look. "No, why?"

"I could swear I saw you the night we were at the Rutledge Inn. I thought that you were considering staying there, too."

Cowboy turned to the table and poured himself more coffee, his hand shaking. Was it because of his heavy drinking or because of something she'd said? Kara wondered.

"I never stop at those kind of places."

"That's what Jake said."

Slowly Cowboy turned to face her. "You told Jake you saw me?"

Kara thought she saw a flicker of fear in his eyes, but it was gone so quickly she couldn't be certain. "I told him I saw someone who looked like you. Jake went to check the parking lot, but he couldn't find anyone."

He gave her a smirk of a smile. "Must have been your imagination playing tricks on you. So, what plans have you and Jake made?"

"Plans? I don't follow you."

"I thought maybe he'd had enough driving, especially after that scare. I figured he might move back to California, work for the family company, even get married. Seems like you two are pretty close."

"Jake's not the marrying kind, Cowboy." Despite her best efforts to remain untouched by his words, Kara felt her spine stiffen under his penetrating gaze. "As for the runaway truck scaring him, if you think that, you surely don't know the man."

A scowl appeared on Cowboy's thin face. "I know him, all right. He's stubborn. Maybe too damned stubborn for his own good."

Kara felt the sudden metallic taste of fear in her mouth. "What do you mean by that?"

Cowboy set down his still-full cup and replaced his hat. "With all the problems Santini Trucking has had, it might be dangerous to be too stubborn. I'll see you around, Kara." He turned and walked down the hallway that led to the truckers' lockers.

Thoughtfully Kara watched him go. There seemed to be an angry air to his departure. Had she overplayed her hand? she wondered, going over their conversation in her mind. At best she was a lousy amateur sleuth. The clatter of coins dropping into the pay phone down the hall roused her attention. Quietly she left her chair and walked to the archway. Cowboy was on the phone, his muffled voice low, his words indecipherable. A moment later he slammed the receiver onto the hook and marched toward the back door. This time there was no mistaking the anger in his movements.

Hurrying to the side window, she watched Cowboy striding toward his rig. He looked for a long moment up and down the lot. Reaching into his shirt pocket, he stuffed a big wad of tobacco into his mouth. Chewing, he leaned against the cab, glanced at his watch and then stared at the driveway as if waiting for someone.

Kara felt a little silly crouching by the window, spying. What if she were wrong? She could endanger a friendship that went back more than ten years. No, too many things didn't add up. Even Pauly thought so. Something had changed Cowboy. Someone with a weakness was probably involved, Jake had said. Cowboy had several. Even without any real evidence, she sensed that she was right to seriously suspect him. What she needed was proof.

Peripherally a movement caught her attention. Steve, another trucker, walked toward Cowboy, and the thin man didn't look pleased to see him. As Cowboy glanced again toward the drive, Kara quickly went to the rear door. Opening it a crack, she looked about before she slipped outside. She was certain that she was right. Cowboy was waiting for someone, someone he didn't want Steve to meet.

Circling around the wide, cinder block office building, she crept along the pavement in her sneakers. When she came to the side of the truck yard, she peeked around the corner. Cowboy and Steve were still in conversation. Hoping they wouldn't notice her, she darted across the yard and scooted behind the shelter of Cowboy's rig.

A slight summer breeze rustled the leaves of the large maple tree by the fence line. Kara hoped the sound covered the crunching noise of the small stones beneath her feet as she moved closer to the truck and peeked through a sliver of space between the cab and trailer. She saw that Steve had left and Cowboy was alone again, pacing nervously in a tight circle, his jaw moving furiously as he chewed on his tobacco.

The quiet hum of a powerful engine signaled the approach of a sleek, black Cadillac. It stopped on the other side of the truck, directly in front of Cowboy. Kara crouched down and watched closely. Nervously Cowboy spit onto the ground and glanced about before moving closer to the car.

A middle-aged man with silvery-white hair emerged from behind the wheel. "So what's the problem, Cowboy? You sounded pretty upset on the phone." He puffed on a long, slim cigar and watched Cowboy through the smoke.

"It's not working, that's all. Not this time and not this guy. I don't know if Louie's on to me but Murphy might be. He doesn't scare easy. I've tried everything, and he's still nosing around. With this last maneuver I'm just lucky the girl wasn't hurt. You've got to help me, Whitey. We've got to think up another plan."

The man blew a thin trail of smoke out of the side of his mouth. "You're getting soft, Cowboy."

"Listen, Whitey, I've done everything you asked me to do—and more. I got the papers you wanted. I cinched the Monroe deal for you, and I put a guy you can trust into Acme Trucking. But I told you from the start, I don't want anyone seriously hurt." Cowboy took off his hat and wiped his brow with a shaky hand.

The stocky man smiled menacingly at Cowboy. "You're in no position to make any demands, Cowboy. I don't have to remind you how much money you owe the boys. And they're getting mighty tired of waiting for you to deliver. Now I'm going to tell you one more time, and you listen real hard. The Demetri brothers want Santini Trucking, and the only way they can get it is by making Louie so nervous he'll gladly sell—for peanuts. You said you could do it if they'd tear up your gambling debts. We made no deals as to *how* you'd do it or who would or wouldn't get hurt. That part's up to you." He opened the car door. "You got till Friday to get Murphy out of here so we can move in on Santini."

With a pointed finger Whitey tapped twice on Cowboy's shoulder then jammed his cigar in the corner of his mouth. "You don't deliver by then, Cowboy, and you got a lot more to worry about than the money you owe, if you get my meaning!" He swung behind the wheel and slammed the door.

Kara swallowed hard and tried to stand perfectly still, scarcely daring to breathe. Slowly the Cadillac moved out of sight. Putting his hat back on his head, Cowboy stared after the car then leaned against the cab, seemingly lost in thought.

Quietly Kara inched her way back along the first line of trucks. At last she had the information she needed. She'd been right about Cowboy. Though Jake would be upset about the chance she'd taken, he could now question Cowboy and get to the bottom of whatever mess the veteran trucker was involved in. Pauly would be hurt and disappointed, but more was at stake here than one person's feelings . . . much more.

Anxious to locate Uncle Louie and Jake, Kara began moving faster. As she reached the end of the row, she came to a sudden stop. Her heart in her throat, she stared into the cold, blue eyes of Cowboy Adams. He was not smiling.

Louie Santini drove his spotless four-year-old station wagon the same way he ran his life, cautiously but with firm determination. As he exited from the freeway and turned onto the road that led to his office, he fleetingly glanced at Jake's unsmiling profile. Jake was worried and that bothered him more than his own anxiety. They'd had a long breakfast together discussing their various options. Though Jake took a businesslike approach to their problems and seemed confident of the outcome, Louie sensed an underlying uneasiness. "You really think our plan will work, Jake?" he asked, for the third time since they'd left the restaurant.

"I think it's got a good chance," Jake answered guardedly. After months of talking with dozens of truckers across the country, he'd narrowed down the possibilities to the one man who he felt quite possibly was sabotaging Santini Trucking. There were more, he knew, but perhaps this man could lead them to the others and ultimately to whoever was behind it all.

"From what we've put together, we're probably right," he told Louie. "We've known for a while that both Tennessee and Cowboy had reasons, but after our discussion today, I agree that Tennessee isn't capable of attempted murder. Cowboy's another story."

Louie shook his head sadly. "You know, he's been with me from the start. I don't know how this could have happened. If he had problems, he could have come to me. But to do these things . . ."

"Sometimes we don't know people, Louie. We just think we do. Probably Cowboy got in over his head and, in his muddled thinking, he thought this was the answer."

"Thank God Kara has agreed to stay in the office. I shudder to think what would have happened to both of you if you hadn't found that sandpile."

There was a grim edge to Jake's voice. "You just schedule me with Cowboy this next run. We'll smoke him out. I've got a score to settle with him personally as well. It's one thing to come after me or the other men, but to endanger Kara . . . well, just schedule me with him. I think it'll be his last run."

They both grew quiet. Louie glanced again at Jake, something else on his mind.

"Since you won't be scheduled till at least tomorrow, maybe you'd want to take Kara out to lunch," he said, turning into the drive leading to the office.

Recognizing a matchmaking attempt in the works, Jake decided to decline. He'd guessed over the past few weeks from several things Louie'd said, that he was in favor of a union between Kara and him. The trouble was, Louie didn't know all the facts, and Jake was in no mood to explain.

"Louie, I don't think so. Kara and I have—" Jake cut his words short at the sight of a truck rushing past them, Cowboy behind the steering wheel. As he maneuvered the cab toward the back exit, Jake caught a fleeting glimpse of someone slumped next to Cowboy. Someone with a white face and a long, black ponytail. "Stop the car!" Jake yelled. He jumped out and ran toward the truck.

Reaching the yard gate at a dead run, his heart thudding in his chest, he stopped as he saw the big rig head for the highway. On foot he'd never catch up with them. Signaling Louie to pull alongside, he opened the car door, hurrying the man out from behind the wheel. "Call the police, fast! I'm going after them." He scrambled into the driver's seat, scarcely taking time to close the door as he zoomed out of the lot.

Cursing inventively for letting Cowboy have such a head start while he'd foolishly chased his truck on foot, Jake ground his teeth in frustration. That's exactly what he was—a fool. A fool in love, and the woman he loved was in grave danger. Taking a deep breath, Jake forced himself into an attitude of icy calm. This job had put him in dangerous situations before, and he knew that he had to put his emotions aside and think with a clear head.

What had happened between Kara and Cowboy that he was driving away with her like a bat out of hell? Had she inadvertently stumbled onto something that had exposed Cowboy's involvement? Had she baited him, causing him to lose his temper? Where was he taking her, and how could he think he could get away with this, especially after he and Louie had spotted them leaving? Was the man so desperate? He'd have to stop him. There was no time to lose.

Speeding down the expressway ramp, he zipped around another car and merged into the stream of noonday traffic. Spotting Cowboy's cab barreling along in the passing lane, Jake zigzagged from lane to lane, trying to maneuver closer. He swore to himself. Where were the damn police when you needed them? he wondered angrily. Stepping on the gas, Jake shoved forward and strained to peer into the truck.

Cowboy sat high, gripping the wheel, staring straight ahead but, try as he might, Jake couldn't spot Kara. His heart filled with fear. *Did Cowboy have her tied? Had he hit her?* A white sheet of rage burned behind Jake's eyes as his mind pictured several gruesome possibilities.

Reckless now in his anxiety, he drove closer to Cowboy's cab, bouncing the side of the wagon against it. The car boomeranged back into its lane. Again, Jake banged the car against the cab to force it off the road. The big rig held to the pavement, swerving only slightly. As Jake made a third attempt, he heard the blaring of a siren. In his rearview mirror he saw the police car's flashing red light. Louie'd gotten through in the nick of time. At last Cowboy slowed the vehicle to a stop on the highway shoulder.

While the policeman pulled Cowboy from behind the wheel, Jake opened the passenger door. Like a rag doll Kara literally fell into his arms. Carefully he gathered her to him and walked to the grassy area with her. Checking her pulse first, he breathed a huge sigh of relief when he felt it beating steady and strong under his fingers.

Nearby the police handcuffed Cowboy and read him his rights. Jake sat down and cradled Kara in his lap. Gently he brushed the hair back from her face then lightly patted her cheeks, murmuring her name. With a soft moan she moved her head slightly. As he saw a dark, angry bruise on her forehead, flints of anger danced in

Jake's steely gaze. Cowboy *had* hit her! Kara's sudden movement gentled Jake's angry thoughts.

Blinking her eyes against the glare of sunshine, she struggled to sit up. Jake cradled her tighter. "It's all right, babe," he said softly. "You're safe now."

"Jake, what happened?" she asked, bringing a hand up to hesitantly touch her forehead. "Where's Cowboy? I tried to—"

"Shh, never mind. The police have him in custody. It's all over, Kara." Hugging her, he pressed his lips against her temple. Yes, it was over, he thought sadly. In more ways than one.

Chapter Eleven

Jake sat in a wooden chair watching the balding policeman complete his report. After making sure Kara was all right, he'd revealed his insurance credentials to the two police officers who'd arrived on the scene. By the time they'd reached headquarters, Cowboy had been ready to talk. He'd badly misplayed his hand, and he knew it. Perhaps he'd decided that prison was the safest place for him to be right now.

During Cowboy's interrogation Jake had stood by, feeling anger stir as he thought about what might have happened to Kara. While the police booked Cowboy on kidnapping and attempted murder charges, other officers were sent to pick up Whitey and his men for serious questioning.

Glancing over, Jake saw Louie talking with the police detective at the next desk. With a sad expression Louie shook his head in disbelief over Cowboy's involvement with organized crime. The detective had informed them earlier that the Demetri brothers were involved in illegal activities in Michigan and throughout the Midwest. Their recent gambit was infiltrating small trucking companies from within. Using saboteurs like Cowboy who were indebted to them, they forced companies to sell at a loss.

Jake had known of the Demetris from Rob Carter and had explained that they were suspected of planning to combine several small companies and merge them into a large corporation. That corporation would appear legitimate thereby giving them excellent mobility for transporting stolen merchandise cross-country.

Louie looked over at Jake. "Poor, gullible Cowboy must have actually believed that if he did this one more job for them, they'd erase his debt, and he'd be clear," he said.

Remembering their narrow escape in the runaway truck and Kara's kidnapping, Jake felt less charitable toward Cowboy. He looked over at Kara seated in front of a nearby desk. She was quiet, only talking when she had to answer questions. As she informed the police officer that she was returning home to California as soon as possible, her eyes found his. He saw sadness in her and very little hope. He'd known she'd leave as soon as it was over. Yet he had to try one last time.

"Sergeant, are you finished with me?" Jake asked, rising.

"We just need your signature on this, verifying your statement," the sergeant said, shoving the paper toward him.

After reading the form and signing it, Jake walked over and stood near Kara, waiting. When she was free to leave, they exchanged a quiet look, and he guided her with a firm hand on her back to the hallway outside the detective division.

"I feel so sorry for Pauly," Kara said as they walked, her voice filled with empathy. "I've got to go see her. She loves Cowboy, you know. It's so very hard to give up someone you love."

Jake knew she was talking about more than just the relationship between Cowboy and Pauly. As they reached a windowed alcove, he touched her arm and turned her to face him.

His face was serious as he studied hers. "It doesn't have to be that way for us, Kara. I have to finish up some paperwork here on this case, and then I've got some free time before I go out again on assignment. Come with me, Kara. Let's take a trip together, anywhere you say. We could get to know each other better, maybe start all over. Don't let what we have go so easily."

Easily? Is that what he thought? Averting her gaze, she shook her head. "I can't, Jake. I've been away from my business too long. Lord only knows how much work is piled up there waiting for me. My staff depends on me, and so do my clients. My...my house needs work before the autumn rainy season. I've neglected it badly." She moved from him, turning to stare out the window, her back to him. "And Nona needs me. She's growing older, failing. I shouldn't leave her alone so much."

Jake went to her, gently placed his hands on her shoulders and forced her to look at him. "*I* need you. Doesn't that count for anything?"

Kara swallowed hard and dropped her eyes. He wasn't going to make it easy for her, she thought. She took a step closer, put her arms around him. His touch on her back was light, without pressure. "Of course it counts. It's just that...the timing is bad. Maybe one day, when you no longer have this need to travel so much and my life is more in order..."

If she would just offer him one small sign of encouragement, one tiny ray of hope, maybe... "Do you honestly believe that day will come, Kara?" he asked, speaking softly into her hair. He felt her arms tighten about him.

Afraid. She was so damned afraid. If she gave in, and he came home with her, how long would he stay? Until the restless need to wander returned. She couldn't face another goodbye. "I don't know," she answered.

It wasn't the answer he'd wanted to hear. Jake dropped his arms from her. "All right, go back. Go to your all-consuming work and your wonderful house by the sea." He sighed audibly. "I hope it all makes you happy. Evidently *I* can't."

Her brown eyes, filled with anguish, turned to him, pleading with him. "Please, Jake, try to understand. I can't just leave all that I've worked so hard for for all these years. I do care for you, but..."

"But not enough," he finished for her. He saw the color drain from her face, but he didn't feel like softening his words. Silently she turned back toward the window, her shoulders looking small and defeated.

"I have to call Rob Carter," he told her, "let him know what happened here today. I'll be right back. Wait here, and I'll drive you to Louie's place."

Feeling drained, Jake turned toward the detective's office. Absently he rubbed his beard as he walked. The attraction between Kara and him was strong, the love they shared real. But they both seemed incapable of compromise. The only answer he could see was separation.

At the door he glanced back at the woman he loved. Despite the pain he knew she was feeling, she stood straighter now, looking tall and proud and capable. And she was. He knew he wouldn't ask her again to go with him. And she knew it, too.

When he'd finished his business call, she was gone.

It was time to move on, Jake thought. There was no one to keep him in Michigan any longer. He'd wind up this case in the next few days and then leave. He had some time off coming. Maybe he'd take a couple of weeks' vacation. Wearily he walked to the bank of elevators and pressed the down button.

"He didn't intend to hurt you," Pauly said, her voice anguished. "He was scared, his back to the wall. It was almost like he didn't know what he was doing, you know?" Her red-rimmed eyes pleaded with Kara for a glimmer of understanding.

Kara patted her friend's thin shoulder as she sat with her arm around her on Pauly's couch. A sticky night breeze ruffled the drapes at the window behind them. Lord, but it was hot and she was bone tired. "I know, Pauly," she said.

"Did you tell Jake that Cowboy didn't hit you, that you bumped your head on the dash?"

"Yes, I did, when we were filling out the reports." She had, for all the difference it had made. Jake's eyes hadn't softened the slightest at that piece of news. Kara sat back as Pauly dabbed ineffectually at her eyes. "But let's remember, he did shove me into his truck. What was he planning to do with me? How was he going to keep me quiet? When he started off so quickly, and I fell forward and hit my head, I didn't have a chance to talk with him, to ask him anything. I admit he didn't strike me, but

Pauly, you've got to face some facts here. We weren't out for a Sunday drive either.''

"I know," Pauly moaned, grabbing Kara's hand and squeezing hard, her face pinched as she fought a new rush of tears. Why, oh, why hadn't she been able to get through to Cowboy? she asked herself for possibly the hundredth time since learning of his involvement. She'd known for some time that he was troubled. She'd never in her wildest dreams guessed how deeply.

"If you'd have seen him like I did tonight, Kara. He looked like a crumpled man. But you're right, he's guilty. There's no question about that." A small sob escaped from her throat.

Kara shook her head sadly, wishing she could find the right words to comfort Pauly. The image of Cowboy's cold eyes and rough hands came back vividly to haunt her. And what would have happened if Jake and Louie hadn't come along when they had? Or earlier, if Jake hadn't found the runaway truck ramp? They might both be dead, she thought with a shudder. She wanted to be compassionate, yet she wondered just how much good was left in Cowboy.

Reaching for the glass on the low table in front of them, Kara took a long drink of the iced tea Pauly had fixed for them. After leaving Jake at police headquarters, she'd talked to Louie awhile then packed her few things into her car. Tomorrow was Tuesday, and she planned to start her drive for California early in the morning. With any luck she'd be in her beach house by Friday afternoon. She was anxious to get going, to put all this behind her. But she couldn't leave without stopping in at Pauly's. Shifting concerned eyes back to the distraught woman, she tried to ease her friend's mind.

"Do you think Cowboy can be rehabilitated? They have wonderful programs these days for alcohol abuse. Even a Gamblers Anonymous. Maybe if he got help..."

"Yeah, maybe. If he'd *accept* help."

"Pauly, he doesn't have much choice. You talked with Jake. What did he say?"

She shrugged, looking as discouraged as she felt. "He didn't offer a lot of hope except to say that Cowboy's record before he got mixed up with the Demetris would be in his favor. And he was none too pleased that you wouldn't sign the kidnapping charges against Cowboy. Jake was mighty scared for you, honey. I see his side, too."

Kara sighed. "I didn't see any point to it. Cowboy's already under arrest for attempted murder plus serious vandalism, and the feds will probably charge him with racketeering and Lord knows what all else. How much worse can it get?"

Pauly squared her shoulders and took a sip of tea. "I've got some money put by. Louie said he'd help me find an attorney." Her empty eyes swung to Kara, who was watching her. "I know he's sick. I can't just turn my back on him. He's all I got, Kara. All I care about."

Gently Kara moved to embrace her. "Of course you can't walk away," she said, silently praying Cowboy would be worthy of this strong yet fragile woman. "A lot of men have turned their lives around because of one woman's faith in them." She leaned back, meeting Pauly's eyes. "Let's hope that happens with you two."

Rising, she glanced at her watch. "It's late, and I want to get an early start in the morning. I hope to be home by the weekend."

Pauly stood and walked to the door, opening it. "You sure you want to leave just yet, honey? I thought you and Jake would work out your problems."

Swinging back to face her, Kara shook her head. "I thought so, too. Lousy timing, I guess. Maybe one day." She enveloped Pauly in a last brief hug. "Keep in touch. You know if you need anything, I'll be there. Promise you'll call?"

Through her resuming tears, Pauly nodded. "Take care of yourself, honey."

"You, too," Kara said, then turned and left, closing the door behind her.

Pauly leaned against the frame, wrapping her arms around herself. Neither she nor Kara picked men to fall in love with very wisely, it would seem, she decided.

Early-morning sunshine poured through the window of the trucking office as Jake sat at Pauly's desk. He'd deliberately come to the office before she or Louie would arrive. Tired from several restless nights, he didn't want to talk anymore. It was Friday, four days after Cowboy's arrest and the day he'd wrap up his paperwork and move on. Picking up his pen, he forced himself to concentrate on finishing the last of the endless forms.

At last he made a notation on the final page and walked to the filing cabinet. Shutting the cabinet drawer, he closed his manila folder. As he shoved it into his briefcase, the office door opened, and he looked up. The one man Jake had hoped to avoid this morning strolled in. He put on a tight smile. "Good morning, Louie."

"You're here mighty early," Louie said, walking over to the coffee table. "Glad you put the pot on." He poured himself a cup, took a seat across from Jake and regarded him with his dark, intelligent eyes. "You've been avoiding me all week, Jake," he stated, as if it were a fact that they were both aware of.

"Not really," Jake answered without looking up. "I've had a lot of work to finish up."

"Why'd you do it? Why'd you let her go?"

Jake didn't move a muscle, lifting only his gray-green gaze to Louie's face. He didn't have to ask who the older man meant. "You've been a friend of my family for years, Louie, and I've gotten to know you much better these past few months. I like you a lot. But I don't want to discuss Kara with you." He returned his eyes to his writing.

Louie took a long swallow of coffee. "Jake," he went on as if he hadn't even heard his warning, "you're a man who likes challenges, excitement, maybe even danger. There are a lot of ways to risk your life, but loving someone is the most dangerous. You can get hurt and left with more permanent scars than a physical injury would ever leave. But loving is also the most rewarding of risks. Don't think because I'm not married that I haven't loved someone as deeply as I know you love Kara."

Jake threw his pen onto the desk, scattering the papers, and leaned back in his chair. The eyes he raised to Louie's were devoid of hope. "I don't think you understand. I'm not afraid to risk loving Kara. I admit that I love her. But she wants too much."

He sighed deeply. "She's ambitious. She'll succeed at any cost and if that price tag happens to be the happiness we could have together, so be it. She'll sacrifice. I've asked her to come with me. I'm far from poor, Louie. I make damn good money. She wouldn't lack for a thing, and she knows it. But she turned me down. She wants it all *her* way. Well, I'll go a long way for the woman I love, but I don't knuckle under easily. I won't give up my life and go live in that damn house she's so afraid to leave."

"Jake, listen...."

"No, hear me out." Jake shook his head bitterly. "Kara's just like my father was—driven! And like my ex-wife—always looking for more. Not for material things in Kara's case, but *something*. When will it ever be enough? When will the time be right for *us*?"

His gaze moved to the window as he stared unseeingly at the cloudless sky. "For years I watched my father. All he could think of was work and more work. Pile up the dollars. And Cindy was the same, always pushing me to do more, promising me that when I did what *she* wanted, then we could start to live. I vowed a long time ago, Louie, that I wouldn't get caught in that trap again, and I won't. Not even for Kara."

Louie set down his cup, shaking his gray head. "If you're finished, I'd like you to listen to me a minute. Jake, you're the one who doesn't understand. You know that I've known your family since your father and I were both young men growing up in the same small town. Tom Murphy was dirt poor and saw his father desert his mother, leave her penniless. He had to quit school, go to work at an early age, hustle to put food on the table when he was just a boy. When he met your mother, and they fell in love, he... he wanted to give her everything. He didn't want that hard life for his wife, and, later, his sons.

"Sure he was a workaholic, driving himself. There never could be enough for Tom. But he did it for your mother and you and your brothers and your children to come. He didn't work for the sake of piling up money for himself. It was all for his family because he couldn't forget his own struggling youth."

Jake's face was bleak, unconvinced. "You weren't there, Louie. He neglected us all. Even after my mother got sick, he wouldn't quit pushing."

"I don't say he was right. In a lot of ways he was wrong. He overdid a good thing. He didn't understand that his time away from you while you were growing up would keep you from being close and eventually contribute toward driving you away. But he didn't intentionally neglect your mother. She had a weak heart—that's why she died."

"But she died alone!" Jake said, his voice full of anguish.

Louie sat back in his chair, his eyes suddenly sad. "It was just a stroke of bad luck that no one was around the day she had that last attack. She was always frail, even as a young girl...frail and very beautiful. I used to tell Tom that he didn't appreciate what he had, but you know what a stubborn Irishman your father is. Ann never blamed him, Jake. She understood him and she knew what drove him. And she loved him. She *always* loved him."

Jake sat very still a long moment, studying Louie's stooped shoulders, the loneliness etched in his features. How clear things become, he thought, if we only stop and really listen. "You loved her, didn't you, Louie? *She* was the one you said you loved deeply."

Louie shrugged and turned to stare out the window, his eyes suddenly nostalgic. "Yes, she was the one. It was a long time ago. I was a young man, living in California at the time. Your father and I both loved her, but she chose him. After the wedding, I...I moved, finally settling in Michigan. I never found anyone quite like her. She always loved Tom. And in his own way he cared very deeply for her. It nearly killed him when she died. But his stubbornness wouldn't let him show it. He blamed himself, put himself through hell. Yet he wouldn't share his grief with you boys.'' Louie allowed himself a small smile. ''I don't suppose you've ever noticed how stubborn an Irishman can be?''

Jake didn't speak, but his eyes ruefully registered agreement.

Louie leaned forward, his gaze suddenly intense. ''Don't let that happen to you, Jake. Don't let yourself get out of touch with your feelings.''

''I'm not,'' Jake protested, but his voice held little conviction.

''Aren't you? Your father loved you then, and he loves you now. Why don't you go to him before it's too late? Maybe he can't speak anymore, but he can hear. Make your peace. Don't make the same mistakes he did, Jake!''

After a long pause Jake gave him an affectionate smile. ''You're quite a man, Louie. I'm sorry you didn't find someone else to share your life with. You have a lot to offer.''

''For some men, Jake, there is only *one* woman. I think maybe you're like that, too. Cindy wasn't that woman even though you may have thought so at first. I think Kara is. She loves you, and she's not a woman who gives her heart easily. She's spent years running away from relationships, afraid she'd turn out like her mother. She doesn't want to be a dependent person who sees herself only as an extension of some man. Kara couldn't stand that image, so she tried to be as different from it as night from day. But I know that girl. Inside is a woman longing for love. She saw man after man walk away from her mother. She needs reassurance that the man she commits herself to won't do that.''

"I don't know, Louie. There's still that ambition of hers. She'll work nonstop to get what she wants. She's obsessed with that house, decorating it, filling it."

Louie smiled indulgently. "You still don't see it, do you? It's not just a house to Kara. It stands for all she didn't have as a child and a teenager growing up in shabby apartments over smelly storefronts. It's her declaration of independence. It tells the world she's somebody—not the nobody she felt like while my sister dragged her around like a piece of baggage."

His voice was filled with emotion, pleading Kara's case, love in every line. "She's afraid, Jake. Afraid you'll take away that independence. Afraid if she trusts you too much that you might one day walk away like all those men did from her mother."

Jake leaned toward Louie, his eyes silvery and intense. "I would *never* do that to her, Louie. It's not her independence I object to. It's her desire to do everything alone. She doesn't seem to know how to take, to receive. She thinks there's a price tag to even a small gift. She's got to know that, with me, loving means trusting."

Louie smiled at Jake, almost in a fatherly way. "Teach her, Jake. Show her. Would it be so terrible to give in a little? She'll meet you halfway, I know. Don't give up the woman you love. We both know it's a risk, but take that risk. Grab that moment. None of us know how many moments are left to us in this crazy life."

Draining the last of his coffee, Louie looked a little embarrassed at his long, somewhat impassioned speech. Getting up, he paused beside the younger man sitting in Pauly's chair. Placing his hand on Jake's shoulder, he patted him affectionately. "Think about what I've said, Jake. You have so much to gain." Quietly he went into his office.

The morning sun was still climbing as Jake finished up. Briskly he snapped his briefcase closed. He'd come to a decision. If he hurried, he'd have time to make the mid-morning nonstop flight to L.A. He'd be in California by afternoon.

Loose ends . . . he had a couple of loose ends to tie up. For some years now he'd been unafraid of taking risks. That hadn't changed. He was about to take the biggest.

Louie was right. It was time for him to let go of the past, to stop allowing Cindy's painful influence affect his love for Kara. It was time, as Louie had pointed out, to try to make peace with his father, to make Kara understand that he cared enough to let her be free. Maybe she would realize that the strongest ties that bind us are woven from love and trust. Jake picked up his case and walked toward the door, not looking back.

Chapter Twelve

Patches of the coastal road were still flooded, Kara noticed as she turned onto the four-lane highway that ran along the rim of the seashore. The storm had abated for now, but an angry gray sky laden with heavy clouds hovered over the churning ocean. Mother Nature was resting before she let loose with Act Two, she thought. As one who'd grown up in the area, she was well aware of the awesome power of the sea during a squall. Nervously she gripped the wheel with one hand and fingered her gold apple with the other, fearful of driving any faster on the wet pavement yet eager to see her house. In the darkening twilight of Friday evening, she inched toward her home, her sanctuary.

Wearily she rubbed the back of her neck. She'd made the drive from Michigan in four days, not something she'd recommend to anyone considering such a long trip. Unable to sleep anyhow, she'd driven mile after mile on

coffee and nerves and very little else, tired but incapable
of turning off her troubled thoughts. She felt sunburned
and windburned having driven much of the way with her
convertible top down. But it was up now. The radio had
warned of early autumn storms brewing along the California coast. She'd fervently hoped they wouldn't arrive
before she did, but she saw now that at least one had.

Uneasily she peered through the windshield at the dis-
mal sky. This had come so early, she thought, not allowing her time to prepare her house, to secure it against the
beating it might receive. People who lived along the shore
knew you had to be ready, knew that the wind and sea in
tandem could heap destruction for miles on end. With a
sinking feeling Kara rounded the bend and turned into
her winding driveway.

An involuntary cry escaped from her as she saw the
young olive tree she'd recently planted, lying bent and
broken on the ground. Several larger trees leaned pre-
cariously from the effects of galelike winds. She pulled
the car up as close to the side of the house as she could
and, fumbling with her keys, moved swiftly to the door.
A light drizzle had resumed and the wind whipped at her
thin, cotton blouse as she managed at last to open her
door.

Her hand automatically went to the lamp switch. The
room flooded with light. "Oh, God, no!" Kara cried out,
slumping back against the wall. The large living room
just past the entryway was in near shambles. The far wall
that faced the sea was composed almost entirely of glass
sliding doors that led out onto a large bricked patio. She
crept closer and saw that evidently the force of the wind
had hurled a redwood lounge chair through the door.
Glass shards and fragments lay everywhere, dotting the
long, wheat-colored couch and marring the terrazo floor.

she'd been so proud of. Pieces of the chair were scattered nearby like broken matchsticks. The wind whipped at her drapes through the jagged opening, causing the drenched fabric to swirl about in a macabre dance.

A sudden noise from the direction of her bedroom caught Kara's attention, and she moved quickly toward it. Turning on the light, she gasped at the sight that met her shocked gaze. That doorwall hadn't survived the storm, either, and broken glass was sprinkled on her pale blue carpeting, remnants scattered onto her white bedspread.

Carefully Kara picked her way to the bookcase along the side wall. Tears of frustration filled her eyes as she saw how the driving rain had reached some of her favorite books, her mementos, her photo equipment, saturating all that it touched. She scarcely felt the moisture stream down her cheeks as she picked up an old photo album and pulled open its soaked cover to reveal the few pictures she'd cherished from her childhood, all ruined. A five-by-seven studio photo of her mother, taken during her happier, younger days, smiled back at Kara through the streaks of water that dripped from the edges of the album.

Unmindful of broken glass crunching under her shoes or the chill wind blowing about her, Kara walked around the room she loved, touching the shattered pieces of her dreams that lay scattered about her. She picked up a broken piece of glass, what had once been a lovely bowl of cobalt blue that Nona had given her years ago, crushed now. Her books, her paintings, her pictures. God, why did this have to happen? she moaned. It just wasn't fair! She was just getting it all together and . . .

Through the whistling wind Kara heard a pounding on her door, but she simply didn't have the strength to move.

She slumped down on a corner of her bed, pieces of the bowl still in her hand.

"Kara! Kara, where are you?"

It took some time for her dazed mind to recognize the voice. No, she thought foggily. It couldn't be him. It was just because she needed him so much right now that she imagined she heard him calling her.

Jake's footsteps crunched along the hallway as he moved toward the the rear of the house and into the bedroom. He saw Kara sitting on the bed, looking lost and bewildered. "Thank God, you're all right," he said, rushing to her.

Gently he took the broken glass from her hand and pulled her up into his arms. He held her against the warmth of his body and closed his eyes in a rush of relief and love. Wordlessly she sagged against him, allowing him to comfort her.

He'd made his flight with minutes to spare, arriving in the late afternoon just as the rains were beginning. Picking up his car, he'd driven directly to the hospital and spent an enlightening hour with his father.

Leaving, he'd noticed how quickly the weather had changed and imagined that along the shoreline, it would be much fiercer. He'd decided to drive to Kara's, wondering if she'd arrived home yet. As he'd driven, the skies had darkened, and his fears for Kara's safety had increased. He'd seen her car as he'd pulled up, but he didn't know how long she'd been home. As fanatical as he knew she was about her house, it didn't surprise him she was still here.

The damage was terrible and quite extensive. They had to get moving because it was getting brutal outside again. There was more to come, probably worse than before.

They'd have to make arrangements to clean up and salvage what they could afterward.

Thank God Jake had arrived in time to help her, Kara thought. Pushing out of his arms, she looked up into his face with eyes suddenly bright. "I'm so glad you're here. I need your help so badly." Moving quickly, she took his hand, pulling him along the hallway. "I've got some lumber in the carport storage area. We can board up the broken windows. Go get them, please, Jake, and I'll find my hammer. Then, we can—"

Abruptly he stopped, turning her to face him, his hands firm on her shoulders. "Kara, have you looked out at that sky? It's black, and the waves of the sea are higher each time she rolls in. Another storm is coming, worse than the last. I just hope we have time to get out of here before it hits."

She shook her head wildly. "No! We have time. I know we do. I can't . . . I *won't* let everything I've worked so hard for be destroyed."

"Are you crazy?" he shouted above the sound of the wind, which had picked up momentum and was now shuddering through the house. "You've lived near the ocean all your life. You *know* what a storm like this can do." He grabbed her, propelling her toward the door. "You're coming with me whether you like it or not."

With a burst of strength rooted in pure adrenaline, Kara pulled free of him and ran toward the carport. "If you won't help, then get out of my way," she raged at him. A fresh gust of wind nearly knocked her over as she opened the storage room door of the open-air carport. She hit the light switch but it flickered momentarily and died.

Cursing inventively at the storm, the fates, whatever, she braced herself as she hunted frantically for the lumber she knew was in there somewhere. It was really pitch dark now, and her hair was wet and getting in her way. Impatiently she brushed at it. She had to do this. Why couldn't Jake understand? Suddenly strong hands around her waist whirled her about.

"What kind of an idiot would get herself killed over a stupid house?" Jake yelled at her. His angry gaze took in her wild eyes, her tear-streaked face. God, how was he going to make her see? he wondered.

"It's not a *stupid* house. It's *my* house. Mine. I found it and bought it. No one...nothing is going to take it away from me. Not this time. Not you, not this storm!"

"Dammit, Kara, stop! It's only a pile of wood and stone. We can buy another, or repair this later."

"A pile of wood and stone! Not to me, it isn't. Get out of my way! You don't understand."

She turned away to rummage again in the darkened shed. He saw her struggling but refused to aid her. Not in this madness.

Suddenly she cried out, and he saw her sit back on her haunches on the cement floor. Leaning forward, she frantically searched about with her hands.

"What is it?" he asked.

"My chain broke," she answered, her voice ragged, almost at a breaking point. "It caught on something. I can't find it. My apple's gone. I can't lose that, too. Please, Jake, help me!"

He thought he felt his heart break. Was it with hope? He went to her, moved her aside and leaned into the shed, hunting with probing fingers on the cement floor. At last he found it, the chain broken, the gold apple intact. "I have it," he said, showing her.

A shaft of light from the open door fell on her, and he saw gratitude reflected in her luminous eyes. "Oh, Jake, thank you. I don't know what I'd have done if..."

Roughly, to cover his own emotions, he pulled her into his arms. He held her, just held her as she clung to him, her chest heaving.

"Kara, please, come with me now." He was practically begging her. Yet he felt her stiffen. Desperately he searched his mind for something that would penetrate her obsession. "What about Nona?" he asked, his voice sounding very reasonable and calm.

Slowly she got to her feet and looked at him. He saw confusion and fear mingle in her eyes as they sought his.

"Oh, God! I've never seen one of these storms go as far inland as the little cove where Nona's house is. Yet..."

His voice was filled with gentle persuasion. If he could get her as far as Nona's, he'd have a chance to calm her. "I came up that road, and it was very bad already. The weather reports say this storm is one of the worst in years. It could have reached as far down shore as her place already."

He saw the decision register on her face, the love and concern for her grandmother winning out. He tried not to let her see the relief he felt as he guided her to his car.

The screeching winds buffeted Jake's station wagon as they inched their way down the flooded coastal road. The windshield wipers struggled to reveal a small clearing in the rivers of water washing over the car windows as Jake drove slowly and carefully. Beside him Kara was silent, her anguished eyes straining to see through the torrents of water. She clutched her trembling hands together in her lap, her mouth a white line.

They could see the picket fence surrounding Nona's garden as Jake turned into her drive and pulled close to the house. Kara was out and running toward the door almost before he'd come to a full stop. Quickly he followed her onto the porch.

They found Nona sitting quietly in her rocker in a corner of her kitchen. Figaro leaped from his place beside her and ran to greet Kara with wet licks. Overcome with emotion, Kara ran to Nona and knelt before her, placing an arm about the thin shoulders in a fierce hug. With her free hand she scratched Figaro's head.

"Nona! Thank God you're all right," Kara said. "We were so worried."

"You shouldn't have come out on such a bad night, Kara," Nona said in her usual, calm voice. "You know you catch colds easily. And look at you...you're all wet. Go get a towel and dry off, and I'll make some coffee. Jake, it's nice to see you again."

An amazing old woman, Jake thought, shaking his head. He could see where Kara got her strength. "Nona, we don't have time for coffee now. The storm is getting worse and headed this way. Get your coat, and we'll take you out of here before the roads are impassable."

Nona looked from one to the other, puzzled. "This is my home. Why would I leave it?"

Kara grabbed her hands and held them tightly between her own, her brown eyes beseeching. "Nona, you must. The storm is the worst I've seen. My...my house was already hit." She couldn't bring herself to tell Nona how extensive her own damage was. "It'll get worse before it dies down. We'll take you to Mrs. Harrison's, and, as soon as it's safe, we'll bring you back." Nona and Mrs. Harrison had been friends for years, even though the little widow lady lived almost at the city limits of Los Angeles.

The old woman looked about, frightened. "But my things. If I'm not here to guard my things, something might happen." She gave them a small smile. "You go on. I'll be all right. I want to stay with my things. I've lived here over fifty years. I can't just walk away." Figaro moved to sit beside her, and she reached out to stroke him as if for reassurance.

Must run in the family, Jake thought, this damn stubborn streak. He walked to look out the window that faced the sea and peered out through the curtains. The raging winds tangled with the high waves as they thundered farther inland with each wild thrust. Already they were up past the fence line and rapidly moving closer. He turned, determined to get the two women into his car even if he had to carry them bodily.

"We haven't any more time to waste arguing," he told them, losing patience. "We have maybe ten minutes before those huge waves will be knocking at the door. Please Nona, Kara, let's go!"

Nona's deep brown eyes pleaded with him as she looked up. "You don't understand, Jake. I raised two children in this house. My husband died here. It's filled with so much that's important to me. But especially my memories. Don't you see? I can't leave."

"Nona," Kara whispered softly, her worried face hovering close to her grandmother's, "no one can take away your memories. Probably nothing will happen, but we can't take a chance. *You* are what is important in this house... nothing else. You're the one who taught me, Nona. It's people who count, remember?"

Slowly Kara turned and looked up at Jake, her eyes swimming with unshed tears as her own words echoed back at her. So much had happened lately. So much to absorb. She spoke to Nona, but her eyes never left Jake's.

"A house is wood and stone. We can build another, or fix this one up if it comes to that." She swung her gaze back to Nona. "Nothing's more important than the people we love—not a house or anything in it. Things can be replaced. People can't." She stood and held her hand out. "Please, Nona."

As Kara waited, her grandmother patted her moist eyes with a small handkerchief. She knew that adjustments were hard at Nona's age—maybe at any age. At last, Nona put her hand in Kara's and rose, clasping her granddaughter briefly to her.

"I'll get my coat and my handbag," Nona said.

Jake watched the old lady walk to her bedroom. He turned to Kara, his heart in his eyes. God how he loved this fragile, brave, lovely woman. How far she'd come tonight, and how proud he was of her. "I know how hard that was for you. I hope you believe you did the right thing, for her and for yourself."

Kara's eyes spoke volumes as she continued to gaze at him. "I love you, Jake," she whispered, so low he had to lean forward to hear. She took one step and moved into his arms, handing him her love and trust. It was the biggest step she'd ever taken in her life.

It was close to ten o'clock in the evening when Jake pulled into his parking space alongside his apartment building on the south side of Los Angeles. Here, in the heart of the city, the rain continued, but without the ferocity of the sea's close influence. He switched off the ignition and turned to look at Kara, asleep next to him.

Despite recent exposure to the sun, her face was paler than he'd ever seen it, and there were dark smudges of fatigue under her eyes even in repose. Her long black lashes contrasted starkly against the pallor of her cheeks.

Her hair had been wet and windblown, yet it lay wild and beautiful, framing her oval face. How very much he loved her, Jake thought with an intensity of feeling that almost overwhelmed him.

They'd driven Nona to Mrs. Harrison's, a ride that had taken the better part of an hour under stormy conditions. After the initial fuss about leaving, Nona had been quiet and subdued, oddly calm. They'd settled her and Figaro there and turned down her friend's invitation to remain also. Despite the fact that he knew it would take another hour to drive to his apartment in the rainy weather, he wanted to be alone with Kara. And the look Kara'd given him had told him she shared his feelings. She'd fallen asleep almost immediately, the deep sleep of the exhausted. He hated to wake her, but he'd make it up to her. He'd let her clean up, and then he'd put her to bed. There'd be time tomorrow to talk. Gently he shook her shoulder.

Jake's apartment on the tenth floor of a highrise had been picked out more for convenience of location than roominess. He seldom spent much time there. Kara preceded him into the living room and looked about. Beige, rich browns, muted golds. Big, comfortable furniture, a huge bookcase stuffed to overflowing and a surprisingly vibrant framed print of a New England seacoast during a raging storm. She moved to sit on the wide corduroy couch and leaned back, feeling the weariness deep in her bones.

"I know you're worn out. Why don't I run you a hot bath?"

"I'd like to rest for a few minutes. Come and sit beside me."

"In a minute." He moved to a small sideboard and poured both of them a snifter of brandy. Walking back, he sat down beside Kara, handing her a glass. Silently they toasted one another, then sipped.

She set her drink down on the low side table and turned to him. "I think we should talk."

"It can wait until morning. You're tired."

Even in this he was understanding. Kara felt a warmth spread through her and knew it wasn't just from the liquor. "I'm not that tired."

"Then let me go first." Jake took one of her soft hands into both of his. "I've learned a lot these past few days, Kara. Some of it has been a long time coming. I had a serious talk with Louie before I left Michigan. He's quite a man, you know. I never realized."

Kara smiled. "I always thought so."

"He told me some things about my father. I don't know if you're aware that they attended the same college together years ago. Louie made me see my father in a different light. All these years I've been blaming Dad for a lot of things. Some of them justifiably so, but I still didn't have the right to judge him. I should have tried to understand him. He's made mistakes, and he's paid a bitter price tag for them. I went to see him in the hospital as soon as I arrived this afternoon."

"He needed that visit, Jake, but so did you."

"I know." Jake rubbed his tired eyes. "God, it seems like days ago instead of just a few hours ago. He's not fully recovered from his stroke, probably never will be. He's sick and old and alone. I haven't been the best of sons, but he didn't press that point. His speech is slurred but understandable. We talked today, *really* talked, for the first time in years. I guess there has to come a time when you stop blaming your parents for things you feel they've done wrong and accept them as human beings who made some right decisions and some wrong ones.

You have to believe that they did the best they could with a given set of circumstances. I think that today Dad and I took a step in that direction.''

Kara reached up and ran her fingers along Jake's beard, her touch loving. "I'm glad you went, Jake. It was time.''

"Yes. And I learned some other things from Louie. He knows you pretty well and he loves you very much." He moved closer, his arm sliding around her, his eyes on hers. "I know, Kara, how much your house means to you. I know how rootless your childhood was, and I know that the house is important because it symbolizes your independence."

"It's not important any more..."

Jake went on, intent on explaining, her words not registering. "Of course, the damage may not be as bad as it looked. We can get it repaired. I swear to you, I'll fix it. Or build you another one. I—"

Swiftly she shut him up with a soft, sweet kiss. Leaning back again, she looked deeply into his eyes a long moment before she spoke. "It doesn't matter any more. Not like I thought it did. I learned something today, too, Jake. I meant what I said at Nona's. In trying to convince her, I saw it so clearly. *People* are what matter, not a pile of stones and wood."

She looked down at their entwined hands and idly traced a jagged pattern along his wrist with one finger. "I won't pretend I don't hate the thought of losing some of my things. I don't expect you'll understand, having lived all your early years in one house. But Mother and I were always moving, trying to get away from nosy neighbors, bill collectors and jobless men. Small, stale apartments where countless others had lived. Used furniture, hand-me-downs and the smell of other people. Nothing of my own except a handful of books and a satchel of worn clothes. No place we were in ever felt like a home. I loved being with Nona, but even there, I was surrounded by *her* things. I wanted—I *needed*—to feel that the things around me were mine. Things I'd earned and paid for that no one had the right to take from me or the right to make me move on to another place if I didn't want to go."

He stroked her face gently. "I do understand. You've got to believe I have no intention of robbing you of your things or your independence. I know how important they are to you."

She shook her head, placing her two hands around his face. "*You*. You're important to me. *The* most important thing. Compared to you, the house and everything in it can wash out to sea. Everything I hold most dear is right here between my two hands. I can always get more things. I can't replace you. I love you, Jake Murphy, with all my heart, with everything I have to give."

His smile lit up his face. "I'll take it," he said, "but only because it comes in such a delectable package." He met her mouth with his own. Fatigue was forgotten as his lips roamed her face, reacquainting him with her taste, her scent. His hands moved over her body, the familiar feel of her igniting the passion that lay smoldering under the surface, waiting for her touch to release it.

Kara leaned her head back as Jake's lips found the pulse point at her neck. She felt comfort at his touch, a sense of peace, a feeling of trust. With this man, wrapped in the wonder of his love, she need look no further. She had found her home.

And she'd almost pushed it away. Stupid. She'd been stupid to think she could arrange life to suit her. As a child she'd dreamed of having a loving mother, a caring father, a real home. It hadn't worked out that way, so she'd postponed her happiness.

She'd set it all up, trained herself to be good at something she liked to do, saved her money, bought herself things that gave her pleasure then sat back and commanded herself to enjoy. What a Pollyanna she'd been!

Tonight she'd learned how quickly the things she'd thought so important could be lost. For life was never perfect, and only fools thought it would be. There was only here and now, snatches of happiness, a perfect day, a man who loves you—always realizing it could all disappear tomorrow. If we didn't allow ourselves to live today, how could we be certain there'd be a tomorrow? Thankfully she'd learned that before it was too late. Wherever Jake was, that was home. How had she ever thought otherwise?

Leaning back, Kara captured his eyes. "I just want you to know that wherever your work takes us, that's where we'll go. We can still fix up my house, use it as a base between your assignments. My studio's well on its way to running itself. I can work anywhere, as long as I'm with you." She smiled lovingly. "Have camera, will travel."

Jake didn't bother to hide the surprise on his face. "You'd do that for me, after telling me how you hate to travel, to live in places others have occupied?"

She shrugged. "That was different. I *had* to do it then. Now, I *want* to do it. Where you are is home—and I want to be with you."

Jake shook his head wonderingly then let a slow smile form. "Well, lovely lady, I have a surprise for you. I've come to a few realizations myself. At heart I'm a homebody, too. I left California and started roaming about because I had lost what I considered home should be. I wanted to be free, independent—or thought I did.

Now—" he ran his hands slowly up her arms "—traveling holds no more appeal. I want a home, Kara, here with you. I want us to rebuild your beach house together. I want children, a bright little boy and a sweet little girl like in the pictures you took by the sea. Only they'd be ours, yours and mine."

Kara's eyes glistened with unshed tears. "I want that, too, Jake. But your work..."

His fingers played with a lock of her dark hair. "Yes, well, I've given that a lot of thought lately, too. I've been fair with Rob, given him full measure for every day I've worked for him. But I think he always knew that one day I'd have my fill of that life-style. It's a single man's job."

"You want to stop investigating, to stay—"

"Here, with you. Yes, that's exactly what I want."

With an air of disbelief Kara let out a ragged sigh. "I can't believe what I'm hearing. But what would you do? Wouldn't you miss that life?"

"No. I've got you." He smiled then let out a deep breath. "As to what I'd do, my father seems to feel I'd be most welcome back at Murphy Trucking, said it would make him and my brothers pretty happy."

Her eyes grew serious. "What about you—would that make *you* happy?"

"I always did like working there, until I used it to escape from my muddled home life. This time I'd have a whole lot of reasons to hurry home after a day at the office—someone who wouldn't let me overwork, I hope; someone who would make me very happy if she'd marry me. Will you, Kara?"

"Yes," she answered, her face reflecting the love that filled her heart. More... he was giving her more than she'd dared hope for. Kara sought his lips then for a kiss of hope and promise. And, as always when their mouths met, her needs grew, and the kiss went on, deepening as Jake's hunger matched her own.

Pulling back, Kara murmured into his neck. "Mmm, I really should take that bath. I'm pretty grimy."

Gray-green eyes smiled into hers. "How about a shower? It's quicker." He stood, pulling her up with him. "I'll even wash your back."

"Maybe you could join me. It saves water. I've always been interested in water conservation, haven't you?"

Jake's grin widened as he led her toward the bathroom, already tugging off his shirt. "Not until today I haven't, but I think I'll become a strong advocate if it involves shared showers with you."

With his finger Jake traced the red mark along her neck left by the breaking off of her necklace. "I'll get your gold chain fixed for you tomorrow," he said, placing a soft kiss on the spot.

"Thank you."

His smile was filled with feeling. "That's when I knew you cared more than you thought you did, when you got so upset over breaking the chain I'd given you."

"I've never been without it since you put it on my neck. I don't think I realized what it came to represent. When it fell, I suddenly felt I'd broken the last link with you, that I'd lost you, too."

Jake moved her into his arms, his hands rubbing her back. "You will never, ever have to worry about losing me. I love you, Kara. I'm never going to let you go."

"I'm going to hold you to that," Kara said, raising her lips to kiss the man she loved, secure at last in the knowledge that she'd found the only home she'd ever need.

* * * * *

COMING NEXT MONTH

#445 THROUGH ALL ETERNITY—Sondra Stanford
Upon colliding with luscious Lila Addison, big Jeffrey Chappel found the former model kind to strangers but cautious about commitment. He vowed to win her precious trust, but could he truly offer her his own heart?

#446 NEVER LET GO—Sherryl Woods
Though Dr. Justin Whitmore acted hard as nails, hospital psychologist Mallory Blake had glimpsed his softer side. As professional awe turned to personal ardor, Mallory longed to crack Justin's icy facade—and rush right into his heart.

#447 SILENT PARTNER—Celeste Hamilton
Fiercely independent Melissa Chambers needed bucks, not brainstorms, to launch her new restaurant. But headstrong Hunt Kirkland, her far-from-silent partner, was full of ideas...for passionate teamwork!

#448 THE POWER WITHIN—Dawn Flindt
Strongman Joe Rustin had saved Tina's life. He then became her exercise coach and devoted companion—but *not* the lover she longed for. How could she convince Joe to unleash his powerful inner passions?

#449 RAPTURE DEEP—Anne Lacey
When lovely, treacherous Stacey reentered Chris Lorio's life, buried rage surfaced...as did memories of rapture in each other's arms. For the long-ago lovers, the past held bitterness, secrets and, somewhere, sweet promise.

#450 DISARRAY—Linda Shaw
In small-town Finley, Arkansas, little went unnoticed—especially not "good girl" Barbara Regent's canceled wedding, compromised reputation and budding romance with a mysterious, untrusted outsider.

AVAILABLE THIS MONTH:

#439 CATCH A FALLING STAR
Brooke Hastings

#440 MORE THAN A MISTRESS
Joan Mary Hart

#441 THE PRIDE OF HIS LIFE
Bevlyn Marshall

#442 LOOK HOMEWARD, LOVE
Pat Warren

#443 HEAT LIGHTNING
Lynda Trent

#444 FOREVER SPRING
Joan Hohl

Silhouette Intimate Moments

THIS MONTH
CHECK IN TO
DODD MEMORIAL HOSPITAL!

Not feeling sick, you say? That's all right, because Dodd Memorial isn't your average hospital. At Dodd Memorial you don't need to be a patient—or even a doctor yourself!—to examine the private lives of the doctors and nurses who spend as much time healing broken hearts as they do healing broken bones.

In UNDER SUSPICION (Intimate Moments #229) intern Allison Schuyler and Chief Resident Cruz Gallego strike sparks from the moment they meet, but they end up with a lot more than love on their minds when someone starts stealing drugs—and Allison becomes the main suspect.

In May look for AFTER MIDNIGHT (Intimate Moments #237) and finish the trilogy in July with HEARTBEATS (Intimate Moments #245).

Author Lucy Hamilton is a former medical librarian whose husband is a doctor. Let her check you in to Dodd Memorial—you won't want to check out!

IM229-1R